Stronger than the Rest

MacLarens of Fire Mountain

SHIRLEEN DAVIES

Book Four in the MacLarens of Fire Mountain Series

Other Books by Shirleen Davies

Historical Western Romance Series

MacLarens of Fire Mountain

Tougher than the Rest, Book One

Faster than the Rest, Book Two

Harder than the Rest, Book Three

Stronger than the Rest, Book Four

Deadlier than the Rest, Book Five

Redemption Mountain

Redemption's Edge, Book One
Coming fall of 2014

MacLarens of Boundary Mountain

Colin's Quest, Book One
Coming in 2015

Contemporary Romance Series

MacLarens of Fire Mountain

Second Summer, Book One

Hard Landing, Book Two

One More Day, Book Three – Coming summer of
2014

For more information about Shirleen Davies and her books visit: www.shirleendavies.com

For permission requests, contact the publisher.
Avalanche Ranch Press, LLC
PO Box 12618
Prescott, AZ 86304

Cover artwork by idrewdesign

Book design and conversions by Joseph Murray at 3rdplanetpublishing.com

ISBN-10: 0-9896773-3-8

ISBN-13: 978-0-9896773-3-2

Description

"Smart, tough, and capable, the MacLarens protect their own no matter the odds. Set against America's rugged frontier, the stories of the men from Fire Mountain are complex, fast-paced, and a must read for anyone who enjoys non-stop action and romance."

Drew MacLaren is focused and strong. He has achieved all of his goals except one—to return to the MacLaren ranch and build the best horse breeding program in the west. His successful career as an attorney is about to give way to his ranching roots when a bullet changes everything.

Tess Taylor is the quiet, serious daughter of a Colorado ranch family with dreams of her own. Her shy nature keeps her from developing friendships outside of her close-knit family until Drew enters her life. Their relationship grows. Then a bullet, meant for another, leaves him paralyzed and determined to distance himself from the one woman he's come to love.

Convinced he is no longer the man Tess needs, Drew focuses on regaining the use of his legs and recapturing a life he thought lost. But danger of another kind threatens those he cares about—including Tess—forcing him to rethink his future.

Can Drew overcome the barriers that stand between him, the safety of his friends and family, and a life with the woman he loves? To do it all, he has to be strong. Stronger than the Rest.

"If you're a reader who wants to discover an entire family of characters you can fall in love with, this is the series for you." – Authors to Watch

Dedication

This book is dedicated to a group of wonderful friends who have encouraged and supported my writing efforts. My sincerest thanks to Rayma-Lew, Sue, Don, Marilyn, Linda, and all those who have watched this journey unfold. Their enthusiasm has been a true blessing.

Acknowledgements

I want to thank my editor, Regge Episale, who has been a beacon through my writing journey.

Thanks also to my beta readers, including my wonderful husband, Richard. Their input and suggestions are insightful and greatly appreciated.

Finally, many thanks to my wonderful resources, including Diane Lebow, who has been a whiz at guiding my social media endeavors, and Joseph Murray who is a whiz at formatting my books for both print and electronic versions.

Stronger than the Rest

Stronger than the Rest

Chapter One

"Get up, MacLaren," a tall, burly man sneered before yanking him out of his wheelchair, kicking the contraption against a wall, and breaking a wheel. "I knew you could make it up—one way or another," his attacker smirked and turned to the others at the table. "See? He can stand all right." The last was said as the man landed a blow to Drew's jaw and released his shirt. Drew crumbled to the ground.

His driver had taken him to the saloon after a long day at the office, then reluctantly left when Drew directed him to return in an hour. He'd been working since seven that morning and needed time to unwind. Cards, whiskey, and the bustle of Charley's saloon sounded good—at least that's what he'd thought.

It hadn't taken him long to win fifty dollars from the brawny stranger. The man had lost several rounds, bellowing his frustration, and accusing Drew of cheating.

Now Drew lay on the saloon floor, rubbing his jaw, and working himself into a sitting position before repositioning his worthless legs. His attacker still stood a foot away glaring down at him.

"That's enough, Luther. Wouldn't want the gentleman to think we're inhospitable to our guests." A clipped, smooth voice sliced though the smoky air without creating a ripple. Movement stopped and those who already stood parted to let a medium build man in a dark suit stroll up with an outstretched hand. "Connor, get a chair for this gentleman and coffee for Luther," he called over his shoulder before turning back. "May I give you some help up, stranger?

Drew just stared at the unfamiliar face. He'd been coming to this saloon for months and had never seen the man who stood a foot away.

"Thanks, I appreciate it." Drew knew he was dead weight and expected him to call someone else over to help, but with one strong pull the much shorter man had Drew up and in a waiting chair. Drew adjusted his legs before peering up. "Where's Charley?"

"Well, let's just say Charles made an unwise bet with the wrong person. Poor fellow had no cash to settle his debt, so I am now the proud owner of the Denver Rose." He swept his arm in an arc around the room. "Ira Walsh at your service. And you are?"

Drew glanced around the saloon and for the first time realized that none of the current workers were familiar. Not one. He'd known Charley was having problems, but never thought he was about to lose a business he'd built for more than ten years. "Drew MacLaren."

"Mr. MacLaren, allow me to apologize for Luther and his poor behavior. I'm afraid he drank more than usual. And, he isn't used to losing. He'll no longer bother you. What may I do for you to make amends?" Ira's smile was broad but there was something amiss about it, and the man.

Drew studied him. Ira was around five-feet-eight with wavy hair the color of sticky, brown mud after a spring thaw. His sallow skin had a slight yellow tinge—as close to white as you'd see in a country where many still made their living outside. His mustache matched the muddy brown of his hair. He wore black dress slacks and a jacket with velvet lapels and collar. The white shirt blended into his pale skin. What struck Drew the most was the total lack of mercy behind his eyes. They were a flat gray without a hint of compassion, and no warmth spread from his smile to those dead eyes.

"Perhaps you could arrange for transportation back to my office since my normal means of travel has been destroyed," Drew suggested. He looked at his broken wheelchair. He held no love for the contraption but he was stranded without it—dependent upon others—a situation he despised. His office was only a block away but it might as well have been on the other side of the city. At least he had a spare wheelchair and access to a buggy and driver. His boss, Louis Dunnigan, made sure he received all the services needed for a man in his "temporary condition," as Dunnigan was fond of saying.

"My pleasure, Mr. MacLaren. Connor, see that our guest has transportation to his office and any assistance he requires," he ordered the gent who stood a few feet away. "I hope this incident will not discourage future visits." Ira extended his hand once again.

"I appreciate your hospitality, Mr. Walsh, and look forward to seeing you again," Drew lied with the same ease as his host.

It took little time for Ira's men to deliver him into his comfortable office at Dunnigan Enterprises. It was a massive stone structure, five stories high, and took up the majority of a city block.

Drew was glad for the second wheelchair and other conveniences, even though he cursed the need for them every day. His boss had installed a private facility inside Drew's office so that he didn't need to go far to take care of his often unexpected needs. Another aspect of his new life he cursed on a daily basis.

Terrence, his efficient and formal secretary, arrived within minutes and stared at the sight before him. Like several of Dunnigan's employees, he'd been provided with an apartment in the building. Terrance had heard voices below his window and looked out to see his boss being carried into the building by two burly men.

"Mr. MacLaren, sir, you look rather, uh, disheveled."

Drew had to smile at his secretary's dry tone. Although he wouldn't have selected him if the choice had been up to Drew, he'd grown to appreciate Terrence's loyalty and discretion, especially over the past several weeks.

Drew had left town almost three months ago on a mission to help his twin brother, Will, but had returned with a bullet hole in his back that had left him paralyzed from the waist down. *Temporarily*, Drew thought as he looked up at his secretary.

"I had a run-in with a gentleman who took great exception to my winning at poker, Terrence. Fortunately he took most of his anger out on my chair and not my body."

Terrence looked him over thoroughly. Satisfied that the damage was primarily to Drew's clothes, he stepped back to open the door. "Very well, then. May I get you anything, Mr. MacLaren, before I leave?"

"No, Terrance, go ahead, but I'll need transportation home in an hour." Drew turned his chair toward his desk, and settled behind it to review the latest documents that had materialized during his brief absence. His usual routine was to work until six at night, have supper, then return to the office until nine before going home, or at least what he called home, until he figured out his future. He glanced up when he heard his office door swing open.

"Oh Drew, I heard what happened and just had to come to make sure you were all right."

Patricia Dunnigan swept into the room like a hurricane. At twenty, she had taken one look at Drew and convinced her father that no one else would do as her husband.

Drew understood then, as he did now, that her attraction to him was as superficial as the dresses and jewelry she wore. Patricia no more loved him than she did any other man. What she did love was the lifestyle her father had provided. Dunnigan had made no secret of his desire to someday include Drew as a partner, not just an employee. Patricia took this as an indication that the young attorney would one day be wealthy, and therefore, a suitable husband. Drew wanted no part of that type of union.

When Drew's mind did wander to thoughts of love and marriage, the image that came to him was that of Tess Taylor, not the self-absorbed female who now stood in front of him. Tess was the only woman he wanted, and he thought she felt the same. He'd go to her if he regained the use of his legs, but not before.

"Well, as you can see, I'm fine." Drew held out his hands, palms up, and gestured toward his body. "No additional damage, except to my chair, which is easily corrected. There was no need for you to come out tonight."

"Agnes was serving dessert when the message came to us. Father wanted Clarence to drive us here right away, but of course I had to change out of my dinner clothes. I'm sure you understand."

6

He didn't understand but let her comment stand and nodded toward a tall cabinet against the wall. "May I get you a sherry?"

"If Patricia wants a sherry she can walk over and get it herself." The voice of Louis Dunnigan proceeded the man into the room. "Patricia, I told you there was no need for you to come to the office. I'd have sent for you if it were needed." Drew's boss rarely showed impatience. Although he tended to indulge his only child, he'd been frustrated with her on several occasions over the past few weeks. Patricia had become a self-absorbed, pampered young woman, and Louis saw this as clearly as everyone else.

"But, Father..." Patricia started, but stopped at her father's raised hand.

"I understand your concern, but as you can see, Drew's fine. Next time I'll expect you to do as I ask." Louis offered his daughter a slight smile as he walked over to one of the large leather chairs. "I've asked Clarence to drive you home. He's waiting downstairs."

A pout formed before Patricia masked it with a half-smile of her own. "If that's what you want, Father, of course I'll leave. Drew, please let me know if there's anything I can do for you."

"I will, and I do appreciate your concern."

She left with the same self-possession as when she had arrived. *Subtle and Patricia would never be used in the same sentence,* Drew thought as a chuckle escaped his lips. When he looked up, Louis had settled into one of the guest chairs, his eyes

7

still fixed on the spot where he daughter had stood not a minute before.

"She's a good person, Drew, but she's got her own ways and I'll admit, I sure don't understand most of them." He took a sip of whiskey from the glass he'd brought with him. "I ask that you give her some time before you decide if you want her hand. You know, I won't hold it against you if you decide you don't love her—and I suspect you don't. You're important to Dunnigan Enterprises, and I'm not willing to lose you over this."

Drew could only stare at the man who'd been more than generous. After the shooting, Dunnigan and his daughter had taken the train from Denver to Great Valley, then a carriage to Cold Creek, home of the Big G ranch. They'd escorted Drew back to Denver in their opulent private train cars and set him up not far from the office in a small, but nicely appointed house that came with a twenty-four-hour-a-day personal attendant, wheel chair, and full use of a carriage and driver. Dunnigan had also provided the best medical care available west of Boston. All he'd asked was that Drew continue his legal work at Dunnigan Enterprises for as long as he chose.

"Mr. Dunnigan, you've been very generous and it's not my intention to let you down," Drew began.

"The only way you'd let me down, young man, is if you married my daughter out of obligation to me and not out of love. She deserves love. Do you love her, Drew?"

Lying to Dunnigan never occurred to Drew. "No, sir, I don't."

"That's what I thought, but perhaps in time you will."

Silence enveloped the room for a moment as each man focused on the last words spoken.

"Now, the real reason I stayed to speak with you. I'm still interested in range land in western Colorado. I hear the Bierdan place may be for sale as well as a couple of other ranches in the area. I've heard rumors that Grant Taylor may have an interest in selling, also. Doubtful, as Grant expressed a desire to expand his ranch when I was in Cold Creek, but the rumor needs to be checked out. Assuming we are able to purchase land, someone must work through the legalities, perhaps travel to Cold Creek, and negotiate the deals. That someone is you."

Drew's face had become more set with each word. He'd known as soon as Dunnigan said he still wanted the land that a finger had been pointed at him. It was the last thing Drew wanted.

"I'm always ready to represent the company, you know that. I have a good grasp of the complications involved and know the people, but are you sure I'm the right person to travel to Cold Creek? It may be best for me to handle the legal issues here, in Denver, and let Thompson make the trip. He's eager to get your eye, and I trust him."

"Don't feel you're man enough for it?"

Drew's eyes narrowed and he glared at his boss. "Excuse me?"

"You heard me, MacLaren. Are you man enough to go or are you going to settle back and rely on others now that your legs don't work right?"

"Don't work right? Hell, they don't work at all," Drew snapped.

"Then it doesn't matter if you're behind a desk, on a train, or riding a carriage. Your brain still works fine, and that's what you get paid to use. Not your legs. I'll provide whatever you need to travel, if it comes to that. Could be as early as next week. Be ready." Dunnigan downed the last of his whiskey, raised himself from the big chair, and walked out of the room, leaving a slack-jawed Drew to stare after him.

A minute passed, maybe two, before Drew sat back in his chair and laughed. He'd been wallowing in self-pity for weeks. Perhaps Dunnigan was right, it was time to move on and prove to himself and everyone else that he was still the same man he had been before the shooting. Maybe he'd walk again, maybe not, but he sure as hell could use his brains and education to make Dunnigan, and himself, wealthy men.

First, he'd prepare himself for any other encounters such as the one at the saloon. Drew opened a lower desk drawer and pulled out two Remington double-barreled derringers. Each held two .41 caliber bullets. He placed the guns in custom designed holsters, secured at his waist, that he could cross-draw. They weren't as powerful as his Colt Peacemaker, but they'd do the job.

He leaned forward and began to review the papers on his desk. A fleeting image kept disrupting his thoughts. A memory so vague that he tried to force it to the surface. Drew's mind wandered back to the saloon and the man who had hovered not five feet away, ready for any command that Ira Walsh dispensed.

Drew's eyes had drifted to Connor, the man who had been one of those who transported him back to the office. Tall, lean, with broad shoulders, and the look of a man used to handling difficult situations.

But Drew's gaze had frozen on his features. The face, coloring, all were familiar. Jet black hair, moss green eyes, and squared jaw. He'd seen those eyes before. Drew sank into his chair and tried to remember where but his efforts went unrewarded. It would come. The memory of where he'd seen Connor before would surface and when it did, Drew knew it would be significant.

Chapter Two

Fire Mountain, Arizona Territory

"Any word, Niall?" Aunt Alicia had asked the same question every week when her oldest nephew stepped into the house from his trip into town.

"No, nothing." Niall's frustration wasn't lost on the others in the room. His brother, Jamie, sat holding the newest addition to the MacLaren clan, Caleb, while his wife, Torie, worked in the kitchen.

Will MacLaren, one of the youngest brothers, had just walked in from the barn and taken a seat on the divan. He and Amanda Taylor had married only a couple of weeks before, but Will's thoughts had been on his twin brother, Drew, for most of the time since he'd returned to Fire Mountain.

"One of us should go to Denver and find out what's going on," Jamie said.

"I'll go," Will said. "It's my fault he's still in Denver and not here with the family."

"Don't say that, Will. We all know this has everything to do with Drew's decision to help you and Amanda's family in Cold Creek. We all know you feel responsible, but Drew did what he felt he had to do, as did Jamie. No use wasting time on guilt," Aunt Alicia scolded him. "Besides, I've already made up my mind that I'm going."

"What?" Niall and Jamie spoke in unison.

"You heard me. I've already packed my trunks and plan to leave on the train north tomorrow."

"Alone? You plan to travel to Denver alone and just show up at Drew's home?" Niall asked.

"And why not? I'm his aunt. The woman who raised him and the rest of you three, as I recall." Her crisp voice echoed through the large living room. "However, I plan to stop in Cold Creek and visit Amanda's family on my way to Denver. I sent a message off to Eleanor and Grant Taylor last week. They replied with an invitation to stay as long as I want." She smiled at the way she'd gone around her nephews to make sure her plans remained her own, at least until she was sure she would make the trip.

"And you never thought to discuss this with us?" Niall asked from where he stood, leaning against one wall, his arms crossed over his broad chest.

"I knew you'd just try to talk me out of it, or plan to come with me, Niall. This is a trip I need to make. Besides, it will only take a day to reach Great Valley, where Grant will meet me. I'll stay with the Taylor's a few days before visiting Drew. I'm actually looking forward to the trip."

Niall's wife, Kate, walked into the room with Torie in time to overhear the final part of the conversation. Will's wife, Amanda, stepped in to stand next to them. The three looked at each other then back to Alicia.

"Of course you should go, Aunt Alicia," Kate said, ignoring the scowl on Niall's face. "You never travel anymore and the trip will do you good. The Taylor ranch sounds wonderful and it was obvious you and Eleanor Taylor got along well. I know it's been a long time since you've been to Denver. It may also put your mind at ease as to Drew's condition. Perhaps you'll be the one to persuade him to come home."

"I don't know about putting my mind at ease," Alicia responded, "but at least I can speak with the doctors and find out what Drew's future looks like. Caleb McCauley has done research in the area, actually worked with patients suspected of having temporary paralysis. Caleb says there's no real diagnosis except that no apparent reason for the paralysis can be found. He says it can last for weeks or months, then one day the patient starts to get feeling back."

Caleb McCauley had taken over the medical practice from the town's long-time doctor. Jamie and Torie had named their second son after him. He'd arrived in Fire Mountain the same day as Niall's wife, Kate Garner, and the town sheriff, Sam Browning. All had been victims of a stagecoach accident.

"Are you sure about this?" Jamie asked.

"Yes, Jamie, I am sure. I don't know much about Drew's condition, but one thing I do know is that he needs family around him. People who understand him and his moods. None of you can go," she put up her hand when they started to protest. "None of you *should* go right now. Too much is going on. I'm the best choice."

Niall, Jamie, and Will knew she was right even though they didn't like it. They also understood that once she'd made up her mind, there wasn't a person on earth who could stop her.

******

Cold Creek, Colorado

"Alicia, it's so good to see you!" Eleanor Taylor walked onto the front porch and down the few steps to hug their guest. "We are so pleased to have you here."

"Believe me, Eleanor, I'm very happy to be here." The women looped arms and walked into the house, leaving Grant and one of his men to bring in the trunks.

"Let's get you settled and rested. Supper will be ready by the time you come down stairs. I'm anxious to hear how Amanda's doing and what your plans are while in Denver." Eleanor was more than a little curious about Alicia's trip. Drew had been staying at their ranch, helping them rid the area of a gang of rustlers, when he was shot. They owed him a great deal.

Supper was a grand meal. Eleanor had gone overboard to prepare dishes from her native England, and Alicia had enjoyed everything.

15

Amanda's sister, Tessa, and brother, Joey, had joined them along with their long-time foreman, Jake. Alicia had caught them up on Amanda and Will, how happy they were, and what a great addition Amanda was to the MacLaren family. Then the conversation turned to Drew.

"Has he written to you at all?" Eleanor asked.

"Only at first, before Amanda came to Fire Mountain. All other messages have come from Louis Dunnigan. They've been informative, but I need to hear what's happening from Drew, not from his boss."

"Has Mr. Dunnigan expressed any concerns for Drew or told you about his progress?" This came from Tess, Amanda's sister, who was approaching twenty. She and Drew had formed a special bond while he'd been at the ranch, a bond she'd shared with few people, and no other men outside her family.

"Not really. Just that Drew still has no feeling in either of his legs."

The table fell silent as each person reflected on the strapping young attorney and rancher who'd helped them rid the area of cattle thieves. He'd touched each of their lives, but none more than Tess's.

"I thought I'd rest here a few days then take the railroad on to Denver. He doesn't know I'm coming but Louis did mention in his messages that there are three guest rooms at Drew's home and several at Dunnigan's. Of course I plan to stay with my nephew."

Grant had remained silent for most of the meal. He felt responsible for Drew's injury even though no one else blamed him. "It's a few hours to Denver by train. Do you have help once you arrive? If not, I'd be happy to send one of my hands with you or go myself—just until you get settled at Drew's."

Alicia appeared to consider the idea for only a moment. "Thank you, Grant, but I'm sure I'll do just fine."

"I'll go."

All eyes shifted toward the quiet voice but no one else spoke.

"I mean, if you would like some company, Mrs. MacLaren."

Amanda had spoken with Alicia a couple of times about her sister, Tess, and Tessa's friendship with Drew. Amanda had never said it, but Alicia had gotten the impression that Tessa's feelings for Drew were much stronger than the young woman wanted to admit.

"Why Tessa, I'd love to have you join me, if it's all right with your parents?" Alicia glanced at Grant and Eleanor to judge their approval.

"I think it's a marvelous idea," Eleanor replied. "Tess loves to travel and she's only been through Denver a couple of times when on her way to visit her aunt and uncle in Chicago."

"Then it's settled. But I'll expect you to call me Aunt Alicia and not Mrs. MacLaren." Alicia smiled at the young woman's expectant face.

"Thank you, Mrs...I mean, Aunt Alicia. You don't know what this means to me."

But Alicia thought she did.

Chapter Three

Denver, Colorado

The associate circled the darkened building twice before opening a back door and slipping through. It was Sunday, just past midnight. The deserted streets were muddy from recent rain. He kicked his boots against the wall to loosen some of the caked dirt, then pushed his coat behind the handle of his revolver, exposing it for quick access. Even though he'd yet to encounter anyone else in this part of the building, he wouldn't take any chances.

He made his way through the basement to a hidden door. It opened without a sound, exposing a staircase that few knew existed. The area was pitch black but he knew the way by heart and proceeded with caution up the narrow stairwell. Gun drawn, he worked his way to the top floor of the building and stopped, listening. When he was satisfied that no unwanted guests were in the office, he opened the door and peered inside. The only occupant was the one he sought.

"No one saw you?" the occupant asked.

"What do you think?" the associate responded. He'd done this same thing for weeks without anyone suspecting, yet his boss on the other side of the desk always asked.

"What have you learned?" The occupant of the desk had not looked up from the papers he scanned.

He's a confident son of a bitch, the associate thought. "He's careful of what he says in front others. None of his people know all the details on any of his businesses. On the surface, he appears to be a legitimate businessman, but I agree with you. Something isn't right. He's too secretive—too vague with his orders. I did find what may be another set of books. They were in his wall safe along with a list of what appear to be names."

"Appear to be?"

"They're written in a code. It'll take time to figure it out."

"What do you think you'll find?" The boss looked up for the first time. His razor sharp gaze pierced his visitor.

"Perhaps what we need to finish this job."

Satisfied with the answer, the boss glanced back down at his papers. "What do you need from me?"

"The best decoder available. He's in Baltimore but would come out here if I asked."

"Ask him." The boss stood from his desk, grabbed the overcoat hanging on a rack, and slipped it on. He followed the same procedure at the end of each visit—an obvious dismissal.

The associate turned, opened the door to the staircase, and left the way he had come.

******

20

Connor walked into Ira Walsh's office and plunked down in one of the empty chairs that faced the desk. Walsh stood with his back to his newest—but perhaps most important—hired hand. Connor hadn't been with him long, but he'd been recommended by a business contact that Ira had known for a long time. The one irritant to Ira was that Connor did not use a last name. No one seemed to know it. But Connor was a man with connections who got results, and didn't care much about how he got them.

Ira stared out the window to the street below at the constant march of horses, buggies, and wagons. It was early winter, but commerce never seemed to slow down in the booming city of Denver. Everyone was there for a reason—land, money, power, a new start—and everyone arrived from somewhere else.

"Any news on the Widow Bierdan?" Ira asked Connor.

"It's only been a few weeks since her husband died, but yes, I hear she has spoken of selling the ranch." Eloise had moved out from the East to marry Gordon Bierdan, a man twenty years her senior. Most of the good ranch hands had left after her husband's death. Connor figured it wouldn't be long before Ira would send someone to Cold Creek to negotiate a sale by whatever means available.

"And the ranch on the other side? The Langdon spread?"

"He's struggling. Grant Taylor has shown an interest in both the Bierdan and Langdon ranches, but I've heard of no offers. It would be a sizable investment for Taylor. He'd need to borrow heavily." Connor threw this last out more to gauge Walsh's reaction than as a statement of truth.

"Which could play in our favor," Walsh said as he stroked his mustache. "If he doesn't have the men or capital to take on two additional ranches, he'd still need Bierdan's place for easy access to the Langdon land. If nothing else, Taylor could go after the widow's property for the timber."

What Walsh said was true. Gordon Bierdan's ranch had supported him and his wife but there had never been enough money to expand. Sixty percent of the land was mountainous, with miles of excellent timber but little area for grazing. Gordon hadn't had the vision to see the goldmine he held in lumber but Grant Taylor had. Unfortunately, Bierdan's pursuit of vengeance against perceived wrongs by Taylor had tainted his judgment and ultimately lead to his death. No, Ira's partner in the "cattle relocation business," as Ira preferred to call it, had failed. Now he was left to expand his wealth and holdings without the deceased rancher.

Thinking it over, Ira believed Bierdan's death had been the best possible outcome. Cattle rustling on a large scale could be profitable—had funded most of Ira's operations—but was drawing more attention from the likes of Tom Horn and other Range Detectives. It was time to expand his existing businesses, such as the acquisition of land.

"Have you confirmed Dunnigan's interest in the land?" Walsh asked.

"He's still as interested as you are in the Cold Creek area. Has had his attorney, Drew MacLaren, send correspondence asking for a meeting once Mrs. Bierdan is over her mourning."

"Yes, our crippled patron." Ira knew of the MacLarens, and knew what had happened to Louis Dunnigan's attorney in the Cold Creek shootout. He'd known almost from the day it had happened.

"Send a message to Mrs. Bierdan. Express my interest in her property and ask that she not accept any other offers until I've had a chance to present my terms. Let her know that I will be quite generous if she decides to sell to me."

"Will you be the one handling the negotiations?"

"Yes, but from a distance for as long as possible. I may have someone ride ahead, scout out the situation, and learn if there are others interested in her land besides Dunnigan and Taylor. One can never be too careful. Isn't that right, Conner?"

Connor raised his eyebrows, but nodded, then shut the office door behind him.

******

"Excuse me?"

Connor looked down at the pretty young woman who stood before him. "May I help you?"

"I hope so. We've just arrived on the train and are looking for this address." Tessa Taylor held out the worn piece of paper.

Connor scanned the address, then paused at the name written at the bottom. *Interesting.* "Yes, I do know this address and would be pleased if you'd allow me to accompany you and ...?"

"My aunt. Well, she's not actually my aunt. She's Mr. MacLaren's." Tessa nodded toward a woman who stood a few feet away on the train platform. The woman looked to be in her fifties. Her brown hair was streaked with gray and pulled into a neat bun, all tucked under a wide bonnet. She stood ramrod straight and her eyes widened a little as they locked on the man speaking with Tessa.

Connor's gaze lingered on the older woman for a few moments before returning to the young lady. "I'd be happy to escort you and your aunt to Mr. MacLaren's. I'm Connor." He tipped his hat to Tessa.

"Pleased to meet you Mr. Connor," Tessa began.

"Just Connor, ma'am."

"Well, all right then, Connor. I'm Tessa Taylor and this is Mrs. Alicia MacLaren," she responded as they walked over to stand beside Alicia.

"Mrs. MacLaren." Connor made a slight bow to Alicia.

"Connor is it?" Alicia continued to scrutinize the stranger, not sure if she felt grateful or wary. There was something familiar about him. "You know the address. Does that mean you know my nephew?"

"I have had the pleasure. Now, if you're ready, I'll see to your trunks and we'll be on our way."

"Is Mr. MacLaren a relative of yours, Miss Taylor?" Connor asked as a way to spend the time while the buggy moved along.

"No. A friend. He visited us not long back and helped us with some problems at our ranch." Tessa glanced at the handsome man. He wore his tan colored greatcoat over black slacks, white shirt, and black vest. His head was shielded from the sun by a black western style hat that was common in this part of the country.

"Tessa decided to accompany me, and since she knows my nephew—was present when he was injured—it seemed like a good idea," Alicia added. She didn't know why she felt the need to elaborate, but something about Connor made her want to prolong the conversation, see if something he said would help her figure out why he seemed familiar.

"I see," was all the reply she got.

It wasn't long before Alicia and Tessa were walking up the stone steps to Drew's home, leaving Connor to guard the buggy. Tessa smoothed her skirt and tried to force down a case of intense nerves that had assaulted her when they pulled in front of the house. She took a deep breath as Alicia knocked once, then twice.

The door flew open and a deep voice greeted them. "May I help you?"

Tessa blinked at the tall, mature gentleman who answered the door. But he was no old man. He wore tan slacks with a white high-collared shirt, thin black tie, and tan vest. His coat was black with long tails that draped to within a few inches of the back of his knees. The hand that held open the door was large with thick fingers. He stood at least six-feet-six-inches tall and appeared to be solid muscle. There was a thin, jagged scar that ran from his left ear to the edge of his mouth.

"I believe you can," Alicia answered. "We're looking for my nephew, Drew MacLaren. We were given this address."

"Ah, Mrs. Alicia MacLaren, correct? Yes, Mr. MacLaren speaks of you and his brothers often. I'm Mr. Jericho, his manservant. And you are?" He looked at Tessa.

"This is Tessa Taylor, Mr. Jericho. She is a friend of my nephew's." Alicia answered when it became apparent that Tess was still locked in her perusal of the large man.

"Pleased to meet you, Miss Taylor. Mr. MacLaren is still at his office but I'm sure he'd want you to make yourselves comfortable. I'll inform him of your arrival as soon as I see to your bags."

Alicia and Tessa walked into the spacious front room as Mr. Jericho continued outside and crossed the few steps to the carriage.

"Connor."

"Jericho," Connor responded.

"You know who the women are, correct?"

Connor nodded as he lifted the trunks off the wagon. "How is MacLaren doing?"

"I work his legs every day and make sure he soaks in a hot bath each night, as the doctor recommended, but nothing yet. He's frustrated but hasn't given up."

Connor settled on the carriage seat and took hold of the reins. "Let me know if there's any improvement."

******

"How are you doing, Mr. MacLaren? Any feeling at all?" Doctor Garland lifted one of Drew's legs and began to poke, attempting to illicit a response.

"Nothing."

Jericho had been working on Drew's legs each day and night, applying the liniments and oils the doctor had prescribed, working them into his useless muscles. A couple of times Drew had thought he'd felt a twinge, but that was over a week ago, and nothing since.

"Helen, help me turn Mr. MacLaren over," Doctor Garland instructed the middle aged woman who stood by the door. Drew had seen her on each visit, but she'd always remained silent. "Everything has healed fine. Not as much scarring as I'd expect. The doctor who did the surgery had a skilled hand. You were fortunate," Garland said as they rolled Drew to his back.

"Fortunate?" Drew's sarcasm escaped before he could contain it.

"Yes, young man, fortunate. You could be dead." The doctor turned a stern yet sympathetic gaze at his patient. He wouldn't say it, but the doctor had a strong feeling that Drew would beat this and walk again. Few patients worked as hard at recovery as this young attorney. "As it stands now, there is still hope that feeling will return and you'll be able to walk again, if not like before then at least with a cane. It's only been a few weeks, well within the timeframe of temporary paralysis."

"Yeah, I suppose you're right, but I expected to be up and about by now, not being taken care of by a manservant and numerous others." Drew shook his head in disgust. "Is there anything else that Mr. Jericho or I can do to move my healing along?"

"You're doing all that can be done at this point. I've read everything I can get my hands on and have corresponded with specialists back East. Be patient, continue with the treatments, and let nature take its course."

Doc Garland was a good man, used by most of the influential residents of Denver, and considered the best in this region. Drew knew he was getting the finest treatment available, but that still didn't relieve his frustration.

"I'll do my best, Doc. I'm just damn tired of sitting in this chair." Drew's face reddened a little when he glanced at the nurse. "Sorry, ma'am," he added.

"No need to apologize, Mr. MacLaren. You're doing much better than you know and handling it well. You're much stronger than you realize. I've seen patients throw fits of frustration and others give up completely. They don't even try. You aren't either of those types. If anyone can walk again, you can." Her smile was broad and her tone conveyed that she believed what she said.

"Thank you, ma'am. I'll try to remember that."

******

"The message says another of the Bierdan ranch hands quit. She can't have more than seven or eight men left." Drew set down the piece of paper with the latest update from Frank Alts, their contact in Cold Creek.

Alts was a former Colorado Ranger. He'd helped clear out the rustlers at the Taylor Ranch, and had been there the day Drew was shot. Alts had already made up his mind to quit the Rangers, find another job in Denver, and raise his son, Aaron. The death of the previous sheriff had left an opening for an experienced lawman, and the people of Cold Creek had wasted no time offering the position to Frank, along with a house and monthly account at the general store.

"And the Langdon ranch?" Louis asked.

"Frank says he's struggling. Langdon was a farmer back East and is trying to make a go of it as a cattle rancher. Frank says he works hard but just doesn't have the skills for it. It's just a matter of time."

"Do we know if Grant Taylor is interested in either of these ranches?"

"I haven't heard of it, but that doesn't mean he's not."

Louis contemplated going against Grant for the same land. It didn't sit well with him, but he was a businessman, and he wanted the Langdon and Bierdan ranches. "It's time to make an offer to both Eloise Bierdan and Langdon. You'll have to be the one to go." A knock on the door interrupted Louis.

"Excuse me, Mr. Dunnigan, Mr. MacLaren, but Mr. Jericho is outside. He says he must speak with you right away, Mr. MacLaren." Terrance stood at attention, waiting for a response.

"Please, ask him to come in, Terrance."

Drew never ceased to be amazed at Jericho's size. He filled the doorway, ducking so he wouldn't hit his head, and stood with his hands at his sides. "Mrs. Alicia MacLaren and Miss Tessa Taylor are at your house, Mr. MacLaren."

"They're here, in Denver?" Drew's brows furrowed. His surprise was apparent but he gave no indication as to whether the news pleased or angered him.

"Yes, sir. Both are resting at the house."

"Well, Drew, it appears our conversation must be put off until a more appropriate time. Go ahead and see to your guests." Louis Dunnigan excused himself as Jericho moved to assist Drew with his papers.

"Terrance," Drew called for his assistant while Jericho wheeled him to the elevator.

"Yes, Mr. MacLaren?"

"Make reservations for three at The Regency. At six. My guests are used to eating supper early."

Chapter Four

"That's enough. Anymore and you'll kill him," Luther's voice pierced the quiet night as he watched his partner, Vern, haul the bloodied man up. The others in their group stood around, unmoved by the brutality but making no effort to join in the beating.

They'd been sent to Cold Creek to encourage the men of both the Bierdan and Langdon ranches that they'd be better off working somewhere else. If words weren't enough, they'd been instructed to use whatever level of persuasion necessary to achieve the results Walsh expected, and the man's expectations were high. "Get him some water."

Clint Thayer bent over, coughing up blood as he tried to take a breath. He'd attempted to fight but couldn't handle both Luther and his partner. He was twenty-five and hoped he'd make it to twenty-six.

"So, what's your answer, Thayer?" Luther slapped Clint on the back, hard enough to pitch him forward before Luther caught his arm.

Clint straightened and stared, first at Luther, then at Vern. Luther was a brute, but Vern stood about five-foot-seven. Clint would like one more chance at both, but without the rest of their gang hanging around.

"No," Clint spat out. "I won't ride out on her." His right hand moved to the butt of his gun, but a blow to his side had him staggering. Another to his face forced him to the ground.

"Not what we want to hear, boy." Vern's hardened face focused on Clint's. He wondered how much more time they should put into this before putting a bullet in the man. The sound of approaching horses stopped his thoughts as he and Luther glanced behind them to see riders a couple hundred yards away.

"We're not done with you, Thayer. I expect the right answer from you or you'll find yourself in the same place as Dawson," Luther sneered, then mounted his horse and joined the rest of his men in escape.

Clint continued to lay on the ground, rubbing his beaten face as Luther's words rolled in his head and wondered if Dawson, another of Mrs. Bierdan's hands, had left voluntarily or was forced.

"Clint? That you?"

"Yeah, it's me, Jay." Clint pushed his battered body up as Jay walked over to help him stand.

"What the hell happened?" Stan, another of the Bierdan wranglers asked as he bent to grab Clint's dust covered hat.

"A couple of men took exception to my decision to stay at the Bierdan ranch." Clint's gaze focused on the trail taken by the retreating men. He wondered who they worked for and why it was so important to run Eloise off. "Mentioned something about Dawson, but can't say I know what they meant."

"Seen them before?" Jay asked.

"Never." Clint mounted his horse. "But, from their threats, I'm guessing they'll show up again."

******

Hard pounding at the front door interrupted Eleanor Taylor's reading. She returned the book to the table and walked to the door, grimacing at the constant hammering. She opened the door to an angry young woman, covered in dust, and breathing hard. "Hello, Eloise. Are you all right?"

"No, Eleanor, I'm not all right. I want to see your husband. Someone ordered the beating of one of my men and I want to know if he had any part in it."

Eleanor's eyes moved over Eloise Bierdan's face and saw that the woman believed what she said. "Eloise, now you know Grant would never order a beating. Never. But, let's find him so you can explain what happened." Eleanor reached for her bonnet and led Eloise toward the back corral where the men worked one of the two-year olds, a beautiful colt—black with a white blaze—much like the horse Will MacLaren had ridden when he came to help them with the rustlers.

Grant turned at their approach and started to move toward them. "Eloise, what a nice surprise," he started but wasn't allowed to finish.

"Did you order your men to beat up one of mine?" Eloise was only inches from Grant's face, hands on her hips as she glared at him.

Grant glanced at his wife, but she shook her head and looked back on Eloise.

"I have no idea what you're talking about. Who was beaten?"

"Clint Thayer. By two men. One named Vern and another named Luther."

"Never heard of them. Clint tell you what happened?"

"No, two other ranch hands did. Clint wouldn't say anything. Wouldn't answer any questions." Eloise shook her head, frustrated at Clint's lack of trust in her ability to handle unwelcome news. "Jay Bellows and Stan Clark found him last night, near Rock Creek. He spoke with them but wouldn't talk with me or my foreman."

"He said their names are Vern and Luther?"

"That's what he told Jay and Stan."

"I can tell you for a fact that I never ordered any of my men, at any time, to rough up your men." Grant leveled his gaze at Eloise.

The young woman paced a few feet away, took a deep breath, then walked back over to Grant and Eleanor. "Who would do this? Why Clint?"

"You having troubles with anyone? Threats?"

"Not anything that would warrant this." Eloise thought of the last weeks, the offers to buy her land, the insistent tone of the bank manager encouraging her to consider the offers. "I've lost a few men, but it's normal for ranch hands to move around, isn't it?"

"How many have left?" Grant had heard rumors about several men taking off and he doubted it was just for a change of location.

"Four over the last few weeks."

Grant considered that as his mind worked over the possibilities. Four was quite a number. His ranch, the Big G, would lose one, maybe two each year, but never as many as four.

"Sounds more like they're trying to send you a message. But, like most cowards, they're not talking directly to you but passing it through others by force." He turned to his foreman, Jake. "I'm riding over to the Bierdan ranch. You look after things here."

"Sure thing, Boss." Jake had been at the Big G a long time and was more a part of the family than an employee.

"Let's go, Eloise. I'm riding back with you. Maybe Clint will talk with me."

It angered Eloise to think she needed another man, from another ranch, to get the straight story from one of her own men. No one seemed to think she had a brain in her head or any ability to run a ranch, which was a constant source of irritation to the young woman. But now was not the time to let pride push away an offer of help.

"Thanks, Grant. I'd appreciate you telling me and my foreman anything you learn from Clint."

******

It was noon when Grant rode up with Eloise. The Bierdan wranglers were just finishing dinner and getting ready to ride out.

Jefferson Burnham, the foreman, walked over to shake Grant's hand. He was a tall, rangy, Southern man. He'd fought for the South in the War Between the States, but moved west a few years afterwards to find peace, at least that's what he'd told Eloise Bierdan when he'd hired on two months ago. Jeff was soft-spoken, had considerable experience, and the men respected him.

"Grant, what brings you out here?" Jeff asked after a quick glance at his boss, Eloise.

"Heard about Clint and asked Mrs. Bierdan if I could speak with him. Try to find out what happened."

"He sure doesn't want to speak with me about it. Don't know why," Jeff shook his head. He had a good relationship with the men, but Clint had closed him out of this discussion. "He's in the barn. I'll get him for you."

"No need." Grant walked toward the large barn. He spotted Clint at the back in one of the stalls, grooming a young mare. He stood a few feet away, waiting for Clint to acknowledge him, not wanting to spook the young horse.

Clint ran a hand from the withers, along the back, and down one thigh. He had a soothing hand that gentled the horse. "What can I do for you, Mr. Taylor?"

"Nice mare. Had her long?"

"Mrs. Bierdan bought her from Langdon a few weeks ago. Jeff spotted her and spoke with Mr. Langdon. The next we knew, we had ourselves a beautiful horse." Clint walked out of the stall, securing the gate as he turned to Grant. "You here to chat or have something on your mind?"

"Last night. I'd like to know what happened, what you remember."

Jeff had followed Grant into the barn, hoping to learn the truth of the bruises and cuts on his ranch hand.

Clint had thought it over while working with the mare. He needed to talk to Jeff about the threats. The foreman had a right to know. Might as well tell it once to both men.

"Not much to tell. Two men I'd spoken with in the saloon a week ago rode up to me last night with a group of other men. Asked if I'd thought about what they'd suggested. I told them I had and I'd be staying at the Bierdan ranch. Next I knew they'd pulled me to the ground. I got in a number of good punches, but the one was too big. He landed a blow to my jaw, then the other one took over. Didn't stop until the big guy pulled him off me."

"And the others?" Jeff asked.

Clint shrugged. "Stood and watched. Guess they knew the odds were already against me."

"Mrs. Bierdan said their names are Luther and Vern. That right?" Grant asked.

"That's what they told me."

"So what did they ask you to think over?"

Clint punched both hands in his pockets and looked at the straw covered dirt floor. He didn't want to stir up trouble, which he'd always been pretty good at. He wanted to stay on at the Bierdan ranch, get beyond his reckless past and thoughtless actions. This was the first place that felt solid, secure.

"Look, Mr. Taylor. I don't want to stir up more trouble for Mrs. Bierdan. She's got enough to deal with. She doesn't need to concern herself with my problems."

"Is that how you see this, Clint? As just your problem? Perhaps you're forgetting that she's lost four men in the past few weeks. She told me three rode out, and one just disappeared. Ever think their leaving wasn't voluntary?"

Clint looked up. He shifted his gaze from Grant to Jeff, paced a few steps away, grabbed a halter, then walked back to join the two men.

"They asked me to ride out. Offered me three hundred bucks if I did."

"That's a lot of money. I'm guessing almost a year's wage for you." Grant knew what it took to get a good wrangler, and from what he'd heard, Clint was better than good.

"About right."

"And you declined. Why?"

"I like it here, Mr. Taylor. Jeff's a good foreman and Mrs. Bierdan is trying to make this place work. She's already lost enough. The woman needs a break, not more men letting her down."

Grant mulled this over for a minute. "You'd recognize them if you saw them again?"

"The two for sure."

"Good. Let's ride into town. That is, if you can spare him, Jeff?" Grant asked the foremen who nodded in agreement. "We'll talk with Sheriff Alts and give him a description. At least make him aware of the threats."

******

Denver, Colorado

Jericho helped Drew through the front door and into the large front living area of his home. A wonderful aroma wrapped around him and he smiled at the knowledge that his Aunt Alicia had already made herself at home. Stew. He knew it well. He was just approaching the kitchen when his aunt walked out to greet him.

"Aunt Alicia. I'm so glad you came," Drew said, and meant every word. Her arms wrapped around him and squeezed as she placed a kiss on his cheek. A tear slid down her cheek but she wiped it away before he could notice.

"You knew I'd never be able to stay in Fire Mountain with the knowledge that you'd been hurt. So here I am, and I plan to stay a little while if you have the room." Her first look at Drew in the wheel chair had jolted her. Even though she had thought she was prepared, the sight of her handsome nephew, forced to sit in a chair all day, rocked her.

"As long as you want, Aunt Alicia."

"And me?" The soft voice came from behind him.

He closed his eyes and took a slow, deep breath. Even though she visited his dreams and thoughts, he hadn't planned to see her again unless he could walk. He wasn't what she needed, not in his current state. Drew turned the chair towards her. She was even more beautiful then he remembered.

"Hello, Tess." His eyes moved over her features. Her dark brown hair was pulled up into a twist. Soft, caramel-brown eyes settled on him. He could just see the sprinkling of freckles across her nose. She'd told him once that more appeared each year and she'd just accepted it. He'd laughed and told her he liked them—and he did.

"Hello, Drew." She walked forward to stand a few feet away. "I hope it's all right that I've come." Her voice was unsteady, her nervousness apparent.

No, it's not all right. "Of course. I'm glad to see you." *You look beautiful.* He cleared his throat. "Did you have a safe trip?"

"Oh, yes, it was wonderful—so majestic and breathtaking. Sometimes we forget how beautiful some things are when we haven't seen them in a while."

Drew drank in the sight of her. "Yes we do, Tess. We certainly do."

He tore his gaze from Tess and look up at his aunt. "You've found rooms? Unpacked?"

"Yes, we're all set. Mr. Jericho was wonderful when we arrived. He handled the surprise quite well," Alicia glanced at the tall, brawny man who now stood a few feet to the side. He returned her smile.

"Good. I've made reservations at six o'clock for supper at The Regency, if that's agreeable. I think you'll both like it."

Alicia wondered at the sudden change in Drew. His words were stilted, almost formal. "We can do that, but I've made your favorite supper."

Drew wanted the protection of a large restaurant, not the intimacy the family dinner offered, but he loved his aunt and would do whatever she wanted. "Of course. Mr. Jericho, please send word to The Regency that we're cancelling tonight?"

Jericho nodded before walking outside.

"Does that mean he must ride to the restaurant?" Tess asked.

"On most nights there are one or two boys milling around this area. He can usually find one he can pay to run an errand. If not, he'll go himself. It's not far." He didn't look at Tess, but rolled his chair toward the kitchen.

Louis Dunnigan had made several modifications. Work tables were lowered as were the counters. Open shelves replaced cupboards below the counters and a sink had been placed at the perfect height for Drew's use. Another was at a standard height as Jericho often did the cooking. Dunnigan had told Drew everything would be changed back when he was able to walk again.

"It smells wonderful." Drew inhaled and smiled at the memories. Alicia had made stew at least once every week when he was growing up. It had always been his favorite. That and her pies. He looked toward the counter and, sure enough, one sat cooling not three feet away. "How did you manage a pie? Did I keep you waiting that long?"

"Not at all," Alicia replied as she took down plates and found utensils. "Eleanor packed a bag of items she thought I'd need. That woman is a marvel."

******

Drew sat in bed, reading, trying to focus. The food had been excellent. Catching up on the family had been the highlight. Will and Amanda's wedding and the birth of Jamie and Torie's second son, Caleb. But Drew hung his head as other parts of the supper conversation played through his mind.

Tess had taken over many of Amanda's responsibilities at the Big G. She was learning and growing, preparing for the day she'd run the horse breeding program at the ranch. She admitted she had a long way to go, but her enthusiasm showed in her face, her smile, her eyes. She was excelling, doing what she loved, and he was languishing, stuck in his damn chair.

He threw the book he'd been reading across the room. Why had she come? He didn't need or want her here. Aunt Alicia, yes, but not Tess. He needed to concentrate on his recovery, walking again. He couldn't do that with her consuming his thoughts, her image flashing through his mind. She couldn't stay.

First he'd make arrangements for her return to Cold Creek, then he'd tell her.

******

The following morning Drew arrived in the kitchen to find his aunt and Jericho laughing, working together to prepare breakfast. He rarely saw Jericho relaxed, joking like he was now.

"Good morning, Drew." Tess came up behind him and placed a hand on his arm, feeling a slight tensing of his muscles. "Looks like those two are enjoying themselves."

Drew saw her eyes sparkle as she watched them. He'd felt the jolt the instant Tess had touched him. Her soft voice flowed over him as he glanced up to see her amused face taking in the scene in the kitchen.

Jericho wore an apron similar to Alicia's, with slim straps that went over his shoulders. Jericho's ties hung loose—his girth just too much for the shorter ties. Alicia made another comment which caused Jericho to laugh again. It was a deep, rolling sound.

"May we join you?" Tess asked.

Alicia glanced over her shoulder. "Of course. We've just finished. Hope you're both hungry."

Drew backed up the chair and spun the wheels as much as they'd allow, then headed toward the large dining room. "Starving. Come on, Tess. We'll get settled at the table while the cooks finish up."

Tess looked around. The house was quite large for just Drew and Jericho. "It's such a nice place, Drew. Mr. Dunnigan set it up so well."

"He's been more than generous. This is what I found when I came back to Denver. I'm guessing he had Terrance select all the furnishings as they're more east coast than Colorado, but that's fine. I didn't have to figure anything out. It was already finished and ready for me, including appointments with the best doctor in the area."

"I guess it makes the accommodations in Cold Creek seem rather pale."

Drew looked up at Tess. "I don't understand?"

"Well, you have this wonderful home all setup for you, Mr. Jericho to see to your every need here, Terrance to make sure you have what you require at the office, a job you love, and Miss Dunnigan is obviously quite fond of you. I suppose nothing in Arizona or Colorado would seem sufficient after this."

Drew studied her for a long moment. He had every intention of leaving Denver, going back to Fire Mountain, and working with his brothers. Even if he never walked again he knew there would always be a place for him at home. But he would

45

walk again, and when he did, he would ask Tess to marry him, not Patricia Dunnigan.

"None of this is what I want, Tess. I'm grateful for it, but it's not what I dream about."

"What do you dream about?"

"Ok, here you go," Jericho said as he placed heaping plates in front of Drew and Tess. "I made the eggs. I checked the flapjacks, and must admit that your Aunt Alicia does a darn fine job, Drew."

The moment broken, Drew tore his gaze away from Tess. "Yes, Mr. Jericho, she does."

******

Two days had passed since she and Aunt Alicia had arrived in Denver.

Tess pulled the brush through her long hair and separated it into three strands. It had been the same routine every night since she'd first met him and every night after he'd left Cold Creek. Braid her hair, crawl under the covers, and think of Drew. She'd hoped her constant thoughts of him would diminish once they'd seen each other again. Perhaps her memories were flawed, her attraction to him temporary. But it had only gotten worse. Now his image haunted her every minute of every day.

He'd barely had time for her since she and Alicia had arrived. They ate meals together, made small talk, but after that first morning, the easy banter they'd shared before was gone. He had closed up as if he'd erected a wall around himself.

She mourned the loss. Drew had become important to her in the brief time he'd been at the ranch. Although he'd never expressed it, she'd thought he had feelings for her also, but apparently she'd been wrong. The words her sister, Amanda, had said the day of her wedding to Will MacLaren flashed through her mind.

"You go as a friend, not as someone expecting anything from him. His focus is on walking and I'll bet he could use a friend, someone he knows wants nothing from him but to help. That's you, Tess, not Louis Dunnigan and not Patricia. Go to Denver, be his friend. You'll never know what could be until you take the chance."

But she hadn't gone right away. Alicia's decision to visit her nephew had provided Tess with the push she needed to see Drew again. Now she was in Denver, in his house, three doors from his room, and she'd yet to make a move that would express what she felt. Well, that was about to change. She'd find a way to get him alone, talk with him like they used to, and start to be the friend she had been in Cold Creek.

Chapter Five

Cold Creek, Colorado

Grant and Clint walked into the sheriff's office as Frank was pouring a cup of coffee. "Would you gentlemen like some?" He nodded at the cup in his hand. Both men declined. "Looks like you had some trouble, Clint. Have a seat and tell me what brings you here." Frank studied the man's battered face and waited.

"Clint, why don't you tell Frank what happened last night," Grant said.

Frank sat and listened without interrupting, but his mind worked double-time as some pieces started to come together. When Clint was finished, Frank set down his cup and stood. "Come with me." He grabbed his hat and opened the door for the two men.

"Where we headed?" Grant asked as they made their way down the dusty boardwalk. The winds had started, stirring up sand. Clint watched as a tumbleweed made its way down the street, bouncing from one spot to the next.

"Through here." Frank opened the back door to the doctor's office, then led them to another locked room. He pulled a key from a wall cabinet, unlocked the door, and pushed it open. The room smelled of death. Inside were two tables. One appeared to contain a body, covered by a course sheet. Frank walked up and pulled the sheet down. He looked at Clint. "Recognize him?"

Clint looked at the corpse then quickly pulled back. "Yes. It's Dave Dawson. He worked for Mrs. Bierdan. What happened?"

"Don't know. A cowhand found his body a couple of miles from town. Two bullet holes in him."

"Murdered," Grant said.

"Appears so." Frank turned to Clint. "Could be the same men that attacked you last night may have been involved in this. Let's go back to the office. You can tell me everything you know about Luther, Vern, and the men who rode with them."

******

Denver, Colorado

"What's it say?" Louis Dunnigan asked after Drew had read the latest message from Frank Alts.

"One of Mrs. Bierdan's ranch hands was murdered and another threatened and beaten. Seems someone wants the Bierdan ranch enough to kill for it." Drew passed the paper across the desk.

Dunnigan read through it once, then set it down and sat back in his chair. He'd hoped to have more time to pull some things together, but the news from Alts meant a change in plans. "It's time, Drew."

"You want me to go to Cold Creek, speak to Eloise Bierdan and Warren Langdon?"

Dunnigan nodded.

"How far do I go?"

"We'll pay top dollar for the land, cattle, and horses for either place. The foreman at the Bierdan ranch can stay and some of the men. We'll buy her a house in town or wherever she wants to resettle, within reason." He stood and shoved one hand into a pocket as he walked around the desk and leaned back against it. "My guess is Langdon won't take long to accept the offer—unless he's already been approached. If that's the case, let me know who made the offer and the price." Louis thought for another moment. "May be different for the widow. If she insists on keeping the ranch, offer her a partnership where Dunnigan Enterprises receives timber rights on her land plus any access rights we'd need to move the timber. We would insist on first right of refusal if she decides to sell, but regardless, the timber rights must be written to survive any change of ownership."

"Any other help with the ranch operations if she decides to stay?"

"No." Dunnigan replied and pushed away from his desk. "Be ready to leave in two days. I'll have Terrance make the arrangements. Mr. Jericho will accompany you."

"And my aunt and Miss Taylor?"

"That's up to you."

******

It had been a long two days. After the first morning Drew had rarely been at home—there was too much to do in preparation for his trip to Cold Creek. Dunnigan commissioned a second wheelchair for the trip. Terrence worked non-stop to pull together the travel arrangements. Jericho packed what he and Drew would need for the trip. Drew worked with Henry Thompson to transition his responsibilities. The young man was new at Dunnigan, but had worked for a firm in Philadelphia before traveling west. Drew was comfortable that he'd do well with the additional workload.

It would be a full day's journey by train and carriage to Cold Creek. Drew had given his aunt and Tess the choice of waiting for him in Denver or going back. Both had made the decision to leave. Tess had mentioned something about the train ride giving them a chance to catch up.

Tess. His thoughts had rarely strayed from her since she'd arrived in Denver. His decision to send her home had fallen aside with the plans for the three of them to travel to Cold Creek together. It was a blessing. He didn't want to hurt her. She'd been the one to stay by his side those first few days after the shooting, when his brothers, Will and Jamie, had been focused on finding the man who'd shot him and returning the stolen cattle to the Big G. He and Tess had spent hours together. He liked

51

her. Hell, he more than liked her, but she deserved better than a man with useless legs. Her goal was to breed and raise the finest horse stock in Colorado. It was a dream he shared, but now might never realize. She needed someone who would pull his weight, not lean on her for support.

"Mr. Jericho has the carriage ready. Mrs. MacLaren and Miss Taylor are waiting for you outside," Terrance announced as he entered Drew's office. "The train just arrived and they're attaching the Dunnigan cars. You should arrive in Cold Creek late tonight. Are you certain you don't wish me to come along, sir?"

"Thank you, Terrence, but I'll be fine. I know the town and several people, including the sheriff. As long as I have a carriage and Mr. Jericho, I'll get around without a problem."

An hour later Aunt Alicia, Tess, and Drew settled in one of the opulent private cars, and headed west through the middle of Colorado. It was some of the most spectacular scenery he'd ever seen. No matter how many times he saw it, he never tired of the view. Tall peaks rose on both sides of the train during much of the journey. A wild, fast-moving river partnered with the moving machinery for much of the trip. He sat back, closed his eyes, and thought about the last few days.

He spent time thinking about Dunnigan's daughter and her desire to marry. Even though a relationship with Tess was out of the question, a union with Patricia wasn't what he wanted. He'd scheduled a meeting with Patricia before leaving Denver to tell her of his decision.

She'd been devastated by the news that he'd decided not to pursue an engagement. She'd thought they fit very well, while he thought two people couldn't be less suited for marriage.

Patricia smoothed her custom fitted dress then clasped her hands in her lap. "I know I met Tessa only once, in Cold Creek, but she simply does not seem to be the type of woman who would interest you. She's a ranch woman with little understanding of city life. You have an education and are sophisticated. How could you possibly choose someone like her?"

Drew looked away. Patricia was correct but in a different way than what she meant. While she was glamorous in her curls and stylish gowns, he found her to be stilted, detached, with little understanding of those outside her circle. Tess was genuine with a deep caring of those around her. Her lovely but plain clothes fit well and highlighted her soft curves. The image of that softness brought heat to his face and a desire that grew with each thought of her.

He'd sat with Patricia for hours, talking of her dreams, which were few, and what each wanted from a marriage. If possible, he planned to have several children and raise them at the MacLaren ranch in Fire Mountain, Arizona territory. He'd teach them to ride, raise cattle, breed horses, and shoot. Although Patricia listened politely to everything he said, it was the last that got her full attention.

"But, Drew, how can you even think of teaching children how to shoot after what happened to you? Guns are dangerous and have no place in a civilized house."

"Guns are a necessary fact of life on a ranch, as essential as food and water. It would be foolish not to teach my children how to use a gun and handle a rifle."

"Well, I don't understand it. There will be no guns in my house," she stated in a firm tone.

"And that's the major reason why we don't suit. Our lives don't match, not in any way."

After a while, Patricia calmed down and her protests ceased. Drew knew the moment she accepted his decision that they weren't meant to marry. She was stubborn but also smart. The woman knew how to back off graciously. He admired her for it but he wouldn't miss her demanding nature or selfish ways. What a contrast she was to Tess.

Tess loved horses, reading, and her family. It was hard for her to open up and trust people, but she had a big heart, a gentle touch, and beautiful smile. How he cherished that smile. She and his aunt had been quiet during the trip, each enjoying the scenery, reading, or keeping to their own thoughts. That was fine. He'd needed the time alone to gather his thoughts.

"May I join you?" Tess stood beside his chair, ducking to look out the train window. "It's almost too beautiful for words." She watched the fast moving river that twisted and turned, following the railroad's path.

Drew gestured to the seat across from him. "That's one of my favorite sights. The river flows most of the way from just outside of Denver to Great Valley."

Tess settled across from him.

"I wish there'd been more time in Denver for you to see the city," Drew said, and meant it. "You and Aunt Alicia didn't see much during your stay."

"That's fine. We came to see you, not the town. At least that's why I came." Tess didn't look at him, keeping her eyes focused on the rushing river below.

Drew watched her, wondering how much to say, or if he should say anything. There was still so much uncertainty in his life.

"Mother and Father will be glad to see you, as will everyone else. We have a mare ready to foal. You'll be there to watch it." Tess's eyes met his. "You've talked about how much you like watching new foals entering the world. We're hoping for a colt."

"I still plan to return to Fire Mountain someday, work with Will and my brothers to grow the horse breeding program." Drew took a deep breath, letting the air out slowly. "Tess, I don't know how long it will take these legs to start working again or if I'll ever walk. I'm trying. Each day it's like I'm starting over again. I still have no feeling. They're just these useless limbs dragging me down, forcing a life in this chair. It's not a life I want to bring anyone else into."

Tess's heart quickened. She wondered if he was speaking of her, but realized that no, he must be speaking of Patricia Dunnigan—working so hard to walk again so that he could be with the young woman in Denver. Her hopes plunged.

"We're coming up to Great Valley, Mr. MacLaren. There should be a carriage waiting for you."

Drew pulled his gaze away from Tess to look at the conductor. "Thank you." He wanted to speak more with Tess, but now wasn't the time.

Drew found he was looking forward to seeing the doctor in Cold Creek again. He was the one who'd operated on Drew to remove the bullet and had encouraged him not to give up when feeling had not returned within a few days.

Drew had not given up on walking. It had now been several weeks. The doctors in Denver had told him they'd seen people go as long as five to six months before feeling returned and they regained the use of arms or legs. It was rare, but possible. That's all he asked—for it to be possible. Drew suspected the Cold Creek doctor knew more about paralysis than he'd shared. Drew hoped the doctor would consent to help him walk again.

******

"Welcome back, Drew." Grant Taylor extended a hand to help Drew from the carriage and into the waiting chair.

"It's good to see you, Grant. This is Mr. Jericho, my traveling companion."

Grant nodded to Jericho before turning to help Alicia and Tessa down. He pulled his daughter into a hug. She returned the hug before moving to embrace Eleanor. Although she'd only been gone a little over a week, it felt good to be home.

"How was Denver, Alicia?" Eleanor asked as they walked up the front steps.

"It's a wonderful town but much larger than I realized." Their voices faded as they walked into the house with Tess right behind.

Grant turned to Drew once he knew the women were out of range. "Not that we're not glad to see you, but what's going on that brings you to Cold Creek?"

"Louis Dunnigan heard about the troubles that Eloise Bierdan has been having and sent me out. He's had an interest in her place since before Gordon died." Drew paused to look down at his useless legs, the results of a bullet from Gordon Bierdan. He raised his eyes back up to Grant. "Dunnigan wants to see if she'll agree to sell the ranch to Dunnigan Enterprises."

"Won't be easy. That woman's determined to make it on her own. She has a new foreman, some good wranglers, and about as much stubbornness as you'll ever see." He chuckled remembering her accusation that Grant had sent men to rough up her ranch hands. She stood about five-feet-four-inches, but she had been like an angry bull that day.

"Well, I'm here to see if some type of agreement may be reached. Put something together before any more of her men leave or go missing."

"You know about that do you?" Grant was surprised to learn that the news had traveled to Denver. "Alts believes one man was murdered, but hasn't been able to find the men responsible."

"I heard. Greed and power are high motivators for a lot of men. They'll do just about anything to get what they want."

"Does that include Louis Dunnigan?" Grant had only met the man briefly when Dunnigan had come to Cold Creek to accompany Drew back to Denver after the shooting. He'd seemed honorable, but one never knew for certain.

"No. Louis Dunnigan is as honest as they come. He's no fool, but he'll walk away if a mutually acceptable agreement can't be reached. Make no mistake, he wants the Bierdan ranch, but not at the expense of human life." Drew sat back in his chair and pondered whether or not to ask his next question. In the end, it was fair to get it out in the open.

"Dunnigan is interested in the Langdon spread, also. Any thoughts on that?"

Grant's gaze drifted to the young man who'd helped him save his ranch from cattle thieves. He liked him, and suspected his youngest daughter liked him even more.

"Well, you need to know I've spoken to Langdon about his place. Made him an offer which he said he'd consider."

"I see." Drew thought as much. It made sense, even if it was further away than the Bierdan ranch. "But no offer to Eloise Bierdan?"

"No, not yet. Don't doubt that I'd like that land, Drew, but taking on both ranches right now would stretch me a little thin. I can pay cash for Langdon, but need to work with the bank on the Bierdan place. Plus, well, I just don't feel quite right going in right now, given what transpired between her husband and me." Grant's lowered voice and heavy sigh told Drew that Grant was still haunted by what had happened between the two men.

"Understandable. I hope I'm not making a mistake going there myself. Could be she'll shut the door in my face."

"Doubt she'd do that. I'd say it's worth a try. But, I wish you luck because something tells me you're going to need it."

******

Denver, Colorado

The associate made his way to the darkened building as had been the normal routine for weeks. The streets were deserted. He scanned the area to be sure no one was watching, then ducked into the basement. This time the decoder from Baltimore accompanied him. It had taken a couple of weeks but, as promised, he'd arrived to help decipher the documents his companion had uncovered.

The newcomer followed the associate up the blackened stairwell and into the office above. The boss looked up for a brief moment before indicating that both men should take seats. He stared for several moments at the decoder, looked at the associate, then back at the newcomer.

"You're related." It was a statement, not a question.

"Yes, brothers," the decoder answered. "Any problem with that?"

"No. As long you can do the work, deliver results, there's no problem. Have you seen the documents?"

"Looked them over a little before coming here. They're in code all right. Pretty sophisticated from what I could tell."

"How long will it take?"

"Won't know until I get started, which will be tomorrow."

The boss looked at his associate, who'd sat silent during the exchange. "Get word to me as soon as you know anything. Do you understand?" The decoder nodded. "I want this done as soon as possible." He stood, and as was the custom, grabbed his coat. When he looked up, his two visitors were gone.

Chapter Six

Connor walked into Ira Walsh's office and dropped the latest message on the desk. "From Luther."

Walsh frowned as he read the words. "Drew MacLaren is in Cold Creek." He glanced at Connor, who'd already read the missive. "That can mean only one thing. He's there to negotiate a sale for either the Bierdan or Langdon ranch, or both."

"How do you plan to proceed?"

"I'll send both ranchers a message, indicating my interest in their property. Luther will apply more pressure—this time directly to Langdon and Mrs. Bierdan."

Connor's eyebrows came together as his eyes narrowed. "What kind of pressure?"

"Nothing you need to concern yourself with. You have your own issues here, running my saloon and mining interests. Luther can handle the situation for now."

Connor didn't like the answer. He'd hired on with Walsh after being assured all businesses and methods of operation were legitimate. Connor didn't plan to use his extensive network of connections if he sensed it would end with a free-fall down a legal hell hole. He'd assured them when they invested in Ira's businesses that the man could be trusted. Now Connor wasn't so sure.

"I don't agree with threats or violence to achieve goals and neither do my colleagues. If that's your plan, you can count me out." Connor had leaned closer to the desk while fixing his gaze on Ira.

Walsh settled back in the large leather chair, his eyes narrowed to slits, lips pursed. He took his time contemplating Connor's words before a feral smile transformed his face. "Your worry is misplaced. You can rest assured that I have not ordered any illegal actions."

From what Connor knew of Ira's business activities, the comment was at best a half truth. He'd never heard Ira order one of his men to do something illegal, but Connor would bet his last silver dollar that Walsh was aware of illegal actions. Connor needed to confirm this one way or another before he led his associates down a path that could land them in all jail.

******

Cold Creek, Colorado

"Good afternoon, Mrs. Bierdan. I appreciate you seeing me," Drew said as Mr. Jericho helped him into the small front room of the Bierdan home.

Eloise Bierdan stepped back and stared at the chair and its occupant. She'd dreaded seeing Drew MacLaren again. After all, it was her husband who'd shot the bullet that had paralyzed him.

She'd change things if she could. Perhaps if she'd known of her husband's activities things could have turned out differently, but she was as unaware of his illegal actions as most. He'd shared little with her, which also contributed to the difficult times she was having now.

"I'm glad to see you, Mr. MacLaren. May I get you anything? Water, coffee, a whiskey?"

"Nothing, thank you." Drew looked around the room. The home was much smaller than the Taylor ranch house, with little furniture. Grant had mentioned that Mrs. Bierdan had sold some of the nicer pieces to raise cash. He and Eleanor had bought a sideboard from her—not that they needed it, but they'd wanted to help the young woman if possible. It wasn't her fault she'd been left in this sorry state. Drew wasn't sure he felt the same. He'd often wondered if the widow had known more about Gordon's activities than she let on.

"Well then, what can I do for you?" She took a seat across the room from the wheel chair and folded her hands in her lap.

"I'm sure you're aware that I work for Louis Dunnigan, at Dunnigan Enterprises. He's been expanding his operations to western Colorado, purchasing cattle ranches and other businesses that fit with what he does."

"And just exactly what does Mr. Dunnigan do?"

"It's complicated," Drew began.

Her eyes narrowed on his. "I know most people in Cold Creek don't think much of my abilities, but I'm fairly certain I can understand what Mr. Dunnigan does if you take the time to explain it to me." Her slight smile never faltered, although there was no humor in her eyes.

Drew could hear Mr. Jericho cough behind him, no doubt attempting to hide a chuckle. "It's not that I don't think you'd understand, it's just that there are many interconnected businesses. Explaining is more a challenge to me than a statement on your ability to understand."

"Please try."

"All right. Mr. Dunnigan owns businesses that include cattle ranches, mining, restaurants, hotels, and shipping. His main focus, however, is the land." Drew left out Dunnigan's extensive logging operations.

"And just what do you do for Mr. Dunnigan?" Mrs. Bierdan asked.

"I'm his attorney. I work on all the legal transactions within and between all his businesses. Negotiations, contracts, disputes—anything that impacts the legal part of Dunnigan's businesses."

"So that's why he sent you? Not because you have some personal interest in my ranch?"

"Yes, that's why I'm here and for no other reason. Believe me, I had no desire to come back to Cold Creek." His eyes bored into the young widow's. "I'm the person who discusses purchases and establishes the terms of each agreement. Mr. Dunnigan must review and approve what I do, but I work through the preliminary steps."

His tone had her pushing back in her chair and stiffening her back. She truly felt horrible about the damage her husband had done to this man, but she had her own issues to face and was determined not to fail.

"So you're here to offer me a fair price for my ranch, is that it?"

"If you're interested in selling, then yes, we would work toward a fair price."

She stood and walked to a window, drawing back a curtain to watch the men milling around the barn and corrals. Eloise had been in Cold Creek less than two years, but she'd learned to love the small town and admire the people who worked hard to make a success of their ranches. Her husband had gone about it the wrong way. She was determined to do it right.

"No doubt you've heard that the ranch is struggling with a few men leaving. My husband didn't leave me with much, other than the ranch and cattle. But make no mistake, Mr. MacLaren, I plan to keep them and not sell off to some greedy businessman who cares nothing for Cold Creek or its people."

Drew considered her rigid stance, determination, and the insulting comment she'd made about his boss. He understood her desire to succeed, but he couldn't leave without setting her straight about Dunnigan.

"I respect your desire to make the ranch work. Admire it. But I want to make clear one thing before I leave. I've worked for Dunnigan long enough to know that he doesn't cheat or steal. He offers top dollar when he's serious about a purchase, and he's serious about your ranch. Don't make the mistake of lumping him in with those other greedy business people or you'll find you've closed the door to a lucrative escape route, should you ever need it." He tilted his head just enough to catch Jericho's attention and nod. "We'll be leaving now, Mrs. Bierdan. You know where to find me if you're ever in the mood to discuss this again."

******

"Don't seem to me like you have much choice, Bellows. You can agree to ride out or we can send you to a place where it won't matter. Either is good for Luther and me." Vern Tyson, Luther Grimms, and the rest of the men stood over Jay Bellows as he lay sprawled in the muddy banks of the Gundy River. He'd ridden alone to visit the daughter of a neighboring rancher, Warren Langdon, oblivious to the band of men following his trail. It was a full moon and Jay had been daydreaming about seeing Clarisse Langdon again. It was a costly error.

Tyson poked Jay again with the butt of his rifle. Bellows kicked at the offending weapon, shoving Tyson back a few feet and discharging the gun in the process. The men in the circle jumped back and pulled their guns, pointing them at Jay.

"Damn it, boy, this ain't a fight you'll win." Luther held a cocked revolver pointed at Jay's head. "Best you mount up and head out before..."

His words were cut off with the approach of riders who fired into the night sky. "We've got to move," Luther growled, then turned back to Bellows. "This ain't over. You can count on that. Better you leave this area than end up in a box six feet below it." Luther mounted, but just before riding out he took aim and fired.

Minutes later three riders circled Jay as he attempted to stand, blood dripping from a wound to his shoulder. He looked around, dazed, trying to locate his missing gun. He'd known not to ride out without keeping an eye on his surroundings, but worse, he'd failed to let Jeff know he'd be visiting Clarisse.

"What the hell are you doing out here alone, Bellows?" his boss, Jeff Burnham, asked in his slow southern drawl. A drawl that could be misleading. Jay recognized the fire in the foreman's eyes. They'd been warned that ever since Clint's beating, no Bierdan men were to ride alone and Jeff was to know their whereabouts at all times. He'd said it was not open for discussion. They could abide by it or leave. Jay had broken both commands.

"Visiting Clarisse Langdon, Boss."

"Yeah, Clint thought that's where you might be. Good thing he mentioned it. We were on our way to find you when we heard a shot." He turned Jay toward him to look at the damaged arm. "You're lucky it's just a flesh wound. It'll hurt like hell, but will heal fast." Jeff tore off pieces of Jay's shirt to wrap around the injury, then looked toward Clint and Stan Clark, the other man who'd found Clint the night he'd been beaten. "Okay, let's head back, but keep your eyes peeled for those vermin. Jay can tell us his story on the ride. And Jay, this better be good." Jeff nudged his horse into a gallop with the others close behind.

******

Eloise paced the small area of what had been her husband's office. It was hers now. "What do you plan to do with him, Jeff?"

"Haven't decided. Can't afford to lose anyone else since that's what those men want, but I can't let him defy my orders, either," her foreman responded. He swallowed the last of the whisky in his glass, stood, and set it on the corner of the desk. "He'll work a few days around the barn and corrals, not out on the rangelands, and won't be allowed off the property the next two weekends. That should do it. He was invited to Langdon's for supper on Sunday. That won't happen, either."

Eloise turned and looked at him as if deciding whether or not to speak.

"What is it, Mrs. Bierdan?" Jeff asked.

"You know we had visitors today?"

"I heard."

"They represent a businessman from Denver who's interested in buying the ranch." She paused, walked back to the desk, and lowered herself into the large leather chair. "I need to consider it, Jeff."

"Have they given you a price? Any details?"

"No. This was just a first visit. I told them I wasn't interested, but the truth is the ranch is running thin. There's money for a while, but this season needs to be good or I'll be at the end of my resources. I thought you should know."

"You don't have to worry about me leaving, Mrs. Bierdan. I'll stay through the season and we'll talk after that."

"Fair enough, Jeff. I appreciate it."

He nodded before closing the door.

******

Tess had worked all morning in the barn while keeping watch on a mare that was about to foal. It was the mare's first time—a mare that Tess had raised from birth. Some mothers did well, others panicked, which could put stress on the foal and prolong the birth. Tess hoped this delivery would be easy.

She brushed her hands on her skirt, took one last look at the horse, and walked toward the house. Drew had been in the office most of the day. Grant had offered him the use of it for as long as he stayed in Cold Creek. Their guest was making good use of it.

Drew looked up as she walked by the open office door. Their eyes met and held for an instant before she broke the contact and continued to the kitchen.

"Tess?" Drew called after her.

She stopped. Their conversations had been short and strained while she'd been in Denver. They'd spoken little since arriving at the ranch. Tess knew he'd seen Patricia Dunnigan just before they left for Cold Creek and assumed they were making plans to marry. It surprised Tess how much the thought hurt. She knew she wasn't beautiful or rich like Miss Dunnigan, but she and Drew had shared so much in his brief stay before. They'd become close. Friends. She'd dreamed of him since the shooting, but in each dream, he walked, rode his horse, and laughed. She guessed that's why they were called dreams—images she could see but never hold.

"Yes, Drew? Can I get you something?"

"No, I just wanted to see how you were doing with the mare. It's close, isn't it?"

"Any day now by my count." She began to walk away.

"Tess, I'm sorry we didn't have much time to talk in Denver. My work and other obligations made it hard. Then Dunnigan asked me to travel here. I wish we'd had more time together, just you and me."

"It's all right. We knew you weren't expecting us. You have important work, and of course there's your fiancée. But she's probably more of a pleasure to be around than an obligation."

"About Patricia..." Drew began but stopped when Eleanor and Alicia walked into the room.

"I hope we're not disturbing anything," Eleanor said, "but dinner is about ready, Tess, and

70

I wondered if you could locate your father and Jake."

"Of course." She took one quick glance at Drew then left the house.

Drew felt her absence, like a gift that had been ripped from his grasp. He had to find time to speak with her, explain.

"Everything all right?" Aunt Alicia asked as she settled herself in one of the two large, leather guest chairs. Eleanor had returned to the kitchen, but Alicia wanted time with her nephew.

Drew threw his pen down on the desk in disgust. "Could be better."

"I see." Alicia waited for him to explain. Drew always took more time to express his thoughts than his three brothers did. He was a thinker, more introspective than the others.

Drew turned his wheelchair a fraction so he could see outside. Tess was speaking with Grant, who shook his head and yelled to someone behind him. Ranch life. So familiar yet so far from his reach.

He looked back at the woman who'd raised him. He owed her and his deceased Uncle Stuart everything. She deserved to know what was happening.

"I think I'm in love with Tess."

"Of course you are, Drew."

Drew's eyes sharpened, his surprise at her comment apparent.

"It's quite obvious to me and those who know you. It's apparent she feels the same about you.

She's a wonderful girl and you're a remarkable man. I'm just wondering what's keeping the two of you from telling each other how you feel."

He let his head fall back, then rolled it from one side to the other in an attempt to calm his stress, clear his mind. Wasn't it obvious why neither had said a word?

"I'm in a wheelchair, Aunt Alicia. She's an amazing woman with a gift for raising horses, training them. The last thing she needs is a man who is a burden and can't keep up. She'd grow to hate me and I'd grow to hate myself."

"It doesn't seem to concern Tess that you're in a chair. I believe that woman's love for you has grown despite the circumstances." Alicia stood and walked around the desk to place her hand on Drew's shoulder. "Besides, she believes with absolute certainty that you will walk again. There's no doubt in her mind. And she'd help you, if you'd let her."

"And what if I don't walk again?" He placed an elbow on the desk and rested his forehead between his thumb and fingers, massaging his temples, his eyes. What a mess.

"Then you'll help her with the horse breeding operations from your chair, with your brains. Someone else can do the heavy lifting. Just because you can't walk doesn't mean you can't ride. Why, I saw a man in Phoenix once whose son lost the use of his legs in a riding accident. He built the boy a special saddle. I never saw anything like it. Held that boy in place and he rode around the pen like a champion. Even went on trail rides." Alicia took a calming breath before continuing. "I've known you since you were a scared, seven-year-old little boy. But you found your place in our life and never looked back. Whatever you wanted, you worked for until it was yours. Don't tell me you don't have options and can't be with the person you love. I just don't believe it."

Drew's wide eyes and slack jaw were evidence of his complete surprise at his aunt's adamant support of him and Tess. He felt chastised, and rightfully so. Maybe he had been wrong about his future, and what he and Tess could have together.

"I know you just got much more from me than you expected, but I love you Drew, and so does Tess. If you feel the same, don't throw it away before you explore what could be." She placed a kiss on his cheek and walked toward the door.

"Aunt Alicia?"

She turned to her nephew.

"Thanks."

Chapter Seven

"Find anything useful last night?" the associate asked as he walked into the small room.

The decoder, Pierce, had been in Denver a few days working almost nonstop each night to prepare a copy of the documents the associate had discovered. Two different ledgers. Unfortunately, the books had to be returned to the safe early each morning, then retrieved again for the first few nights so that Pierce could make his own copies. It had been dangerous for his brother, but Pierce now had an exact set to work from.

The younger man looked up from his desk where the documents were spread out in an order only he understood. "The books are not the same. Although each has the same dates, the second set contains additional information. Dates, dollar amounts, and what look to be locations that don't appear in the first book. But there's still the possibility that the second ledger is a copy of the original with additional information. Perhaps Walsh is just cautious and keeps a duplicate with more detail in case the original is destroyed or lost."

"It's possible," his brother replied, "but unlikely."

Pierce understood his brothers' doubts after meeting Walsh the one time he'd stopped in at the Denver Rose for a whiskey. Walsh had introduced himself to Pierce before signaling for another man to join them. The other man, Connor, seemed to be in charge of running the saloon. Pierce had no issues with him. But Walsh set off red flags from the moment Pierce had shaken his hand.

"I won't be able to come up with anything reliable until I decipher a significant amount of the writing, but I believe I've discovered the key which is required for decoding. I just need to test it to be certain. Whoever developed the code was good. Very good." Pierce looked through his magnifying glass again to check his theory. He needed the correct key to overlay above the written symbols to decipher the documents.

"How long?"

"A few days, a week, but I will figure this out for you."

******

Cold Creek, Colorado

"How have you been, Doctor Wheaton?" Drew asked as Jericho wheeled him into the examination room.

"Fine, Drew. Glad to see you back in Cold Creek. You planning to marry that pretty young woman, Tess Taylor?" The doctor helped Jericho position Drew on the table.

Drew's eyes snapped to the doctor, his surprise obvious. "What did you say?"

"Well, it just seemed to me there was something special between the two of you. More than just friends, I mean."

Drew laid his head back down on the table and stared at the ceiling. How he wished there was more to their friendship, and that he could act on it. But no, the doctor was mistaken. "No, there's nothing more between us." The regretful tone of his voice wasn't lost on the doctor or Jericho.

"I see," the doctor probed his patient's legs, lower back, and abdomen. "You having any problems with doing your business?"

"My business?"

The doctor nodded to Drew's private area. "You know, using the facilities when you need to?"

"Oh, yeah, that's working just fine."

"Does your body tell you it's time?"

"Of course it does, Doctor, how else would I ...." but Drew's words trailed off when he started to understand the doctor's meaning. He'd had to have help every few hours during the first weeks, just in case it was needed, not because he felt any urge. But over the last five or six weeks those slight urges had begun and increased to where Drew knew what was needed. The feelings had been so gradual that he'd missed the signs. He'd never even thought to mention it to Doc Garland in Denver.

"You think..." Drew started before Dr. Wheaton raised a hand.

"Let's not jump too far ahead. I think it's one sign that something may be happening." The doctor turned to a table and grabbed a sharp instrument. It appeared to be a very slim needle of some type. "Mr. Jericho, please roll Mr. MacLaren to his side."

The doctor started at mid-back, inserting the needle less than a sixteenth of an inch every few inches. "Tell me if you feel anything at all."

Drew acknowledged feeling the needle the first few times as the doctor worked his way down to the lower back and hips—the places where the doctor suspected the paralysis started. He probed several more times without any comment from Drew, but when he inserted the needle into the upper section of one hip, Drew squirmed.

"You feel that?" the doctor asked.

"I believe so. Do it again."

The second and third attempts yielded nothing, but the fourth caused Drew to suck in breath. It hadn't been much, but he'd definitely felt something.

The doctor kept at it until he'd worked his way to Drew's ankles. His patient had felt something four times. "All right, Mr. Jericho, you can help Mr. MacLaren into his chair." Doc Wheaton scratched a few notes and pulled a chair up next to Drew.

"You have some feeling. Not much, but more than what you had right after the shooting. I've been doing some more reading, and there's this doctor back East who is convinced that temporary paralysis can be brought on by trauma to the area surrounding the spinal cord. Now this isn't the same as actually injuring the cord, which didn't happen to you. It's like a ripple effect. Over time, the majority of patients with this type of paralysis regain close to a hundred percent use of their limbs."

Drew had held his breath, not sure what the doctor would say. But the words were so much more encouraging than he'd expected. He felt his throat close as he pushed down the urge to voice his excitement.

"So there's a chance, Doc?"

"I think there's more than a chance but that's not a guarantee." He looked at Jericho. "Keep doing the exercises and use the liniments, Mr. Jericho. But now, I want you to help Mr. MacLaren to stand a little each day, bracing his weight on you and anything else that will hold him. Furniture, bars, fence posts. Whatever it takes to get his body to start understanding that it's supposed to stand and not just sit. Take it slow, don't push it. Drew's body needs to heal on its own, but let's try giving it just a slight nudge. Any questions, Mr. Jericho?"

"How long do you want him to stand, Doctor?"

"Only a few seconds the first few times, then increase it as long as he's up to it."

"Oh, I'll be up to it," Drew responded.

"All right. I want to see you again next week." The doctor stood to open the door for Mr. Jericho and Drew. "And Drew, don't forget what I said about Miss Taylor."

"Ah, yes, sir. Guess I better study that a little bit more." A slight smile formed on Drew's face as his mind wandered over the possibilities if he walked again.

******

Drew pushed up to the supper table, his seat directly across from Tess. Everyone else was still milling around, getting settled. "Good evening, Tess."

Her eyes lit up when her gaze met his. "Hello, Drew. I heard you went to see Doctor Wheaton today. Any news?" She smiled and that one small gesture meant more to him than anything else she could have done.

"The usual. Keep working my legs, use the oils, and don't give up." Drew didn't want to share the doctor's prognosis of a possible recovery. He didn't want anyone, including himself, to get their hopes up, but Drew felt more positive than he had at any time during the past two months. "He did say that there is still time, same as the doctors in Denver. But I do intend to walk again."

"Of course you will, Drew. We're all sure of it," Eleanor Taylor chimed in as she took her seat.

"How did your meeting with Mrs. Bierdan go?" Grant asked.

Drew looked around the table at Aunt Alicia, Grant, Eleanor, Joey, Tessa, Jake, and Jericho.

There was no reason to keep the conversation from any of them. Dunnigan's desire to buy the Bierdan land wasn't a secret.

"It was a starting point," Drew began, then took several minutes to relay the conversation.

"She's a stubborn one, that's for certain," Grant said.

"How long do you think she has, Grant?" Drew asked.

"If Eloise doesn't have a good season, she's through. That's about four months off, but you know the cycle as well as anyone." Grant was well aware of Drew's ranching background and his knowledge of cattle operations.

The table became silent as each tucked into the meal the Taylor cook, Maria, had prepared. She'd been with them for years, had helped to keep Joey safe the day of the shootout with the rustlers. The same day Drew was shot.

"Maybe she'll make it, but if not, Dunnigan will offer her top dollar. I believe he may also retain some of the men, and he'll make sure she gets settled wherever she likes."

"You like Mr. Dunnigan, don't you?" Tess asked.

"Yes, I do."

"And his daughter?" Tess wished she could pull back the words as soon as she'd spoken them. *What was I thinking?*

Drew's fork stopped midway to his mouth. He set it down and trained his eyes on Tess's. "I like his daughter fine."

"Oh," was all Tess could get out.

"But I have no plans to marry her." His eyes never wavered.

Tess showed no response except the appearance of a slight smile. Her eyes sparkled and it was all Drew could do to contain the frustration he felt at not being able to stand and walk around the table to her. He'd never felt anything like the pull he felt toward Tess at that moment.

Grant and Eleanor looked at the two young people, then at each other. So, their other daughter was smitten with a MacLaren. Somehow they weren't surprised. And each noticed that Alicia didn't seem surprised either.

Alicia sat near them with a serene look as she watched the young people. She didn't say a word, but prayed that her nephew and Tess could work through whatever held them back and build a future.

"How's the mare doing?" Drew asked Tess, hoping to move the conversation in another direction.

"I expect she'll deliver anytime. She's a small horse, and it's her first foal, but she should do fine. After supper I plan to check on her, unless you need help on the accounts, Father."

"No, you check on the mare," Grant said. "Come back in and help me when you're satisfied she's all right. Maybe Drew could look at her, give you his opinion."

Tess looked at Drew. He could see the hesitancy in her eyes.

"I'd like that, if you can use the company." Drew wanted nothing more than to share time with her. "Mr. Jericho usually does my therapy right after supper, but I'm sure he can wait a little bit. Right?" He looked to Jericho.

"That is fine with me, Mr. MacLaren."

They went to the barn right after supper. It took Drew just a few minutes to concur with Tess that the foal could come at any time. "She's healthy. You've done a good job with her. I'd expect a fine foal from her."

"You really think so?"

"I wouldn't say it if I didn't mean it."

"No, I guess you wouldn't."

Drew watched the light from the lantern she held play over her face. Over the months he'd known her, Drew had seen her scared, timid, determined, angry, resilient, and happy. But tonight he saw sadness. His gut told him he was the cause. Drew wanted to tell her how he felt, how important she was to him, but wasn't ready to say the words, make a commitment, until he could walk. He reasoned that if he could stand, he could walk, then he could ride. Drew knew she'd wait for him. *Wouldn't she?* Suddenly he wasn't so sure. What if she was being courted? Certainly there were men in this town who were attracted to her.

"Well, I guess it's time to head in. Father needs some help with the accounts and I'm trying to learn as much as I can. Amanda used to do the books, but it's been up to him since she left." Tess walked behind Drew's chair to help him back to the house. "I miss her."

"I'm sure you do, but I'm pleased for Will. He deserves some happiness after everything he went through, and Amanda's his perfect match."

"Will you go back there soon? To Fire Mountain, I mean."

"Not as soon as I'd like, but yes, I'll go back."

"You need any help, Miss Tess?" Jericho called out from the porch.

"No, we're doing fine, Mr. Jericho," Drew answered for her. "Guess he's anxious to put me through some more torture." He tried for a light tone, but failed.

"Does it hurt much?"

Drew could hear the concern in Tess's voice.

"No, not really. In fact, I'd welcome pain, the more the better. Anything to tell me my legs are starting to react somehow. But it will happen." He looked at Tess. "If I have any say in it at all, I will walk again, Tess."

******

It had been a quiet day. There was nothing to indicate that the menace that had plagued the Bierdan ranch the last couple of weeks was still lying in wait. The men circled the buildings each morning, then rode out in groups of two to four to check cattle and fences. Two men were posted each night as guards. There had been no sign of further danger.

Eloise lowered herself into a chair in the kitchen. Some nights Jeff Burnham would join her to discuss ranch business, but tonight she was alone. She liked the solitude. It gave her a chance to think about her options, about her past.

She laid her head back against the slatted wooden kitchen chair and closed her eyes. It had only been a few years, but Eloise was determined to never go back to the life in the East. The life Gordon Bierdan had rescued her from.

She'd grown up in a home for children, with little education and fewer prospects, but she'd come to the attention of a wealthy woman who'd volunteered at the home. When she was sixteen, the woman had offered her a position in her home, cleaning and working with the children when the governess was not around. Eloise had jumped on the opportunity, and it had been everything and more. They'd let her sit in with the children's tutor. She learned to dance, and was even allowed to take piano lessons—a thought that would have shocked many in Boston. As long as she was loyal and did her work, the family was willing to help her with what they could.

Gordon had swept into her life five years later. He'd been a guest in her employer's home. She'd been around him little during his brief stay, but when the time came for him to leave, he'd asked the family for her hand. It had been unexpected, but she'd said yes. It was hard to leave the family but an easy decision to leave Boston.

The trip west had been an education, as had being Gordon's wife. She was twenty years younger than her husband. At times he treated her more as a daughter than a wife, but he was always kind, generous, and made her feel cherished. She'd had no idea of the vengeful parts of him. Not until it was too late.

Eloise was pulled from her memories by a loud crash in the front of the house, followed by a couple of smaller ones. She sprang from her chair and raced toward the sound of the noise. Glass was everywhere. A broken picture frame lay on the floor. She flew to the entry and grabbed her shotgun before shoving the door open. No one. She moved further onto the front porch, by the steps. She could just make out a rider heading away towards the east.

Shouts erupted from the bunkhouse and several men ran towards the house, pistols drawn. Jeff was the first to arrive, a rifle in his hand.

"Are you all right, Mrs. Bierdan? Did you see anything?" Jeff asked as he came to a stop beside her.

"Yes, I'm fine. I didn't see anyone specifically, just a man riding away toward the east."

"Clint, Jay, Stan, mount up. See if you can catch up with him," Jeff ordered.

"Yes, sir," the men responded. Clint took an extra moment to glance at Mrs. Bierdan, hesitated a moment, then joined the other two.

Jeff turned to the two who'd been posted as guards. "What the hell happened?"

"I didn't see anything, Boss. I was making a turn around the barn when I heard the crash," one of the men responded.

Jeff glared at the second man. "And you?"

He was young, maybe sixteen. His fear that he'd failed was transmitted to Jeff by his wide eyes and shaking hands. "Sorry, Boss. I..."

"Did you see or hear anything?" Jeff asked, his voice low, unhurried, but firm.

"No, Boss, nothing." The young man hung his head, dejected at his incompetence.

Jeff closed his eyes and shook his head. It'd do no good to chastise the kid. The foreman could see the boy was already doing enough of that himself.

"Come on, Mrs. Bierdan, let's check inside. Maybe we can find something that will help us figure out who did this."

Jeff walked behind her into the house, looking for anything that would help them determine the identity of the rider. He set his rifle aside and followed Eloise into the front room. It was a mess. Broken glass lay everywhere. It wasn't just a small rock the rider had thrown into the room but a long piece of lumber and several pieces of what appeared to be discarded horseshoes. Jeff bent down to pick up the wood and turned it over.

"You'd better see this, Mrs. Bierdan."

She stood by her foreman and read the words burned into the lumber.

Get out or we'll be back for you.

Eloise gasped and took a step back. Her heart raced as she mentally absorbed the meaning. It was a clear threat, directed at her.

"Must be the men who threatened Clint and Jay. Don't know of anyone else who'd do something like this. Unless it's that man you met with from Denver. MacLaren?"

"No, I'm certain this isn't the way he operates. He's a businessman, not a thug." Eloise responded. She'd spent enough time with the Taylor's over the past weeks to learn a great deal about the MacLaren family. This didn't fit with what she'd learned.

"As soon as the men return I'll send a couple of them to town to get Sheriff Alts. He needs to know what's happened," Jeff said. He'd go along with her judgment on MacLaren, for now, but he wasn't willing to take a chance on Eloise's life by ruling anyone out. "Don't move anything until he's had a chance to look around."

Chapter Eight

Frank Alts looked around at the damage and re-read the note burned into the wood. He knew in his gut who was most likely behind the attacks, the vandalism, but he needed proof.

"You see anything at all, Mrs. Bierdan?" Frank asked.

"No. I was in the kitchen when I heard the crash. By the time I got outside whoever did it was riding out. It was too dark and he was too far away for me to see anything more." But she sure wished she had.

"Jeff, you or your men see anything?"

"Nothing. We were in the bunkhouse. Mrs. Bierdan was outside by the time we made it to the house."

"You both think it could be one of the same men who attacked Clint and Jay?"

"That'd be our guess, Sheriff." Eloise replied.

"Unless it's that MacLaren fellow who came here earlier today." Eloise's head swung up to Jeff's at his comment.

Frank appeared to consider the possibility for a moment before replying. "Doesn't sound like anything MacLaren would do, Jeff. I know the MacLaren men, worked with Jamie MacLaren in the Marshal Service. This isn't their style." He knew for a fact it wasn't Drew, or Louis Dunnigan, but remained quiet about his connection to the Denver businessman.

"We're looking for the men Clint and Jay described. They'll turn up somewhere, sometime. No one can stay invisible for long. Mrs. Bierdan, I want you to be especially vigilant. Don't go anywhere alone and make sure you're armed. You do know how to handle a rifle or handgun, right?"

Eloise gave him a scathing look. "Of course I can handle a gun, Sheriff. That was one of the first things Gordon taught me when we married." The thought of her dead husband caused a dull ache in the area of her heart, not because of her love for him, but because of the damage he'd caused. "But I understand what you're saying and won't intentionally make myself a target."

Frank's eyes narrowed on the pretty widow. She had spunk, he'd give her that, but did she have the common sense to keep herself out of harm's way or kill a man if he came at her? He'd have to wait and see.

"I better get going."

"I'll walk out with you, Sheriff," Jeff said and followed Frank outside.

"Keep an eye on her, Jeff. She's determined that no one's going to take the ranch from her, no matter the consequences, and that kind of thinking can get her killed."

"Understood. I'll split up the boys so one group is always available to keep watch on her and the ranch. Wish she could afford more men, but I know she's at her limit. It's been an interesting couple of weeks." Jeff turned his gaze from the sheriff to check out their surroundings. There were enough trees around the property to provide cover to anyone who wanted to lie in wait. He only had ten men, including himself, and that just wasn't enough for what they were up against. He hoped his decision to stay put and support Mrs. Bierdan wasn't a bad one. Jeff had no intention of dying in this southwest Colorado town.

******

"Tess? I wonder if you'd like to go outside for a bit?" Drew's voice was hesitant, hopeful. He'd spent the last hour with Jericho, and even though he was tired, he wanted to see her, spend time with her. Hell, he wanted to just be around her. Their short time in the barn just wasn't enough.

"I'd like that." Tess set down the book she'd been reading and grabbed a shawl. She stepped back to let Drew precede her onto the front porch and closed the door. Her hands began to shake, from nerves or the cold she wasn't sure, but either way, she grabbed the ends of the shawl to wrap around her so Drew wouldn't notice. Tess walked over to the swing and Drew maneuvered his chair next to her.

"We haven't had much time together." Drew said.

"No, we haven't." Tess was rocking the swing with a slight motion. It was enough to help hide her nervousness at being alone with Drew. She'd felt this way in the barn, but the mare had been a distraction. Tess had no distractions now.

They sat in silence for a few minutes, enjoying the quiet and the clear night sky. "Are your sessions with Mr. Jericho going all right? Does it help?"

"If nothing else, the liniment and massage relaxes me. I can't say for certain they help, but doubt that they're causing any more damage." He tilted his head up to gaze at the stars. "I missed you, Tess."

"You did?" Her surprise wasn't fake. She hadn't believed he'd thought about her at all since leaving Cold Creek for Denver.

"You thought I wouldn't?" Drew turned to look at her.

"Well, I know you've had to focus on other things. I didn't think you'd have time for much else. Except perhaps your fiancée."

"Ah, I see." And he did. He'd left the ranch after the shooting when Louis Dunnigan and his daughter, Patricia, had arrived. She'd identified herself to everyone as Drew's fiancée, and Tess had believed it.

"She was never my fiancée. I never courted her, Tess. I cleared that up with Patricia before I left Denver."

Tess let that roll around in her head. *Is he trying to tell me something or just making conversation?* "Are you courting someone else?"

He chuckled. "No, I'm not courting anyone. Are you being courted?"

"Me?" she squeaked out. She knew her family would find the question humorous, not because they saw her as unattractive, but because of her total disinterest in meeting someone, making friends outside of the family. "Of course not. Who'd be interested in someone like me when there are so many beautiful women with more to offer?" There, the words were out, and she meant them. Let him know that she didn't expect that any man, especially someone like Drew MacLaren, would find her attractive or interesting enough to court. She sank lower into the swing and continued to rock.

The disbelief Drew felt at Tess's words grew until he wished he could stand, draw her to him, and tell her how wrong she was. How could she think of herself as unattractive or uninteresting? She was a beautiful woman with a kind heart and quick mind. Her radiant smile and uninhibited laugh brought joy to those around her.

"Tess, look at me." Drew's soft voice broke the silence. Her head turned in small increments toward him until their eyes met and held.

"You are, without a doubt, the most beautiful woman I have ever known. There is so much about you that I admire." His words were soft, but the intense look in his eyes told her that they were from his heart. "I find it hard to believe that no one is courting you. There must be a great many fools in Cold Creek if no one recognizes the jewel right in front of them."

Tess was so stunned by Drew's words that she found herself unable to respond. She stared at him as tears welled in her eyes. She swiped at them before breaking contact and looking down into her lap. When she looked up, Drew saw the most magnificent smile he'd ever seen. He wasn't sure, but thought his heart may have missed a few beats in that moment.

He reached over and placed his hand on Tess's. She turned hers to fit into his large palm. Neither said a word, just enjoyed the night with its brilliant white stars.

******

Ira shoved both hands in his pockets and paced back and forth in the large office. Luther's latest attempts to scare Widow Bierdan and her men into leaving had failed. She was no more interested in selling than she had been two months ago. Luther was a brute but, in Ira's opinion, he hadn't exerted the right kind of pressure. They needed to go after her directly. With MacLaren already in Cold Creek, Walsh had no option but to change plans.

He penned a quick message to the one man he was confident could make things happen, Sabastian Drago. He'd kept him out of this part of the business, preferring for Drago to concentrate on other matters. Ira felt certain that Langdon and

Bierdan saw Luther as a threat. Walsh knew the man was a mere nuisance compared to the fear Drago would inflict.

Ira poked his head out of his office and called for one of his men to take the message to the telegraph office. He didn't like doing it this way—preferred a more subtle approach—but he wanted that ranchland. In the process, he wanted to rid Cold Creek of its most recent arrival. Ira's thinking was like many—MacLaren was only half a man anyway.

******

Eloise walked down the dirt-covered boardwalk and stopped to look at the new merchandise in the window of the mercantile. A yellow calico caught her eye. When her husband was alive she would have gone right in and bought the dress. Now? She had to satisfy herself with looking.

"Hello, Mrs. Bierdan." The deep, masculine voice came from behind her. She looked up to see the man's reflection in the window. An odd feeling passed through her as she studied the sheriff before turning to greet him.

"Good morning, Sheriff Alts. I was just on my way to see you." Eloise always thought him a handsome man, but for some reason, his solid frame and broad shoulders had her heart beating today. It was a new feeling—something she'd never felt with her husband. She had the oddest urge to walk forward and touch him, place a hand on his shirt-clad chest. Eloise was embarrassed at the path her thoughts took, and her face must have transmitted her inner turmoil.

"Are you all right, Mrs. Bierdan? Do you need to sit down?" Frank asked.

"Ah, no, Sheriff. I'm fine. I just felt a little dizzy for a moment."

"Have you had dinner?"

Eloise shook her head.

"Good. I was just heading to the restaurant. I'd be honored if you'd join me." Frank hadn't realized how much he wanted to share a meal with the attractive widow, but the pull he'd felt toward her intensified with each meeting.

"I'd like that, Sheriff," Eloise replied and took the arm he offered.

The restaurant was close, just three doors down. Eloise felt fortunate to have a table by the window. It would give her something to look at other than the gentleman escorting her. He wasn't handsome like the dandies who'd frequented her employer's home in Boston. His face was rugged, weather-beaten, and his nose was just off center, as if he'd injured it. Intriguing was the word she'd use for him.

"The beef stew for both of us," Frank told the waitress and looked at Eloise for approval. "So what brought you to town to see me?"

"You said the MacLarens are well-known to you. You trust them?"

"I do."

"You're sure Drew MacLaren wouldn't harm someone? Absolutely sure?"

"I'd stake my life on it. I trust him and his brothers." Frank sipped his coffee and considered what she was really trying to ask him. "Why don't you come right out and tell me why you wanted to meet today."

"There's another man, from Denver, who's expressed an interest in my land. I've put him off, but under the circumstances I believe I need to at least discuss my options. I don't want to sell, but if I do, I want the best price for the land."

"And the motivation of the person who might purchase your land. Do you care at all about that?" Frank asked, concerned about where this conversation might be going.

Eloise thought about what the sheriff was implying. She hadn't really considered the character of the buyer, just that she'd get a reasonable price for the ranch and a fair deal for her men. "If I decide to sell, I'll want the best price I can get plus assurances that the buyer will continue to employ my men. They've worked hard to keep the ranch going and have stayed when others have left." She stopped to consider what she'd said, then looked up at Frank. "That's reasonable, don't you believe, Sheriff?"

"I believe it is reasonable, but an agreement is only as good as the word of the man behind it. Contracts can be broken, and believe me, I've seen it many times. How hard would you be willing to fight if you sold your ranch, moved away, then discovered all of your men had been fired? Would you come back to fight for them?"

Frank glanced out the window to see two men ride in and dismount in front of the saloon. Each looked up and down the street, then hurried into the building. They fit the descriptions of Luther and Vern. One tall, bulky, with broad-shoulders, the other one shorter and lean.

He picked up his cup of coffee and took a swallow. "I'd feel more comfortable knowing who's behind the beatings, the threats, before you make a decision to sell. Someone is after your land, and the Langdon's, and they're not above using force to get what they want. Now, I don't know who this other Denver buyer is, and he may be as honest as they come, but I'm certain that Drew would never work for a man who used those tactics to entice you to sell." He set his cup down. "All I'm suggesting is that you be sure of the buyer's character before you make a decision." He continued to keep watch on the saloon. Frank wanted to finish dinner and take a better look at the men before they left town, but as the plates were set down the two men emerged from the saloon and walked toward their horses.

"Mrs. Bierdan, you'll have to excuse me but I believe I may have found the two men that threatened Clint and Jay." He moved out to the street in time to walk in front of the men's horses just as the large one mounted.

"You Luther and Vern?" Frank asked as his hand instinctively went to the butt of his pistol.

"Who's asking?"

"I'm Sheriff Alts...." Frank began, but before he could finish, Luther kicked his horse and would've run the sheriff down if he hadn't jumped out of the way. Frank pulled his gun just as the man he believed to be Luther's partner, Vern, started to follow his partner.

"Don't try it, Vern. I'll shoot you if I have to." Frank's gun was trained on Vern's chest. At three yards away there was little chance he'd miss.

Just then Frank's deputy, Eddy O'Dell, came up from the other direction with a rifle pointed at Vern. "If the Sheriff doesn't get you, you'd best believe I will," he said as he raised the rifle and sighted on Vern's head.

Vern dropped the reins and slid off his horse. He looked around to see a sizable crowd milling about. A crowd that included the Widow Bierdan.

"Turn around," Frank ordered and pulled handcuffs from his back pocket.

"What's this about, Sheriff?" Vern asked.

"Go to the Bierdan ranch. Bring back Clint and Jay," Frank called to his deputy, then turned to Vern. "We'll talk at the jail. Come on." He nudged his prisoner forward and came face-to-face with Eloise Bierdan.

"Is this the one who attacked my ranch hands?" She glared at the prisoner, taking in his scruffy appearance as a strong odor drifted towards her. Eloise covered her mouth and coughed at the stench.

"That's what I plan to find out. Now, if you'll excuse me..."

"I'm coming with you," Eloise declared.

"No." Frank retorted.

"You can't stop me, Sheriff. It was my men he attacked. I want to hear what excuse he has for what he did to them."

Frank stared at the widow and let out a deep breath, his frustration with her demand obvious. "You're right, Mrs. Bierdan, I can't stop you from coming to the jail. But I can stop you from talking to him or listening to our conversation." He still had one hand on his prisoner's arm and one on the handle of his gun. "This is no game. I need to get answers, my way, without any distractions or interruptions. Let me do my job. I promise you'll be the first to know if I can find a link to what happened to Clint and Jay."

Eloise considered his words. She wanted to hear what was said, but didn't want to hinder the Sheriff. "All right, but I'll hold you to your word. You'll find me in the mercantile if you learn anything." She took one more disgusted look at the prisoner and turned toward the general store.

Frank watched her walk away before turning back to his prisoner. "Let's go, Vern."

Chapter Nine

Denver, Colorado

Ira lifted his head from the ledgers on his desk when he heard the commotion downstairs. It was a Saturday night and the saloon was full of local cowboys looking to find release in cards, whiskey, women, or a fight. It didn't seem to matter to some of them—one release was almost as good as another.

Another loud crash had him walking out of his office to stand at the balcony. He looked down into the crowded room. A big circle had formed in the center with two men rolling around on the floor, smashing fists into each other's face. His manager stood off to the side, observing but not interfering. Connor was good at controlling these situations and under normal circumstances, Ira wouldn't have interfered. But tonight's hullabaloo added to the building tension he'd felt for several days. Ira let it go another minute before he'd had enough. "Conner!" he shouted down.

Connor looked up at Walsh and nodded. "All right, boys, enough of this foolishness. Time to break it up." He grabbed the arm of the larger gent and yanked him up. One of his bouncers grabbed the arm of the other and pushed him toward the bar. The larger man lunged into Conner and tried to take a swing, but Conner cut him off with a left hook that dropped him back to the floor. "Get him out of here," he ordered some other men. "Let him know he's not to come back in until I say so." Conner bent to brush off the dust from his black slacks and vest. He looked back toward the upper balcony, but saw that Walsh had disappeared.

Ira once again studied the ledger in front of him. It wasn't an ordinary listing of expenses and income. It was a compilation of all his businesses, people involved, and cash transferred. Many were legitimate but others were used to hide illegal—or what some would consider disreputable—transactions. Saloons, retail establishments, and silver mines were supplemented by cattle rustling, brothels, and opium smuggling. All lucrative, but he craved more. His latest focus was on obtaining more timberland by whatever means necessary to clinch profitable deals with lumberyards. His ultimate goal was to own the land, the lumberyards, and the distribution to large cities. These would be used to mask his growing import business.

No one else understood the extent of his illegal operations. Ira worked through intermediaries, offered a cut of the profits, and shielded himself through bogus companies. He hired men without conscious, who were willing to do anything to make money. Walsh set them up to handle the difficult facets of each separate business—actions most men would find repulsive. And they never asked questions. His years on the streets of New York had prepared him well for this life.

He closed the ledger, opened his wall safe, pulled the hidden door at the back, and deposited the incriminating material. Ira kept three sets of ledgers. One for his legal operations. A second one that combined all operations but in a form not as incriminating, and a third ledger, which was hidden behind the unseen door. It held the evidence that could destroy him.

******

Pierce stood from the desk and stretched his tall frame. He'd worked non-stop on the ledgers, comparing what he'd found, and with each hour his frustration increased. The code had been broken two days before but what he found made no sense. Something wasn't right but Pierce couldn't pinpoint what bothered him.

A short knock was followed by the door to his office being pushed open. His brother walked in and threw his greatcoat on a nearby chair. Pierce admired his older brother, understood the demons that drove him, and would do anything he asked.

They'd been inseparable since their journey to the new country years before. At the urging of their father, they'd left their family and homeland behind to build a new life in America. It had been expected that they'd meld with another part of the family who had emigrated over ten years prior but the young men had never been able to locate their relatives and were left on their own. The years had been hard. Both had held many jobs, some they were proud of, some not so much, but they'd done well. His brother eventually became an undercover Range Detective. Pierce, a wild kind in his youth and one of the best thieves in New York, found a home in science and math, knowledge often used to support the work of his brother. It also provided Pierce with occasional entertainment when he felt the urge to return to his wild past.

"What have you found?"

"Nothing that makes sense. It seems what we have is one ledger showing legitimate transactions. The second shows the same entries, but some additional data on operations that appear illegal. But nothing that would send him to prison or ruin him. Why keep another ledger if the information would cause limited damage?" Pierce rubbed a hand over the stubble on his face and sat down.

His brother paced the floor trying to come up with a reason why Walsh would take the time to prepare two ledgers if not to hide significant illegal operations. He came to a stop across from Pierce. "We need to meet with the boss. Tonight. I'll set it up."

******

The boss sat behind his desk listening to the two men explain what they'd learned. In his mind there was just one explanation for what they'd found.

"They're a ruse. Walsh knew someone would try to dig into his businesses, discover his secrets. He setup a second set to throw off anyone prying into his affairs. He hopes that whoever finds it will stop there, think there was nothing else to discover." He fell silent and leaned back in his chair. "There's a third book somewhere. That's the ledger that will tell the full story and seal his fate. I'm convinced of it."

"If there is a third book, it's in his office. Walsh leaves each night with nothing but his coat and hat. I've observed him for weeks, coming and going from the Denver Rose. Everything important takes place upstairs, not in his home," the associate said.

"Find it. Do whatever you have to, but get the information we need to stop him. Time is becoming scarce. Do we understand each other?"

His visitors nodded before standing to leave.

"One more item. I must travel back East. I'm not sure how long I'll be gone. This is where you can reach me." He handed a piece of paper to his associate. "You let me know if you find a third book, and if Pierce is able to learn anything from it."

******

Cold Creek, Colorado

"You're sure that's the man?" Frank asked Clint and Jay.

104

"That's him, Sheriff. I'd recognize that smell and face anywhere," Jay replied.

"Clint?"

"That's one of them. I understand the other one was with him today." Clint walked up to the bars to get a good look at the prisoner.

"He was, but rode off before we could stop him. You want to press charges?" Frank asked.

Both responded in the affirmative.

"All right. I'll be in touch as soon as the circuit judge gets here. Until then, I'll keep looking for the other man, as well as whoever is riding with them. I expect you two will escort Mrs. Bierdan back to the ranch?"

"We will, Sheriff. And thanks for getting one of them," Clint said as he closed the office door.

"Hey, wait a minute, Sheriff," Vern yelled from his jail cell. "I didn't do nothing. Never seen those two in my life." The man had yet to admit a thing, including his association with Luther or information about a boss. They had him on the beatings, but that was all. He'd be kept in jail for now. Eventually he'd crack.

Frank looked at his dusty boots and shook his head. "Vern, you and I are going to get along a lot better if you just stay quiet. Maybe you should consider the sins of your ways. Might be time for you to have a change in direction." He walked to the desk and sat down. He had yet to meet a criminal that confessed his guilt instead of proclaiming his innocence, and the guiltier they were, the louder they yelled. He guessed he wouldn't get much sleep tonight.

******

The loud crash brought Tess and Jericho dashing toward Drew's room. They didn't stop to ask if they could enter, but shoved the door open. What they saw brought a gasp from each. Drew lay flat on his stomach, his chair pushed back to the wall. He had on his pants but the shirt he'd worn earlier was missing.

Jericho bent down to wrap his arms around Drew's chest and haul him up. "You should have called me."

"I would have, Mr. Jericho, but I wanted to try this by myself. It was a damn stupid thing to do," Drew growled as Jericho positioned him in his chair. Then he spotted Tess.

She stood still, her breathing somewhat labored, her eyes fixed on his naked torso. The memory of him—on his side, unconscious, oozing blood from a hole in his back, caked in dirt—assaulted her. It took a moment to remember this wasn't that day months ago. That it was tonight, in her father's home. He'd only fallen. That was all.

"Tess?" Drew asked in a soft voice. When she didn't raise her head, but continued to stare, he repeated her name. "Tess, look at me. Are you all right?"

She took a slow, measured breath to ease her racing heart. "Yes. Yes, I'm fine. How did you end up on the floor?"

He looked at Jericho and shook his head just enough so the man would notice. "Bent too far forward and slipped out of it. Thought it was against the wall, but guess not." He wasn't ready to share with Tess the additional exercises Doc Wheaton had ordered. It had only been three nights and he had a long way to go. "I'm fine now. Mr. Jericho will help me get ready for bed."

"If you're sure," Tess said and backed out of the room. "Goodnight, Drew. Mr. Jericho."

"Goodnight, Tess," Drew's gaze followed her out of his room.

"What were you trying to do, kill yourself?" Jericho asked as he helped Drew move from the chair onto his bed. "If you wanted to do some more of those exercises the doc ordered, all you had to do was call me." His voice was gruff, but Drew knew the irritated sound was due to concern, not anger.

"I needed to try it on my own. Almost pulled myself up but I lost my grip and the chair slipped."

"You want to try it alone, fine, but call me first. Don't want you to go messing up that pretty face of yours, Mr. MacLaren. Miss Tess may not like it." Jericho's comment was meant as jest, but his face bore the expression of a man who understood the impact his words would have on his boss.

Drew didn't reply, but the words stuck in his mind after Jericho had left the room. For the first time, Drew realized most of what he did was so that he could be the man Tess needed and feel he was worthy to court her. The other night in the barn and their time on the porch confirmed his suspicions that she'd be interested in him even if he never took another step. But that wasn't good enough for him. He wouldn't let her know how much he cared about her until he could walk up and say the words. Drew hoped she'd wait.

******

Denver, Colorado

"Vern's been arrested by the sheriff of Cold Creek on some trumped up charge," Ira spat out after he'd read the latest telegram from Luther. "I'll need to send more men." He looked at Connor. "Send Dex and Carl up to see me."

"Sure, but I'll need replacements for them."

"Your decision. Right now I need to work out this mess with Vern."

"Need my help?" Connor asked.

Ira glanced up and considered the offer. But no, that would give Connor too much insight into his operation. That couldn't happen. "No, I'll take care of it."

Connor left the room, already knowing the two men he'd hire. He walked down the hallway to the stairs but stopped at the top. It was midday and the saloon was quiet. Connor looked over the bar, the small stage, and toward the back room.

Nothing caught his attention. He was a cautious man—trust came hard. He knew he must be extra careful around a man like Walsh. Connor's gut told him that no matter what Ira planned for Cold Creek, it wasn't good.

He continued down the stairs just as a man he'd never seen before walked into the saloon. Every stitch of clothing the stranger wore was black, except for a red bandana tied around his neck. He was mid-height and wore matching pistols positioned so the butts faced forward. The hair on Connor's neck bristled.

He walked up to Connor but didn't extend a hand. "I'm looking for Walsh."

"He expecting you?"

The man glared at Connor with the look of someone who wasn't used to being questioned or detained.

"He's here to see me. Let him pass," Ira said from the balcony above.

The stranger brushed passed Connor and took the steps at a slow pace, casting a smirk over his shoulder to the small crowd below. Ira slapped the visitor on the back before escorting him into his office and shutting the door. Connor could hear the lock click into place.

"You recognize him, Connor?" Nelson walked up once the balcony was clear.

"No."

"I do. He's Sebastian Drago. A hired gun and known for doing anything for the right price. Wonder what Walsh wants with him?"

Connor asked himself the same thing. He'd never met Drago but had heard of him, and what he'd heard was worse than most people could imagine. He wondered if Drago's arrival had anything to do with the Bierdan ranch. If so, Walsh had upped the ante tenfold.

******

Drago walked to the window and peered out. No one. He'd thought he'd been followed, but then he always assumed he was being tracked. Over the years his face had been on and off of wanted posters more times than he could count but no one had ever been able to pin anything on him. Had come close, but nothing stuck. He'd kept a lower profile since working for Walsh, running the import business, a business he'd suggested.

"Sit down, Drago. You make me nervous pacing about," Ira said and offered his guest a cheroot and light.

Drago took it as well as a seat across from Walsh. "Why'd you send for me?"

"I've got a situation that needs your attention."

"Where?"

"Cold Creek, Colorado. West of here."

"What's it involve?" Drago took a draw from the square-cut cigar and let the smoke go in a long, slow breath.

"Persuasion."

"Ah. And just who would I be persuading?"

"A young widow. We need her land for the timber operations we discussed."

"Terms are up to me?"

"Of course," Ira said, pleased Drago understood the job.

"When should I leave?"

"Tomorrow. Tonight supper and drinks are on me." Ira crushed the last of the cheroot and stretched his legs out, satisfied that everything he wanted would soon be under his control.

Chapter Ten

Cold Creek, Colorado

Jeff rode up to the ranch house, dismounted, and stomped up the steps, throwing the door open in his haste to find Eloise. He was tired, dirty, and damn angry.

"Mrs. Bierdan, you here?" No answer. He walked through the main part of the house, calling once or twice more before heading toward the barn. He found her there, grooming her horse, preparing to ride out. She peered over her shoulder to see her foreman stalking toward her, anger flashing in his eyes.

"What is it, Jeff?"

"Cattle. About twenty head. Slaughtered."

"What!" She dropped the brush and took a step backward, as if she'd been struck. "Where?"

"Up a canyon. Looks like they were herded in and slaughtered. Last night from what I can tell."

"My God." She placed a hand over her mouth in an attempt to stop the rising bile in her stomach. "Who would do such a thing?"

"It's got to be the men who've been threatening you and Langdon. They're determined to run you off, no matter the carnage." Jeff took off his hat and ran a hand through his short hair. "I need to send someone to tell Frank. I don't expect he can do much, but he needs to know. Don't go anywhere while I'm gone. Stay in the house and have a rifle ready. I'll send Clint and Stan up to keep watch before I leave."

Eloise heard the words but could only nod. It was so confusing. She was just a woman who wanted to run a ranch, build a life, and live in peace. It's all she'd ever wanted. But now someone was determined to destroy her dreams. The realization galvanized her. She would not be backed into a corner—not ever again.

She straightened and walked with purpose into the house toward the gun cabinet. She removed Gordon's rifle as well as the one he'd bought for her, four pistols, and her shotgun. She stacked them up then proceeded to pull out ammunition and load each one. When finished, she placed a rifle and pistol in the study, the shotgun and two more pistols in the front living area, the last handgun in the kitchen, and her rifle in the bedroom. Eloise then poured a cup of coffee and sat at the kitchen table to wait, and think.

******

Denver, Colorado

Ira watched the two new men from his position on the balcony. He'd seen both in the saloon—one several times over the past few weeks, the second man just one other time. Walsh

113

wondered how Conner knew these men and how he'd come to hire them on such short notice. Well, he couldn't dwell on it. There were other urgent matters that required his attention.

Ira returned to his office and the latest reports he'd received on the opium delivery. It would move from Victoria, British Columbia through northern Washington, with final delivery to Walsh's business partner in San Francisco. He'd make three times the money he'd paid the supplier for the addicting drug. From San Francisco, smaller amounts would make their way to other western towns with a final delivery of one hundred pounds in Denver. That delivery would not be resold.

Drago had convinced him to enter this business, saying it would make them both rich, and he'd been right. This had been a standing order for two years, but their next order was for three times the normal amount he ordered from his Victoria supplier. Requests for opium—known to his buyers as joy plant—increased each month in San Francisco, plus new buyers in the city had shown a strong interest in his merchandise.

As always, keeping his involvement quiet was essential. That's why Drago's presence was necessary. They'd grown up together on the streets of New York, both immigrants and both with different skills. They'd stayed in touch and it had benefited both men over the years. Drago was the only person Ira trusted without hesitation.

Ira needed to retain his cover as a legitimate businessman to obtain the financing needed to grow this business and others. So far he'd been successful, but his instincts told him something was amiss. Nothing jumped out as being inconsistent and no one had drawn his attention, but Ira hadn't gotten where he was by ignoring his gut feelings. They'd saved him more than once from making a mistake and trusting the wrong men. He'd be extra cautious until he discovered what continued to eat at him or the suspicions went away. *Trust no one* had been his motto most of his life and there was no reason to change it now.

******

"Wake up, Mr. MacLaren. Miss Tess needs you out in the barn." Jericho stood over the bed with Drew's chair close at hand. It was after midnight, but with Grant and Eleanor staying with friends on the other side of Cold Creek, he thought it best to wake his boss.

Drew shook his head as he used his arms for leverage and pushed his body into a sitting position. "What is it? Has something happened?"

"There's a foal on the way and Miss Tess needs your help."

"How does she think I can help her? She should have Jake or one of the other hands by her side."

"She's been out there a while and is quite insistent. You're the one she wants." Jericho crossed thick arms over his massive chest and waited for MacLaren. His boss could sometimes be one stubborn blockhead.

"Alright. But I'm not sure what she thinks I can do."

It wasn't long before Drew and Jericho entered the barn and moved toward the back stall. Tess was on her knees, trying to reassure a frightened mare who was already on her side, lathered, and breathing hard. One of the hands, a young man not more than sixteen, stood at the side of the stall, unsure of his role.

"What can I do, Tess?" Drew asked in a soft voice.

"She's been working for over an hour, but I can't see enough to tell if the foal is okay or breech. One of us needs to calm her while the other watches for the birth sac. Mr. Jericho, I may need you to help us."

The big man nodded.

"You too." Tess looked at the young ranch hand.

"Mr. Jericho, you'll help me with the birth sac while Tess keeps her calm." Drew looked up to see that Jericho's eyes had grown as wide as saucers. "Have you ever done this before?" Drew asked the man who stood immobile beside him.

"Never."

"Well, then, you're in for an experience." Drew pushed up from his seat and positioned himself to lower his body to the straw covered floor at the mare's back. He didn't want to be caught if she started to kick. "Grab that bench over there and position it behind me for leverage."

Once on the ground, he moved his legs to where he wanted them, and ran his large hand down the mare's back and over her hips. Drew lifted her tail. It was soaked but very little of the sac showed. While he worked, Tess continued to coach the mare, talking in a calm voice, stroking her neck.

Drew had seen times, not many, where mares had become so exhausted that they couldn't push further, their strength gone. In those cases severe measures had to be taken to save the foal, but he didn't believe this would be one of those times. He watched the mare's eyes. They weren't panic-stricken. It was the calm she displayed that made Drew think it would be okay.

Without warning the mare reared her head, snorted several times, and pushed. A few inches of the birth sac appeared. Drew saw hooves, but not the head. The mare pushed one, two more times, and this time the head was visible.

"It's not breech, Tess. I think we may be good. Let's see how much this mare wants to see her baby."

Within twenty minutes there was a new colt in the Taylor stable and one very tired mare. There were also four people who felt a sense of joy at what they'd seen.

Tess looked around the stable at the colt and the men who'd helped with his birth. Her smile was radiant, creating a wave of heat that melted

Drew's heart. She threw her arms around his neck, surprising him with a warm hug.

"Thank you," she whispered in his ear before placing a quick kiss on his check and pushing away.

He wanted to tug her back into his embrace, but now wasn't the time.

Drew knew his calling was to breed horses, had been his whole life, but he'd needed the education and distance from his family to accept it. He'd been fortunate to be selected by Dunnigan for the opportunity in Denver. His legal skills had increased and he'd had access to the best resources available. But when he'd come to help his twin brother, Will, find the killer who'd murdered his brother's wife, it was like coming home.

And there'd been Tess.

It had taken just days for him to realize that if he ever did return to ranching, she was the type of woman he'd want beside him. Hell, she was the only woman he wanted beside him. Then the shooting. But tonight, working with Tess to deliver the foal made him realize that, no matter what, he had to return home to Fire Mountain. Preferably with Tess by his side.

******

"What do you mean, the prisoner's dead?" Frank stormed into the jail after Deputy Eddy O'Dell found him at home, getting his son, Aaron, off to school. Frank and Aaron had been living in town for a few months, and it had been the best months of their lives—until now. He'd thought the threats to Cold Creek were over after Bierdan's death and the arrest of his gang of rustlers. He'd been wrong.

"Found him like this when I went back to deliver his breakfast." Eddy pointed to the body lying on the cell floor, his throat cut. "I was gone a few minutes to get his food. He was fine when I left."

"Did you lock the door?"

"Yes, sir, just like you told me." Eddy was visibly shaken. He'd been a new deputy when the previous sheriff went missing—his whereabouts were still a mystery. Although O'Dell had helped with the cleanup after the rustlers had been apprehended, this was the closest he'd come to seeing a murder.

"Son of a ..." Frank walked into the cell and turned the body over. No other marks. "They were watching for you to leave. Whoever did this didn't try to break him out. They were here for one reason only. To kill our prisoner. Silence him."

"But he just roughed up a couple of men, Sheriff. Why kill him?"

"From what I know, these men are out to intimidate ranchers into selling, leaving the area. Men like him," Frank nodded at the body on the floor, "are the instrument of their boss. When they cease to be of value, or could be a witness against him, they're killed. This is no small game, Deputy."

"I'll get a wagon and take the body to Doc Wheaton. Anything else you want me to do?" Eddy asked.

"Come back here after you deliver the body to Doc. I need to ride out to the Bierdan ranch and let them know what happened. The situation just got a lot more serious."

******

"Murdered?" Eloise whispered. She knew the men were dangerous, but to murder someone—one of their own—signaled a danger that was hard to comprehend.

"Did Eddy see anyone?" Jeff had joined them as soon as Frank rode up. The stern expression on the sheriff's face let the foreman know that this was no social call.

"No one. It happened when Eddy left to pick up Vern's breakfast. He was gone a few minutes."

"So they were watching." It was a statement, not a question.

"That's what I think." Frank turned back to Eloise. He hated to cause the young widow more worry. She'd dealt with a lot since Gordon had died, and now this. He knew her financial condition was weak but he admired her determination to make a go of it with little experience and few men. "Can you afford to hire more men?"

"I don't see how that's possible. I can just make the payroll now." She looked around the

120

room. "I suppose I can try to sell more furniture. Maybe there's some unused tack in the barn...." Her voice drifted as her mind worked the consequences of this latest news.

Jeff and Frank glanced at each other. Both knew she had few options.

"You have some other possibilities that might help save the ranch," Frank offered in a cautious tone. He knew her well enough to understand that pride was one of the few possessions she had left. He didn't intend to damage it.

"Other than selling? I don't see that I have other choices."

"Have you thought about offering some of your land to other ranches to graze their cattle? Maybe bringing in a partner?"

"Maybe a partner, but you know how little good grazing land I have, Sheriff. There's little left to offer once my cattle have gotten what they need." She looked at her foreman. "Jeff, what do you think?"

"You're right about the pasture land. There's not much we don't use." His soft southern drawl seemed to calm the room. "But a partner? That might work for you. Someone who knows ranching, has connections in the area, and money."

The room fell silent as Eloise considered her options. She stood and walked to the window to gaze out at the ranch her husband had built. It had never been her intention to sell or bring in a partner. When he had died, she'd envisioned expanding the ranch, adding land and more cattle.

Then she'd seen the financial state her husband had left her in and knew her dreams would be hard, if not impossible, to realize.

"I'll consider a partner. Either of the Denver businessmen may be interested in that rather than buying it outright." She referred to Ira Walsh and Louis Dunnigan. At this point she had no preference. Eloise turned back to the men. "Do either of you have thoughts on someone local?"

"There's always Grant Taylor. His land butts against yours and he's expressed an interest in expanding. Not sure why he's remained silent," Frank said.

Eloise thought she knew. Grant and Gordon had been partners when they'd started years ago. A rift had developed and the men split up, but her husband had always thought he'd been cheated. It was Grant's bullet that had killed Gordon. She didn't hold it against him—he'd had no choice.

"You're right. I should speak with him and the bank manager. He may have ideas, also." Her voice resigned, she walked to the coffee pot that sat on a nearby table and filled each of the men's cups again.

"The issue now is your safety until a solution is found. Let me ask around in town and see if there are any men willing to work for food and a place to live, maybe a small monthly pay. They may not have much ranch experience, but if they're good with a gun it could be worth having extra people around." Frank knew of a couple of young men down on their luck who might jump at such an offer.

"I'd appreciate that. And thank you for coming here to warn us. We'll work it out, I'm sure of it." Eloise tried to keep a positive tone, but her broken voice betrayed her attempts.

"It's my job, Mrs. Bierdan. Can't say it's a pleasure to deliver warnings, but it's part of what I do. Let me know if you or your men experience any other instances, or see that Luther fellow. I sure would like to find that man."

So would I, Jeff thought as the sheriff left. *So would I.*

******

Pierce watched his new boss work his way around the crowded saloon. Connor had come to him a few days before, offering work at the Denver Rose, and he'd accepted. A man could always use a few more dollars.

Pierce wasn't surprised that Connor had been detained in his journey around the large room several times by different women who worked for him. Each fawned over the handsome man but he extricated himself each time with a soft spoken phrase or subtle remark. He was all business.

Connor made his way toward Pierce and stopped.

"Pierce," Connor acknowledged his new employee.

"Connor."

"You look like you have a comment you want to make." Their eyes met briefly, then Connor's eyes moved back to the crowd.

Pierce wondered what had given him away. "Just wondering how a man keeps his sanity—says no—when surrounded by women offering themselves to him at every opportunity."

Connor's slight chuckle surprised Pierce. "Who says I always say no?"

The admission surprised Pierce. "Well, it's good to know the man many consider a cold-hearted bastard actually does have blood in his veins. Now, if you'll excuse me, I see a fight brewing." He nodded in the direction of a table where the level of conversation had risen over the last few minutes.

Connor watched him walk across the room, still surprised at the comment Pierce had made. He knew many thought of him as cold, unbending, and they were right. There wasn't much place in his life for weakness or lack of conviction. A sharp crack turned Connor's attention to the table where Pierce now stood holding the barrel of his gun and looking at a man on the floor. It wasn't hard to figure out what had happened.

"Nelson, help Pierce escort him outside and order a round of drinks for those left at the table," Connor ordered. Nelson was the other man he'd hired to replace those Ira had riding to Cold Creek. Nelson had been coming to the bar each week for quite a while looking for work. Said he'd do whatever was needed if a job was available. Connor knew him to be fast with a gun and slow to anger—both traits Connor admired.

"Yes, sir, Boss," Nelson replied.

The remaining men at the table nodded their thanks to Connor and continued on with their card game. Nothing like a drunk cowboy on a losing streak to change the mood of a place.

"Good evening, Connor."

The soft voice was accompanied by an arm slipping through his. "Lola. How are you doing tonight?" he asked without making any attempt to disengage himself from her grasp. She was a nice woman, a little older than him, and accommodating. Her makeup was more subdued than most of the girls at the Rose, and her dresses a little more conservative—not much, but enough to set her apart.

"I'm good. A little tired but that's normal, don't you think?" Her light blue eyes lifted to his.

"Yes, I do think that's normal." A slight grin cracked his stern features. She was the only pleasure he allowed himself these days and even that was rare.

"Thought I'd go on upstairs, if that's all right with you. Seems you have plenty of ladies to handle what's needed."

"That's fine, Lola. We're fine down here." He dropped his arm from hers and watched her ascend the wooden staircase. There'd been many women like her in his past and no doubt there'd be more. But there was something different about Lola. Maybe it was her past and that her work in the saloon hadn't turned her hard, bitter, like most soiled doves. Whatever it was, he hoped she'd find someone to take her out of this life and find peace.

Connor continued to trace her steps up the stairs and caught site of Ira Walsh making his way down. He stopped a moment to whisper something into Lola's ear that made her laugh, then continued down and made his way next to Connor.

"You leaving, Ira?"

"I have a supper engagement." Walsh flicked lint from his black suit. "Some new investors traveled to Denver from San Francisco. They're interested in merchandise I'm able to import."

"Will you be back?"

"Not until tomorrow, I'm afraid. I expect the meeting will run quite late."

"Then I'll wish you luck."

Connor watched Ira leave, then searched out Pierce.

"Mr. Walsh is gone for the night. I'll need you to make a sweep of the upstairs area a few times, just to make sure no one wanders toward his private quarters."

Most everyone knew the staircase led not only to Ira's office and lounge area but also to the rooms used by the girls when they worked. The same rooms became their bedrooms when the saloon was closed. Patrons were allowed in the ladies area, but not Ira's. That was invitation only.

"How often should I check?"

"Each hour until we close, then again just before we lock up."

"Anything else?" Pierce asked.

"Nope."

Chapter Eleven

Cold Creek, Colorado

Drew had been working in Grant Taylor's office the past two days, preparing a proposal to purchase Langdon's ranch. He had been caught off guard when Grant told him Warren Langdon had indicated he'd had enough and would welcome a sale on fair terms. Grant's attorney was in San Francisco, so Grant had gone to the only other person he knew who had the experience to prepare the agreement.

Once Louis Dunnigan had approved Drew's request to help Grant, everything moved fast. The amount offered was quite generous considering considerable work would be needed on the property. He and Grant had a meeting with Langdon that afternoon with the hope of finalizing the sale before Ira Walsh got wind of it.

Tess poked her head into the office. She found Drew engrossed in the papers on the desk, murmuring to himself as he read.

"Good morning. You've been holed up in here since before sunrise. Can I help with anything?"

Drew dropped his pen, swept a hand through his hair, and stretched both arms above his head. "Is it still morning?" he teased.

"Just barely. Dinner's about ready. Father told me what you're doing for him." She walked closer to the desk, stopping at the front edge and letting her fingers trail over the polished wood.

Drew watched her fingers graze the desk, wondering what it would feel like to have those fingers move over his arms, his chest. He cleared his throat and forced his attention to the face of the woman in front of him. "I'm glad to do it. He's making Langdon a good offer—one that I expect he'll take and move on." Drew pulled his eyes from Tess to the outside. He'd hardly noticed the sunrise or morning turning to almost noon.

"What can I do?"

Drew's gaze fixed back on Tess. "If you're serious, I could use a set of eyes on this language." He handed one of the papers to Tess. "Read it. Tell me if it makes sense."

She took the paper and read through it twice. "I don't understand what this means, at least not the way it's written." She pointed to a long passage midway down the page. "But I think I know what you're trying to say."

Drew smiled. It was the same wording he'd struggled with for an hour. "How would you word it?"

Tess took a piece of paper and wrote for several minutes then handed it to Drew. He read and looked up, his eyes sparkling with approval. "This is great. I couldn't come up with it, but you dashed it out in a few minutes."

"Glad I could help." Her face lit up at his complement. "Now, come on to dinner, before you miss it altogether." She walked behind the desk and gripped the handles on his chair. "I'd be happy to come back after we eat, if you want more help.'"

"Thanks. I just might take you up on that."

******

Tess and Drew worked together another hour after dinner. She read, made sure she understood what he wanted Langdon to grasp, and suggested changes. There wasn't much but Drew was grateful for her help. Most of all he was glad to have her near him.

"Well, I guess I'd better check on the new foal again." Tess stood and started for the door.

"Thanks for your help," Drew called after her.

Tess turned and walked back around the desk. She bent, and before Drew realized her plans, placed a soft kiss on his lips. "Like I said before, glad I could help." She strolled out, leaving Drew to stare after her, wanting more.

He rolled his chair into the hallway, deciding the only way to clear his mind was through strenuous work.

"Mr. Jericho, I'd like to proceed with the exercises now, if you don't mind."

"Now is fine," Jericho responded and opened the bedroom door for Drew to wheel through. Drew had just entered his room when a shout came from outside.

"Drew, Mr. Jericho, come quick! There's a fire!" It was Tess and she sounded frantic. Jericho made it outside to see Tess pointing to some distant smoke in the direction of the Langdon ranch and barn.

Grant had just returned from town when he saw the smoke. "Jake, get the men and some buckets. We'll head over right away." He turned to Tess. "Eleanor stayed in town with Joey. Let Maria know what's happening. I'll need you to drive the wagon over."

"I'll drive." Everyone looked up to see Drew. He'd made it down the ramp that Jake and a few of the boys had constructed for him. He had no plans to be left behind.

"Are you sure?" Grant asked.

"Nothing wrong with these arms, Grant. Mr. Jericho will be beside me. If I run into trouble, he can take over." He looked at Tess. "You ride with us." It was an order, not a request. He wanted her close in case there was trouble. If it was Langdon's place, the timing was just too coincidental for Drew, and he was a man who didn't believe in coincidences.

Grant looked around at the people waiting for his order. "Let's go."

It was quite a journey to the Langdon ranch, but Grant knew trails that helped quicken the pace. Even with that, over an hour had passed from the time the group left the Taylor ranch to when the Langdon barn came into view. It was in ashes, but the home might still be salvageable.

"What can we do, Warren?" Grant asked as he dismounted.

"I need men to fill buckets. We can form a line."

"Jake, set the men up and let's get started. Mr. Jericho, you handle the water pump. Take shifts with a couple of my men when you get tired."

"Yes, sir," Jericho responded, rolled up his sleeves, and hurried to the pump.

The work was exhausting. Filling buckets, passing them along the line of men, and tossing the water on the fire. Strong winds had spread the blaze from the barn to the house. Sparks landed on dry grass around the entry and caught, swallowing the downstairs in flames. At least the wind had now slowed.

It took another hour before the fire was contained. No one was injured but the house and barn were gone. The horses had been moved to a large corral, and the little amount of tack recovered lay in a heap a few yards from the smoldering remnants of the barn.

"Any idea how this happened, Warren?" Grant asked when the men were able to take a break.

"It was no accident if that's what you're thinking. I saw a group of riders just before the flames erupted. Nothing in that barn would've set off a fire like that. It was intentional." Warren Langdon scowled at the remains of what had been the barn he and his men had constructed the year before. Nothing was left. Not one board-foot. The house was a total loss, but perhaps some furniture and personal effects might be salvageable.

"Papa?" Warren turned to see his daughter, Clarisse, with Jay Bellows standing beside her. Warren wrapped an arm around Clarisse and pulled her close.

"It's all right, Clarisse. Everything will be fine," her father soothed even though his mind screamed at the injustice of it.

Warren walked over to Grant. After a moment the two strode up to where Drew had been pumping water alongside Jericho. Tess stood beside Drew, a hand resting on his shoulder. Like everyone else, she was covered in soot and dirt. Her eyes reflected the pain she felt at the family's loss.

"Is the agreement ready?" Grant asked Drew.

"Yes, sir. It's in your office."

"Then let's get this done," Langdon spat out. "Those vermin hoped to drive me out, give up. They didn't know I'd been interested in a sale to Grant for some time. Selling may anger them even more. You sure you're up for that fight, Grant?"

"I can handle it," Grant responded.

Langdon turned to his daughter. "Clarisse, gather what items you can find and load them into our wagon. We'll follow the Taylor's back and sign the paperwork, then find a place in town."

"No, you'll stay with us, Warren," Grant offered. "You'll want to get back here first thing tomorrow and town will be too far for you. Trust me on this."

"Thanks, Grant. You don't know..." but words failed as the reality sank in. He'd lost the ranch, his home. His wife had died right after they'd arrived. She was buried in this soil. He'd never expected to leave.

Grant clasped a hand on Warren's shoulder. "It will work out. You'll have money for a new start, hopefully here in Cold Creek." Taylor walked away to let his neighbor deal with the loss in his own way.

Warren's head dropped to his chest. He took a deep breath, but coughed as the remaining smoke filled his lungs. He grabbed a handkerchief from his back pocket to wipe his face. Black smudges colored the white piece of cloth. He looked to see his daughter standing several feet away, Jay's arm around her shoulder. He liked the boy, he liked the town. Maybe they could find a way to stay in Cold Creek.

******

Denver, Colorado

Pierce walked the upper balcony. He made his way through the two hallways reserved for the patrons and saloon girls, but found nothing that caught his attention. The back door creaked open as he peered out, but again he found nothing. Walsh's office was on the other side of the upstairs.

The two areas were separated with a door which was left unlocked except when Walsh was gone. Ira owned the only key to it and his office down the short hall. Pierce looked around, saw no one, and checked the knob. Locked. He reached in his pocket to extract a slim object with a point and inserted it into the lock. The gesture was followed by a click and the door popped open a fraction. Pierce pushed it and entered the hallway to Ira's private quarters, then shut the door and locked it.

When he reached the office door, Pierce repeated the same procedure he'd used to access the hall. Again, the lock clicked.

Pierce looked around again and, satisfied he was alone, slipped through the door, locking it behind him. There was a small amount of light streaming through the windows from outside. Not much, but enough that he could see. He knew from his brother that the wall safe was hidden behind a picture. The third one yielded results. It took a few moments, but Pierce opened the safe and looked inside. The main ledger lay on top. He pulled it out and lifted the trap door underneath. The second ledger he'd decoded was beneath. He needed to find the third.

Feeling his way around the inside of the safe produced nothing. Yet he knew the ledger was close—if not in the safe than somewhere close enough for easy access by Walsh.

He tried again. This time his fingers landed on a small catch, almost a miniature ball. He moved it to one side, then the other. Nothing. He pushed upwards on the catch and heard a slight noise. The back wall of the safe opened. Pierce reached in and felt a book. The third ledger.

"What do you mean you haven't seen him?" Walsh's voice was strident, close.

Pierce closed the hidden door, locked the safe, replaced the picture, and looked around for a place to hide. A key clicked in the lock and the knob turned, then stopped. "Find him," Walsh barked, and pushed the door open.

Ira approached his desk while looking about the room. He saw nothing. The papers on his desk appeared undisturbed. He rushed to the picture hiding his safe and pushed it aside. The safe seemed secure, but he opened it anyway. The three ledgers were inside. He closed the safe and replaced the picture before turning at the sound of someone entering his office.

"He was outside, using the facilities," Connor informed his boss. "Everything okay in here?"

"Yes. Nothing seems amiss." Connor watched as Ira lowered himself into his chair. "Your meeting went well?"

Ira looked up, deciding how much to say. Connor had proven himself reliable, trustworthy, but still, Walsh wasn't certain. "Yes, it went well. I'm having my lawyer draw up the necessary papers and hope to make the first delivery within three months."

Connor didn't ask what the merchandise was. He figured Ira would share that with him when the time was right.

"There's another group of investors I must meet with. This time I have to travel to San Francisco. I'll be leaving tomorrow but don't expect to be gone too long. I trust you to take care of everything here."

"I'll handle anything that comes up in your absence." Connor looked about the neat office. "I better get back downstairs. Let me know if you need anything before your trip," Connor said and left Walsh to his own thoughts.

******

"Your new job working out all right?" his brother asked as he entered the room where Pierce worked.

"Yes. I found the third ledger."

"Did you? And where is it?" his brother glanced around but found nothing new on Pierce's desk.

"Still in Walsh's safe. But I can get to it now that I know where it is. The problem, of course, is that it will take days to copy and the book must be returned each night."

"Ira's traveling to San Francisco tomorrow. He'll be gone over a week. You'll be at the saloon and will know when he leaves. That will be your chance."

"Is the boss still back East?" Pierce asked. He knew the man would want answers as soon as he set foot off the train.

"Yes. I expect to get a message from him by tomorrow. He's scheduled to be back next week. That may give you just the amount of time needed to copy the ledger and decode enough to see if it's what we hope."

"Then what?" Pierce asked his brother.

"What do you mean?"

"If Walsh is guilty, like you expect, your job here is done. Where will you go after that?" Pierce enjoyed the work he did for his brother, but he was getting restless. His old life called to him and he was ready to return.

"Haven't thought about it."

Pierce wasn't surprised.

Even though Pierce had been the wilder of the two, his brother had been darker, deadlier. He had a conscious, but held no qualms at all about putting a bullet in someone if they were guilty of a crime. It was his brother's type of justice—black and white—no middle ground.

"I have to get going," he told Pierce. "We'll talk tomorrow." His brother slid out the door without a backwards glance.

******

Cold Creek, Colorado

Warren Langdon read the document once more, signed his name, and extended his hand to Grant, then Drew. "I appreciate your work on this. It's more than I'd anticipated, but you're getting a solid piece of land."

"You know, Warren, there will be a place for you and some of your men once I decide how to proceed with the property. You open to offers or have you made up your mind to leave?"

"Haven't decided. Clarisse wants to stay. You've probably figured out she has something going with Jay Bellows over at Bierdan's place. I hate to break that up by moving away. I guess I'm open to offers if you believe I'd be useful, and I'm certain my men would be open to listening, also. After this is final, they'll be out of a job." Langdon finished his coffee and stood. "Well, I best be getting back to the ranch and salvage what I can. From what I remember of last night, it shouldn't take long."

Drew watched him leave and felt a burden lift. Langdon had made the right decision. He and his daughter were now safe, Grant had an excellent piece of land, and Drew was now free to concentrate on acquiring the Bierdan ranch.

What he wanted to concentrate on was walking again—and Tessa Taylor.

He hadn't told Jericho, but he'd felt sharp painful twinges in one leg yesterday and in the other leg today. Both times the pain had radiated from a foot, up the back side of the leg, to his hip. Each one had been excruciating—and wonderful. The first people he'd wanted to tell were Tess and Aunt Alicia, but he didn't want to give them false hope. Today he would tell Jericho if he experienced the pain again.

Chapter Twelve

Denver, Colorado

"Drop it, Slaughter," Connor's voice sliced through the noise of the saloon, causing everyone to stop what they were doing and stare—not at the man who held the gun on Pierce, but at Conner. They knew he didn't hold with drawing a gun on someone unless you aimed to use it. Everyone knew Connor would use his.

"I ain't leaving until I win my money back," Slaughter hissed. "And your man here ain't going to throw me out, either. He'll be dead if he tries." He continued to point his gun at Pierce's head.

A shot sounded through the room and everyone watched as Slaughter's lifeless body crumbled to the ground—a hole centered in his forehead.

Connor holstered the still smoldering gun. Without so much as a glance at the dead man, he gazed around the room. "Nelson, help Pierce throw the body outside, then go for the sheriff." He ordered another employee to clean up the mess. He felt no remorse, no guilt. The man had a gun pointed at another man's head—Connor's man—and that, in Connor's mind, was a deadly mistake.

He walked over to the bar and stood next to Lola. "Nice shot, Boss," Lola murmured. "That's what? The third man who's pulled a gun since you arrived? You'd think that fella would have heard not to pull a gun in here. Some people just don't learn."

"Each one's been righteous."

"No one's disputing that. Not one person in the saloon has ever said otherwise." Lola studied Connor. He'd be a heartbreaker if he ever let anyone get close. His tan skin, coal-black hair, and clear, moss green eyes set him apart from most men. He'd always treated her well—treated them all well—but there was something dark, sinister about him. His calm exterior and supreme confidence spoke volumes. Connor might be the deadliest man she'd ever known.

"It's all done, Boss," Nelson reported. "Sheriff didn't say a word. Just had someone haul the body away, spoke to a couple of people, then took off."

Connor glanced at Nelson and nodded as Pierce walked up.

"You want me to go up and tell Walsh?"

"He left a few hours ago for San Francisco. I'll tell him when he returns." Connor answered and sipped at the whiskey Lola had ordered. He didn't drink on the job, but tonight he'd make an exception.

"Hey there, Lola. You want some company tonight?" A cowboy about Connor's age walked up and put an arm around her waist, pulling her close and bending to place a kiss on her neck.

She ventured a look at Connor but he was lost in his whiskey and watching the saloon.

"Sure, cowboy. You know the way."

Connor watched as Lola and her companion made their way up the staircase. She was a working girl, knew the good and bad of it, just like he knew the good and bad of his choices. Tonight they'd both live with those choices.

******

Cold Creek, Colorado

"One more time, Mr. Jericho," Drew ordered. They'd been at it for an hour and Drew had yet to feel anything. No twinges, no sharp pain, nothing. He was determined to keep at it until he felt something.

Jericho lifted him once more and helped Drew arrange his feet, then, by inches, let his legs absorb the weight. This time Drew cried out in pain and began to topple. Jericho tightened his grip and lowered him into the chair.

"Are you all right, Mr. MacLaren?" Jericho had lowered his body to rest on his haunches and looked up at his boss. Concern mixed with hope showed in his face. His hands gently moved over Drew's legs, feeling for anything that would elicit such a response.

Drew took a deep breath to steady his heart rate. He'd felt it. Pain. From the heel of his foot to his hip. A sharp, almost searing pain that radiated upwards. It had been excruciating and exhilarating at the same time. Although it hurt like hell, he couldn't contain the small grin that showed on his face.

"You feel something?"

"Yes." Drew pushed himself up in the chair and leaned back. "That's the third time in three days."

"And you didn't tell me?"

"I wanted to be sure before I told anyone. I needed to be sure."

Jericho accepted the answer. He didn't like it but understood Drew's reluctance to voice the hope he knew the young man felt. "What now?"

Drew grimaced as another sharp pain seared through his other leg. "I'm not sure we should do anything more today," he said through gritted teeth. "Maybe a bath? But not too hot. My leg already feels like it's on fire."

"Damn, Mr. MacLaren," Jericho declared. "Do you know what this means?"

Drew just looked at him. This was the first time Jericho had showed much reaction at all to Drew's progress. Of course, there hadn't been much until today. His usually stoic expression had momentarily crumbled and some emotion had peeked through.

"It means we celebrate." Jericho walked over to a cabinet and pulled out an expensive bottle of whiskey. He'd saved it for just this occasion. He poured two glasses of the amber liquid and handed one to Drew. "To you and your recovery, Mr. MacLaren," he toasted.

Drew tipped his glass against Jericho's and took a sip. Damn, it did feel good. He'd just held out the glass for a refill when another severe pain gripped him. The glass slipped from his hand. He grabbed at his leg and began to push his thumbs into it, hoping to relieve the fiery sensation. Jericho pushed Drew's hands away, lifted him onto the bed, and began to massage the area with deep, strong strokes. Drew's relief was immediate.

As soon as the pain lifted, Jericho left to prepare a bath. An hour later, Drew was dry and clothed, and ready to stand.

"I'm not sure this is such a good idea, Mr. MacLaren."

"I want to take advantage while I can feel something. The pain has lessened but there's still pulsing sensations." He placed his hands on the arms of his chair and began to lift himself.

"Ah, hell," Jericho muttered as he moved to stand behind Drew. He lifted him in one steady movement and positioned his legs. But this time Drew was able to help. Just a little, but enough for Jericho to know the muscles were responding.

They continued for another half hour before Drew called a halt to it. He was exhausted and, although he'd never admit it, so was Jericho. Besides it was almost supper time and both were famished.

A soft knock was followed by a quiet voice. "Drew? Mr. Jericho? Supper's ready."

It was Tess.

Drew wanted to throw the door open and shout his good news, but he was determined that when he announced his intentions toward her, he'd do it on two legs.

******

San Francisco, California

"You are certain, Mr. Walsh, that you can deliver that amount within the time agreed?" The businessman looked at Ira and held up a hand when their guest began to speak. "Be sure of your answer. We do not appreciate merchandise that is of low quality or that arrives late. Do we understand each other?"

Ira looked around the room at the six men, all wealthy, all ruthless, and began to rethink his desire to do business with them. In his two days in their ranks they had ordered the death of one supplier who'd failed them, and the severing of another's hand. The second had tried to change his price after the agreement had been signed. In Ira's opinion both men deserved harsh treatment for their stupidity. He didn't intend to be stupid but he was reluctant to become their puppet. Besides, it was much too late to back out now—he already envisioned the wealth he and Drago would make off this new venture.

"Mr. Everts, I assume you checked my references and are well aware of how I run my business. I would not be in San Francisco if I couldn't supply your needs for high quality opium, on time, and at the price agreed."

"You've seen how we deal with those who do not fulfill their promises. As long as we both understand what is expected, our relationship will work out to our mutual advantage." Everts looked at the other five men for their consensus. Each nodded. The deal was done.

Ira walked around the room and shook hands with each man. "I will be in touch, gentlemen."

He walked out of the San Francisco building, one of the tallest in the bustling town of over one-hundred-twenty-five-thousand people, wiped the sweat from his forehead, and settled a black bowler on his head. It was a gift to himself after his successful negotiations with the San Francisco buyers who had visited him recently. He decided to wait to celebrate today's agreement until he was well away from the bustling California port city.

Besides, he didn't want to be gone any longer than necessary from Denver. Something wasn't quite right there. He knew it, but couldn't discover what. Plus, he'd gotten distressful news from Cold Creek while he'd been gone. Langdon had sold his land to Grant Taylor. Well, Walsh hadn't given up on acquiring the Langdon land even if he had to go against Taylor to do it. Drago was in Cold Creek, had already put plans in action, and Ira had no doubt that in time, Drago's work would succeed.

******

Cold Creek, Colorado

Frank had exhausted all of his resources to locate Luther Grimms, the one man everyone believed was responsible for Vern Tyson's murder and the fire at the Langdon ranch. At least he'd been able to obtain their last names and a confession on the beatings before Vern was killed. But Vern had been adamant that no one but he and Luther were involved. There was no boss giving them orders. Alts had known Vern was lying, but had decided to let his prisoner sleep on it overnight and start afresh the following day. It had been a mistake.

Luther was a large man, easy to spot, yet he'd disappeared like a ghost. Frank, Drew, and Dunnigan were all convinced he took orders from Walsh, but without proof, they had nothing to support their suspicions. Langdon had said that more than one man had set the fires at his ranch— he'd seen at least six. That meant that if Alts could catch just one of the group, he had a chance to obtain more information.

He was now on his way to the Bierdan ranch. A telegram had arrived for Eloise while Frank was picking up his mail. He'd offered to deliver it. It had been sent from Denver.

"Sheriff," Jeff greeted him. "You here to see Mrs. Bierdan?"

"I am. Is she in the house?"

"As far as I know. Haven't seen her outside yet today. But the last two days she worked alongside the men and me, wouldn't rest until we did, ate with us, and didn't stop until supper. Woman's pushing herself hard." Jeff removed his hat and swiped a sleeve across his moist forehead. "I know most people in town believe she's a pampered female from a wealthy family back East, but I'm not so sure. She just doesn't behave like someone who's had everything given to her." Jeff looked toward the house to see the curtains pulled back and Eloise looking out. "At least that's what I believe."

Frank took in the foreman's words, letting them roll around to see if anything fit. They did. She'd never seemed like the simpering Eastern society woman, at least not like the ones he'd known. There was much more to the widow than she let on.

Eloise answered his knock and, with some reluctance, asked Frank in. She looked tired, as if she hadn't slept in days. The house was clean, everything in its place, but its owner was disheveled.

"Are you all right, Mrs. Bierdan?" Frank laid his hat next to him on the small divan.

"Just tired. I haven't been able to sleep since Vern Tyson was murdered. I know that Jeff and the men are all concerned and working extra shifts to keep the ranch going, plus guard me. I hate that it has turned to this." She paced the room as she spoke, twisting her hands together.

"I understand you've been working with the men, taking on some of their work plus your own, putting in long hours. It's a lot for a woman to take on." Frank knew it wasn't his place, but there was no one else to say it, plus he'd grown to care about her, more than he liked.

Eloise looked at him and saw concern etched in his strong features. "It's a lot for anyone, Sheriff. This ranch is all I have. I can't lose it without doing everything I can, which includes working with the men." She lowered herself into a nearby chair and gripped the arms. "I can't give up. Not yet. And certainly not because I'm being pressured to sell."

Frank didn't like it but he understood. Most would fight, work themselves to death to keep their land. It was all that many had.

"Have your men noticed anything? Seen any strangers in the area?"

"Nothing. Jeff has drilled into them the need to be vigilant and I believe they understand the seriousness of the threats."

Frank believed Jeff and the men did realize the danger and that much of it was focused on the Bierdan ranch. He hoped Eloise understood it. "I guess I better head out. There was a fire at the Langdon place and I want to look it over, see if anything will help us find whoever set it." He walked toward the door, then stopped when he remembered the telegram. "Almost forgot. This came for you." He handed the message to Eloise.

She tore it open, read it through, and then looked at Frank. "It's from Ira Walsh, in Denver.

He's the other businessman who's interested in the ranch. He plans to travel to Cold Creek and is requesting a meeting, perhaps as early as next week." She sighed, knowing it was best to at least agree to the meeting.

"What will you do?"

"Meet with him. I'd like to talk with him and perhaps Drew MacLaren again before speaking with Grant Taylor. I know Grant won't come to me, given his history with my husband, but if I sell it seems right to have it pass to someone local."

"He's a good man, as is Louis Dunnigan. Either would make you a good deal."

"And Walsh?"

"Don't know him. You'll have to make that call yourself."

They stood in silence for a moment, Frank staring out the window, knowing the struggles she faced. Eloise looking at the message, resigned to the possibility of losing the ranch. Nothing came easy.

Chapter Thirteen

Fire Mountain, Arizona

"How's Aunt Alicia, Niall?" Kate asked.

The oldest MacLaren brother read the latest letter from their aunt. It was a long one. He finished, then passed it to his wife. "She and Tess are back in Cold Creek. Drew went with them."

"He did? That's a surprise."

"You'll read it, but sounds like Dunnigan sent him back on business."

"Alicia says they're having more trouble—at least some neighboring ranchers are."

The door slammed open as Niall and Kate's son, Adam, and Jamie and Torie's oldest son, Isaac, came racing into the house, followed by a scowling Jamie.

"Stop right now." Jamie's stern voice had the intended effect. The boys turned to look at the imposing man who held a baby in his arms. Jamie's younger son, Caleb, was only a few months old, but everyone already knew he'd be a handful.

"What's the rule about boots in the house?" Jamie asked as he passed Caleb off to Torie, who'd stood watching the scene from the kitchen.

Isaac and Adam exchanged sheepish grins, but it was Adam who spoke. "They're not allowed in the house, Uncle Jamie."

Isaac just nodded at his father in agreement.

"That's right. Now march back outside, take them off, and store them in the mudroom. After that, help set the table for dinner." The boys started to protest but he stopped them. "After dinner, both of you will help muck the stalls."

"But, Uncle Jamie..." Isaac started but was cut off by his father.

"You heard your uncle," Niall said. "You broke a rule and you'll muck the stalls. No argument— either of you."

The boys bowed their heads and trudged outside. It was all the adults could do to control their laughter.

"How many times did Aunt Alicia have us mucking stalls for forgetting that rule, Niall?" Jamie asked.

"Don't recall, but I know for a fact you cleaned those stalls a lot more than anyone else." Niall grinned at his wife. She didn't believe a word of it.

"What do you have there?" Jamie walked up and peered over Kate's shoulder.

"A letter from Alicia. She, Tess, and Drew are back in Cold Creek. Guess there's been some trouble at the neighboring ranches. Beatings, threats—mainly toward the Bierdan widow. One neighbor, Warren Langdon, had his barn and house burned down. Alicia says that Frank arrested one of the men, but the prisoner was murdered the next day while in his jail cell." She looked up at the two men. "Doesn't sound good."

"Dinner ready yet?" Will came through the door and started into the kitchen but stopped at the stares from his brothers. They were looking at his feet. He looked down. "Huh, can't believe I forgot," Will chuckled as he walked back to the mudroom and removed his boots.

The change in him the past months had been miraculous. The once hardened bounty hunter was back to his pranks and jokes, just like he had been before the tragedy that sent him on a five year journey of revenge. Everyone believed his wife, Amanda, was the reason for his transition.

"Dinner will be a few more minutes," Torie said, "but there's a letter from Alicia you might want to read."

Jamie finished and handed the missive to Will. A couple of minutes later he raised his head, a grave look on his face.

"I met Langdon a couple of times. Good man but was having a tough go. Sounds like the sale was the best decision for him." He rubbed a hand over his stubbled face. "Doesn't appear that Eloise Bierdan is having an easy time."

The mood in the room had sobered measurably as the letter was passed around. No one blamed the young widow for Drew's condition. It was her husband who'd pulled the trigger. But in Will's mind, the bullet had been meant for him, not his twin brother. Anything having to do with a Bierdan still left a bitter taste.

Niall walked over to Kate and put an arm around her waist. "You've mentioned a couple of times how you'd like to see the Taylor ranch. This might be a good time to go."

Kate's eyes widened. "Why, yes. This would be a perfect time."

"Hold on, Niall. If anyone is going to Cold Creek, it'll be me." Will put his hands on his hips and walked up to his oldest brother.

"Who's going to Cold Creek?" Will's wife, Amanda, had entered the kitchen and caught the last part of the conversation.

"There may be trouble in Cold Creek. Drew and Alicia are there. I don't intend to wait and see how it all unfolds," Will answered.

"Then I'm going, too." Amanda stated.

Niall looked at Jamie and Torie. "You okay here if the four of us go check on Aunt Alicia and Drew?"

"Of course," Torie answered right away.

"No problem. Gus is here, and now that Pete's back, we're in good shape," Jamie assured them. Gus Dixon was the longtime MacLaren foreman, and Pete Cantlin their chief wrangler. He'd left a couple of years before to take care of some business, he'd said, but had returned a few months ago. Pete had been the first MacLaren ranch hand the boys had met on their journey to their Uncle Stuart's and Aunt Alicia's ranch after their parents had been murdered. The first real cowboy the boys had known.

"And Isaac?" Kate asked.

"Isaac's a cinch," Jamie replied. "It's Beth we'll have to keep a watch on."

Beth was Niall's daughter, Kate's step-daughter, and at fourteen she was starting to grow up. Much too fast as far as the adult MacLarens were concerned. Beth was a sweet girl, smart, with a quick laugh, who possessed ranching skills that surpassed some of the wranglers.

Niall clapped his brother on the shoulder. "Thanks, Jamie. We'll let you know what we find."

******

Niall, Kate, Will, and Amanda decided to take the train to Great Valley. It was easier to transport their horses in a stock car than to purchase fresh mounts in Great Valley. Plus they preferred to ride their own horses to the Taylor ranch. It was late the next day when they arrived. There hadn't been time to send a telegram, but Amanda had assured them there was plenty of room at the house for everyone.

Niall and Kate took one look at the massive structure and concurred. It was close to twice the size of the MacLaren ranch house. Lights still burned inside and the front door opened.

"My God, Amanda!" Tess called as she flew down the steps to embrace her sister. "Why didn't you tell us you were coming?"

Amanda drew back to look at her sister. It had been almost three months, but Tess looked more serene, content. "There wasn't time." Amanda looked up to see her parents, Grant and Eleanor, come down the steps. She ran to them and wrapped her arms around both.

"Well, that was quick," her mother said. "I read Alicia's letter before she mailed it. I told her I'd bet any amount of money that we'd see you within a week of getting the letter."

"Two days, Mother. It took two days," Amanda beamed. She loved Will and their life at Fire Mountain, but she missed her family.

Will and Niall had just finished their greetings when both spotted Drew. He was at the bottom of the ramp, waiting, a large, burley man at his back. Kate saw him at the same time, but unlike the men, didn't hesitate to run up and wrap her arms around him.

"Oh, Drew, it is so good to see you. But I'm still miffed you didn't come to Will and Amanda's wedding." She wiped away a tear that threatened and looked up at the stranger behind Drew. "I'm Kate MacLaren, Niall's wife."

"Mr. Jericho, ma'am. I assist Mr. MacLaren with whatever he needs."

By the looks of him, Kate thought the man was capable of handling about anything that came at him. "Mr. Jericho, it's a pleasure."

Niall clasped a hand on Drew's shoulder. "Mighty glad to see you. Wish I'd been here that day, but..." Niall's voice broke at the sight of his younger brother in a wheelchair.

The last memory Niall had of him was during a race they'd had—his horse against Drew's—when the attorney had come home for Alicia's birthday. It hadn't been a surprise that Niall had won on his magnificent stallion, Zeus, but what had been a surprise was Drew pulling up mere seconds behind. They'd laughed and talked for over an hour about Drew's plan to work another few years for Dunnigan, then come home. It hadn't worked out that way.

"Wouldn't have mattered, Niall. What happened, it couldn't have been stopped. No one was looking for it." Drew looked behind Niall to see Will. "And it was my decision to be here. Mine alone," he added for Will's benefit.

Will stepped up and grabbed his brother's hand. He wanted to pull him up in a bear hug, but knew that would have to wait. "You look good, real good."

"Come on, everyone. Let's go inside, get some food in you, and sort out the sleeping arrangements." Grant called out. "Then we can get to the good stuff—whiskey and cigars."

******

Maria put together food for their guests. Afterwards, the men retired to the office while the women settled in the living room.

"How is he, Aunt Alicia?" Amanda asked. The young woman had been at the ranch the day Drew had been shot. It had devastated them all.

"He'd doing well, considering. Works at least twice each day with Mr. Jericho on some exercises his doctors in Denver and Doc Wheaton prescribed. He takes a couple of hot baths and Mr. Jericho massages his legs each day." Alicia sighed. "That boy is stronger than anyone else I know. He won't give up until he walks again. And all the while, he's doing work for Mr. Dunnigan and trying to help around here."

Kate reached over and took her aunt's hand. "We all have faith he'll walk again. It may take some time, but he will."

Tess sat silent during the conversation. She'd met everyone before, at the wedding, and felt comfortable around them, but she wasn't sure how much to share. She was certain Drew had some feeling in his legs. She'd walked by his room and been startled by a crash, then overheard Drew say something to Jericho about a searing pain. She had yet to say anything to Drew. He'd tell her when he was ready.

Grant made his way around the office and topped off each man's glass. "So, there you have it. I now own the Langdon ranch, although I'm sure that won't insulate me from those who've been threatening the ranchers. Mrs. Bierdan is in a financial mess, but determined to keep her place. Two men were run off, one killed, two beaten, and her house vandalized, but she's holding on."

"Has Dunnigan made a formal offer for her place?" Niall asked Drew.

"No. I made his intentions known, but nothing yet. I'll give her some time, then meet again."

"Must be hard for you, her being Bierdan's widow." Will walked to the window and looked out at the blackened sky.

"Not her fault, Will. She was as innocent as any of us. Truth is, I've come to realize, even in this chair, I'm better off than most people." He tossed back the rest of his whiskey and signaled to Jericho for another. "But I will walk again, I guarantee you that."

The room fell silent, contemplating the tragedies that had affected them all, and how none could have been avoided. They couldn't change a thing, only go forward.

"What now?" Niall asked Grant.

"Something tells me the worst is yet to come. Don't know why no one has threatened me or my men. That's a puzzle. But we've got to locate this Luther fellow and those that ride with him. Frank is doing all he can, but it's just him and his deputy. O'Dell's a good man but young, with little experience. What Frank needs is someone with experience." He looked around the room and knew that the experience needed had just arrived on his front step. The MacLarens would do all they could to help, and stay until it was finished.

******

Fire Mountain, Arizona

"Jamie, stop pacing. You're making me crazy," Torie implored as she walked the room with a fussy Caleb. The baby had wakened twice and each time it had taken an hour to calm him.

She watched her husband wrestle with something. Torie was sure she knew what it was but waited for him to say it.

He stopped and ran both hands through his deep auburn colored hair, then crossed his arms and leaned against a wall. He looked up to stare into the eyes of the woman he'd loved since they had shared a desk in the one room school house.

"I should be there."

"Yes."

"What?" Jamie wasn't sure he'd heard her right.

"You're right. You should be there, with your brothers." She shifted Caleb's position, walked up to Jamie, and put her free arm around his waist. "Go. Help them finish this."

He looked as if he would argue, find reasons not to go, but she shut him off.

"I have Gus and Pete, plus twenty other men. Trent Garner and Josh Jacklin are a few miles away, and Sam Browning or Cord McAllister would come if there was trouble. Plus my parents. I can handle the children." She stood on her toes and placed a kiss on Jamie's cheek. "Go. We'll be fine."

Jamie wrapped his arms around his wife and youngest son and, for at least the hundredth time, wondered what he'd done to deserve them.

"Papa?" The door to their room opened and a sleepy Isaac came in, followed by Adam. "What's happening?"

Jamie scooped up both boys in his large arms and held them close. "Everything's fine," he said in a soft voice, then looked at Torie. "Everything is just fine."

Chapter Fourteen

Cold Creek, Colorado

It was late. Jeff had lain on his bunk for hours, unable to sleep. He gave up, pulled on his trousers, and walked toward the door. He stepped into the cool night to the sight of three figures outside the barn. Two held torches, one held the horses. Two more men appeared in the distance, keeping watch.

Jeff heard shots and turned to see Ben, a new wrangler, running toward the trespassers from behind the house, gun drawn. One of the intruders holding a torch screamed and dropped the burning object into the barn. Ben fired again and the outlaw fell to the ground.

Jeff looked back toward the barn, pulled his gun, aimed, and fired. The man holding the horses cursed, dropped the reins, and grabbed at his bleeding arm. The third threw his torch into the barn at the first round of gunfire, and jumped onto his mount. Ben fired again. The rider cursed, but didn't stop. He took off toward where the other two watched, not moving to help. He joined them and left the two wounded men to fend for themselves.

"Stop where you are." Jeff's voice carried through the clear night air. The injured man who had been holding the horses never slowed, but jumped onto his horse and turned to follow his companions into the dark. Both Jeff and Ben fired. Jeff's shot went wide but Ben's hit the mark and the man fell.

Jeff and Ben ran for the barn, ignoring the unmoving figure of the outlaw by the barn and the one who lay shot several yards away. They'd deal with them later.

They led four horses outside while Clint and the rest of the hands filled buckets and tossed water on the fire. Eloise stood near the barn entrance, ready to run inside, but Clint grabbed her arm, and held her back.

"Stop, Mrs. Bierdan. We've got it under control, and the horses are safe. You don't need to go in there—not yet."

She looked at Clint and realized he was right. The men had taken care of everything while she slept. She hadn't heard a thing until the sound of gunfire pierced her fitful dreams. At least no one was injured.

"Did you recognize them, Boss?" Ben asked. He'd been hired just that morning. Jeff knew he was more skilled with a gun than horses, and the young man had just proven how good he was.

"One, maybe. The big one." By the descriptions he'd heard, Jeff was certain the one who fled first was Luther Grimm. If it was, at least he was wounded. But who were the others who had stayed back, watching?

Jeff walked over and knelt by the fallen intruder. He turned him over but his fixed eyes told him it was too late. Ben's shot had been true.

"Clint, Jay. Either of you recognize this man?"

"Never seen him," Jay responded.

"Me either, Boss" Clint said.

"What about that one?" Jeff nodded toward the second man.

"Never seen him, either," Clint said and Jay concurred.

Although not dead, his breathing was labored, and the wound looked bad. The foreman was of a mind to let the injury take its course, but knew he'd never go through with it.

"Stan," Jeff called out, "get some water and see what you can do for this man. If he makes it until morning we'll load him in a wagon with the body of the other one and take them into town. No sense going tonight—it's late and those men may be waiting for us. The rest of you, make sure all the ashes are cold and take the horses back inside."

He looked back at Clint and Jay. "Did either of you get a good look at the one who rode off?"

"He was gone by the time we got close enough to see. Wish we had. He'd be one dead sonofa..." Clint stopped and looked at Mrs. Bierdan.

"It's all right, Clint. I feel exactly the same." Eloise ran her hands over her lightly covered arms, more out of frustration than to stem the cold air. She'd only had time to grab her wrapper in her hurry to get outside. A chill still rippled through her at the thought that more of her men could have been injured, or killed.

"Ben, you okay to stay a while longer tonight?" Jeff asked.

"Sure, Boss. Whatever you want."

"Good. You two," he pointed to the other new men who had been hired in the last two days, "keep guard with Ben. I don't think those men will be back but I'm not willing to take the chance."

Eloise stared at the dead man. She'd never been this close to someone covered in so much blood. He wasn't young, maybe in his late thirties. She'd never seen him before, which meant he was most likely brought in just for the purpose of terrorizing her and her men. *What kind of man would do that?* she wondered.

"Mrs. Bierdan?"

She broke her gaze from the body. "Yes, Clint?"

"You gonna be okay?"

She nodded. "Yes, I'll be fine. Thanks for taking care of everything. I can't thank you and the men enough."

"It's our job, Mrs. Bierdan. Wish we'd gotten out here in time to get all of them but at least there's one that won't bother you anymore." Clint glared at the body without a bit of remorse at the loss of life. The outlaw had it coming.

"We're set," Jeff said as he walked up. "We've got the injured man in the bunkhouse and will do what we can until morning. Three men are on guard and the barn's cleaned up. I'm going to head in if it's all right with you."

"You go ahead, Jeff. See you tomorrow." She nodded at Clint and turned for the house. Eloise thought she should offer to tend the injured man, but knew her lack of skills wouldn't help. Jeff and the others had much more experience with bullet wounds than she did.

Both men watched her enter the house and close the door. Jeff walked one direction around the house, Clint walked the other. They met back at the front and headed toward the bunkhouse. Both were dead tired and angry. All the men had been pushed to the edge with this latest threat, but none would leave. They'd work until they dropped if it was required to save the ranch, and Mrs. Bierdan.

******

"Damn, that hurts," Drew hissed through clenched teeth as pain shot up a leg for the fourth time this session. They'd been working for well over an hour. He was drenched in sweat, but refused to stop. He'd stood for the first time in three months. Three damn months and he wasn't about to sit again until he took a full step. "Again, Mr. Jericho."

Drew placed his hands against the wall as Jericho steadied him. "You ready?" Jericho asked.

"Yes."

Jericho let go but stayed right behind Drew, ready to grab him and start again.

Drew closed his eyes and focused. He thought of walking, riding, anything that involved his legs. He balanced so long against the wall that Jericho thought he'd given up or his body had locked in place. Then he saw Drew take a deep breath and push from the wall. When he was erect, he dropped his hands and stood. One second, two seconds, five seconds. Ten seconds passed and he hadn't fallen. He could feel pulsing sensations up and down both legs, but his body held.

He closed his eyes again and thought of the one thing he wanted more than anything else. Tess. He would walk again, for Tess. Without realizing it he took one step forward, then brought his other leg up alongside the other. He started to take another step but ran into the wall. He was out of room, but he'd done it. He'd walked.

Drew opened his eyes and tried to glance at Jericho over his shoulder. The change in posture confused his muscles and he dropped in a heap on the floor, but not until after he'd hit a table with an arm and sent a vase crashing to the ground.

The door slammed open. Tess stood staring at Drew where he lay on the wooden floor. "Okay, I've had enough. What's going on in here?" Her hands were on her hips, her voice harsh, and an angry scowl replaced her serene features. It was a new look for her, and Drew didn't like being on the receiving end.

"Come inside, Tess, and close the door," Drew said.

She looked around the room, then behind her, into the hall.

"It's okay. Come on in."

This time she did as he asked.

"Sit over there." He indicated a chair on the other side of the room.

Jericho cleaned up the broken vase, up-righted the table, and pulled Drew to his feet.

"You sure about this, Mr. MacLaren?" he asked.

"Yes."

"What are you doing, Drew?" Tess asked. Her heart was beating so hard it felt as if it would jump out of her chest. She squeezed her hands together in her lap and tried not to shake. She thought she knew what was about to happen, and prayed she was right.

"Just watch." Drew's calm voice fortified her, gave her the motivation needed to stay seated and not jump up to stop him.

He stood the same as before, then gave the order to Jericho to let go. Tess's breath caught as Jericho stepped back and Drew used his arms to balance against the wall. A full minute passed. No one spoke.

Just as Tess thought that was what he wanted to show her, he pushed back and stood, balancing his weight on his two formerly useless legs. She almost shrieked with joy. Tears began to form. She didn't brush them away—her eyes remained riveted on Drew.

He took a step. A step! She jumped from the chair but Jericho held up a hand to stop her. Tess waited. She was rewarded with one more step before Drew steadied himself against the wall. Jericho grabbed him under the arms and helped him into the chair. "Enough for today, Mr. MacLaren."

Drew looked up to see tears streaking down Tess's face. Tears she didn't try to stop. They were rolling over the biggest smile Drew had ever seen, and it was for him.

She placed a hand over her mouth in hopes of stopping a sob, but it was fruitless. "Oh, Drew. You did it. You walked." With each word she took a step forward until she stood against his chair. He opened his arms and Tess fell into them, clutching his shirt, and burying her head in his neck.

Drew pulled her tighter and buried his face in her hair. He was vaguely aware of a door opening and closing. He looked up to see that Jericho was gone.

It was just the two of them. She squirmed a little on his lap and Drew felt a slight hardening of his body. He'd felt the sensations for the last few days and hoped they were an indication that his entire body was healing. Relief washed over him as he realized another hurdle was being crossed.

When Tess lifted her face to his it seemed natural to move his lips over hers. It was a soft caress, just a touch. He brushed his lips over hers.

She strained to get closer. His hands moved to the back of her head and deepened the kiss. Her lips parted, and his tongue traced the edges of her mouth. He knew she had little experience and didn't want to frighten her.

Tess melted into his arms. She was totally unprepared for the warmth that swam over her body. She could smell the mixture of pine soap and fresh sweat and couldn't stop herself from running her fingers along his cheek bones, and wrapping her hands around his neck to draw him closer. She never wanted the kiss to stop.

When Drew ran his tongue gently along her lips she opened to him. She had never been kissed before, and no one had ever told her about the fire that could burn and consume her. She wanted to cry and laugh at the same time and found herself pressing against him, wanting to feel his touch on her lips, her throat, her breast.

She turned her body toward his hand until her breast rested under his large palm. She pressed herself against him and felt his fingers caress her.

With a groan he deepened the kiss as he undid the buttons of her bodice. She felt cool air against her skin and then the warmth of his lips on a breast. Heat spread through her until she moaned.

Tess strained to get closer. She could feel a slight hardening beneath her. "More," she whispered into his mouth and squirmed to let him know what she wanted. Blood rushed to his loins and he felt himself harden even more.

She pushed into him with a slow sigh as he took the other breast while his other hand crept under her dress to rest on her thigh. She moaned and squirmed once more in an attempt to get even closer. Her passion amazed him as it also caused him to stop and drop his hand from her leg.

He pulled away from her, gently raised her to a sitting position and slowly buttoned her dress, stopping to kiss each piece of skin before he covered it.

"I want you, Tess, but not here and not like this."

The look on his face told Tess what she needed to know, and she understood.

"Yes, you're right." There was no anger, no censure in her tone. She leaned in to place one more kiss on his mouth before pushing herself up. "But I want more," she said as her hands smoothed down her dress and she walked toward the door. "I don't want to wait long." Tess passed through the door and closed it behind her.

Drew took a long, drawn-out breath and watched her leave. His heart was racing, his body on fire, but not from pain. This time it was from who he knew was in his future. Tess.

Chapter Fifteen

Denver, Colorado

As in the past, the two men entered the darkened basement and found the stairs. They'd had to take more time than usual. A robbery had occurred a block down, someone had been shot, and the streets were teeming with deputies. Each knew their boss would wait. Caution was their guide. Once inside, experience led them upward through the dark stairwell until they were outside the office door, which stood ajar. Behind the desk sat their boss.

"Gentleman. I expect you have some good news for me."

Pierce glanced at his brother, who indicated for him to proceed. "We found the third book. He keeps it hidden in a door at the back of the safe. Clever setup. We were lucky. Walsh was out of town, which allowed me to make a copy." He laid his findings on the desk. "I've decoded the first couple of pages and it appears to include documentation on business dealings not shown in the other two books."

"I see." Their boss picked up the decoded pages and looked them over. His eyes stopped at one entry in particular and he glanced at his associate. "Did you look at this?"

"Yes. And noticed what you did," the associate answered.

"Bierdan."

"It certainly points to Gordon Bierdan as Ira's partner in the rustling operations. From what you've said, Frank Alts," he looked at Pierce to clarify, "the sheriff in Cold Creek, felt certain someone else was involved. A man who held the money, pulled the strings. Looks like Ira was that man."

The boss pointed at another column. "What are these entries, Pierce?"

"I'm not sure. The entries run during the same time period as the cattle thefts, but the contact is in Victoria, British Columbia. It's a purchase transaction but I haven't deciphered the merchandise. He's used a separate code and an abbreviation for whatever it is he purchased. But I can tell you that it was brought into San Francisco through Washington."

"I suspect it can't be legal or there would be no need to code the entries. Correct?" He looked at Pierce.

"Yes, sir. That's my guess."

The boss continued. "So we know he was at least the brains behind the rustling in Cold Creek."

"And Wyoming, Kansas, Nebraska, and northern New Mexico," the associate added. "Plus, notice one other name mentioned regarding the business from Canada."

"Drago." Their boss looked up. "Does that name mean anything to either of you?"

"Only by reputation. He's known to be involved in numerous illegal pursuits, and he leaves no witnesses to his actions. Drago enjoys torturing and killing, and makes no distinction between men and women." The associate walked over to the bar, grabbed the bottle of scotch and tipped it toward the others. Both shook their heads, but he proceeded to pour a shot for himself and down it. "He met with Walsh while you were gone. My guess is whatever Drago is involved in is more sinister and deadly than rustling, and Walsh is in on every single endeavor. Perhaps even calling the shots."

The boss's eyes widened at the extent of Walsh's illegal activities. "Any information on his recent transactions?"

"I'll have that for you in the next few days. It's moving at a fast rate but still takes time. Plus, I need to decipher the exact merchandise coming from Canada. I believe that will be important to us." Pierce had worked non-stop since copying the book. His only breaks from the intense work came at night when he was at the Denver Rose. He couldn't complain. It was that job that allowed him access to Ira's office and the material they now held.

"What of the others? Have you spoken with them yet?" the associate asked.

Pierce's eyes snapped to his brother's at that questions. He was unaware of other men being involved. He thought the man in front of them acted alone.

"We met this morning. They concur with the path we've taken, at least for now. I'll meet with them again once we understand what Walsh is doing."

"Fair enough," the associate replied.

The boss stood and grabbed his coat. "I'll be in touch."

******

Connor watched Walsh pull out a thin cheroot and light it. He found himself wondering, yet again, what Ira was involved in that could spell danger. "I take it your time in San Francisco proved fruitful." It was a comment, not a question.

"Yes. If all goes well it could double, maybe triple that part of my business." He leaned back in his chair and took a long drag from the small, square-cut cigar.

"And what part of the business is that?"

Ira thought a moment and had decided to answer when a sharp rap on the door interrupted him.

"Sorry Mr. Walsh, but we need Connor downstairs. Some man insists that he'll only speak with him." Nelson held the door open as Connor left.

"Did he give you his name?" Connor asked Nelson as they made their way to the saloon below.

"No. Asked if you worked here and demanded to see you."

Connor scanned the crowd. There were two or three new faces, but no one he recognized. "Which one is he?"

"Over there," Nelson pointed to a short, heavy-set man wearing a wrinkled suit and covered in dust. It was apparent he'd been traveling.

Connor walked up to the stranger and extended his hand. "I'm Connor."

The man took a look at Connor then swallowed the last of the whiskey in his glass. "Ah, good, Mr...." but his words were cut off as Connor took hold of his arm and led him outside through the door behind the bar. Once he had him settled in the back alley Connor let go of his arm and stepped back.

"No last name, just Connor."

"Then how do I know if you're the right man?" He pulled out a handkerchief and rubbed it across his face, then shoved the dirty cloth into an inside pocket of his jacket. He glared at the tall man before him.

"Tell me what it's about and I'll tell you if I'm the right man."

"This is most unusual."

"Make an exception."

He seemed to deliberate for a moment before deciding it was best to do as Connor asked.

"My name is Chester Mayfield. I work for Alexander McCann."

"Then I'm the right man. What do you have for me?"

"It's about your sister. We may know where she is."

It took a moment for the words to penetrate Connor's brain. Meggie, his sister. He'd been searching for Meggie for eight years—had been close more times than he could count. Connor was far past getting his hopes up.

"I want to hear what you know, Mr. Mayfield, but not here and not now. Meet me tomorrow morning at this restaurant on the other side of town. Anyone can help you find it." He scribbled a name on a scrap of paper.

"Tomorrow, then," Mayfield took the paper and started down the alley to the street beyond.

Connor watched him leave, wondering if he'd made a mistake in not completing the meeting now. His experiences in the past had led to nothing but dead ends. It was doubtful this information would be any different. No, the meeting with Mayfield could wait until tomorrow—he had other work that needed his attention.

******

Cold Creek, Colorado

Drew and Tess sat across the supper table from each other. It had been hours since the episode in the bedroom, yet Tess was still unable to slow her racing heart or contain her embarrassment. She didn't regret what had happened, not for a minute, but the words she had said as she left made her face grow hot each time she repeated them in her mind. *What could I have been thinking?*

"Good evening, Tess."

She glanced across the table to see Drew's heated gaze boring into hers. Tess recognized the look and her body responded.

"Good evening, Drew" she answered in a husky voice that brought a knowing look from him. She cleared her throat and searched for calm within a body that felt as if a tornado had blown through it. "I, uh, trust you had a good day."

"The best I've had in a long time. It seems I'm discovering new things every day. How about you, Tess? Did you discover anything new today?"

He was teasing, she knew, but she had no experience in this type of situation. It had been her first kiss, her first time in a man's arms. He was right, she decided. It had been a day of discoveries, yet Tess understood she'd only experienced them to a small degree. The thought both thrilled and frightened her.

"Why, yes, I'm sure I did."

Neither noticed that the table had quieted at their exchange. Most everyone else—Grant, Eleanor, Alicia, Niall, Kate, Amanda, and Will—looked at each other, but no one spoke.

Jericho was the first to break the silence.

"I must thank you again for the wonderful food, Mrs. Taylor. I can't think of a time when I've had better."

Tess closed her eyes and said a silent word of thanks to Jericho.

Eleanor's eyes moved from the Tess and Drew to her other guest. "Why thank you, Mr. Jericho, but I can't take the credit. Maria is the person you should thank. I just help out when she needs it."

"Then I'll be sure to do that," Jericho replied.

A knock pulled everyone's attention to the front door.

"I'll get it." Grant opened the door to find the sheriff waiting, hands in his pockets. "Frank, come in. I'm surprised to see you out our way this time of night. We're just sitting down to supper. You'll join us, of course."

Frank followed Grant into the dining room and was surprised to see Will and the others. "Will, it's good to see you again." Frank extended his hand.

"Same goes here," Will replied and made the remaining introductions.

"Well, I finally get to meet the oldest MacLaren. Don't know how you managed to let your younger brothers survive into manhood," Frank joked.

"There were times it wasn't easy," Niall agreed. "Thank God we had Aunt Alicia. If not for her, who knows how we all would have ended up."

An hour later they'd finished dessert and were still discussing the events at the Bierdan ranch the night before. News hadn't reached them until

Frank arrived to ask for their help in canvassing the area for the men who'd ridden out.

"No problem, Frank. Let us know what you need and we'll get to it." Grant looked at Niall and Will. "You two in?"

"Yes, sir," each responded.

"I'll do whatever I can," Drew said. He wasn't about to share his progress at this point, but he needed to be of use in the search for the men who were terrorizing the area.

"Looks like you'll have three MacLarens plus my men. Not bad."

Another knock disrupted the conversation. Grant opened the door. "Well, I'll be damned," he said and extended his hand. "Looks to me, Frank, like you'll have four MacLarens plus my men."

Jamie walked in to see the roomful of people. Will and Niall began to laugh, and Drew sported a full grin.

"Did I miss something?" he asked Grant.

"No, son, your timing is perfect. Have a seat. We'll get you some food while Frank explains what's happening."

It was late when the men walked into the den for whiskey. Everyone else had retired but they wanted to lay out a plan for the following day. All thought it was just a matter of time before the thugs who'd plagued the Langdon's and now caused havoc at the Bierdan ranch would turn on Grant and the others, especially now that the Langdon land was combined into the Big G.

The Bierdan spread was now considered the most vulnerable. There was no reason to believe the sale would stop the actions of Luther and his men. Except, if what Frank said was true, Luther was now wounded. They needed to locate him before he started vandalizing and killing again.

"Any idea where they might hole up?" Niall asked Frank.

"There is one place, but it only makes sense if Luther was somehow connected with the cattle rustling that went on a few months ago. Don't know for sure that I can find it, but it's worth a try. It's an old cabin up in the mountains north of the Bierdan ranch."

Grant rubbed his forehead in concentration, trying to recall possible locations. "Two other places I can think of," Grant said. "One is a line shack on my property. Another is an old cave that used to be the entrance to a mine, long since abandoned. But that's a long shot."

Niall looked at Frank. "Why don't I go with you to check out the old cabin? Jamie and Grant can ride out to the old line shack. What about the cave, Grant?"

"It's on the other side, quite a ways from the other two places. Not hard to find if you know its location, but most have forgotten about it. A wagon could make it without a problem." Grant said, suspecting that the mine would be where Drew would go.

"Will, Mr. Jericho, and I can check the mine." Drew refused to be left out.

Niall's narrowed eyes and pursed lips told Drew how his oldest brother felt about him being involved. Will just looked at Drew, his face a mask.

Jamie noticed the others' reactions. "That's a good idea, Drew. I'd suggest each group include a couple of Grant's men. They know the area plus extra guns would be welcome if someone runs into this Luther fella."

Drew looked toward Grant.

"That works for me. I'll let Jake know. He can select which of my men go with each group. Tomorrow morning, first thing, we'll start." Grant wanted to push the search before Luther had a chance to regroup. No one had any idea how many men they might run into. It made no sense to take chances.

******

Denver, Colorado

Connor stood propped against a wall, arms crossed, and surveyed the occupants of the bar. Pierce was at one end, Nelson at the other. All had been quiet since Connor shot the cowboy who'd threatened Pierce. No one wanted a repeat any time soon.

He tried to keep his focus on the patrons, the gambling, and conversations—anything to stop his thoughts of Meggie. She'd been sixteen when she had failed to return from her job as a maid, and it had been his fault. He was supposed to meet her each night after her shift was over, but he'd been held up at his job on the docks. The overseer refused to let him leave, and forced Connor to work far into the night. When he'd made it back to their cramped room there was no sign of her. That night everything about his life had changed, again. He never stayed in one place more than a few months, never again had a home. His whole purpose focused on finding his sister. But too many dead ends, false leads, and flat out deceits had made him cynical, cautious. Even so, he could still sense a tiny amount of hope at the prospect that Mayfield might have some useful information.

"Connor?" He looked up to see Nelson walking toward him. "Ira wants to see you."

He pushed from the wall and made his way up the stairs. Ira had worked without stopping since his return from San Francisco, but had yet to provide Connor with any further details of the trip—and Connor needed details.

"You wanted to see me?" Connor asked as he closed the door and took a seat.

"Yes. Whiskey?" At Connor's nod, Ira poured another shot and handed the glass to his guest. "You asked me earlier about my meeting in San Francisco and expressed an interest in the business I'm negotiating." Ira took a sip of the golden liquid and let it make its way down his throat. A slow, soothing burn.

"You seemed pleased with the potential. What's it about?"

"Money, Connor. Lots of money." He finished the drink and placed the glass carefully next to the half full decanter, deciding whether or not to indulge further. He decided to wait. "I have an import business. Products come in from Canada for my buyers in California. Purchases by these new customers will almost triple the orders to my supplier."

"And the merchandise?"

"Let's just say it is a highly sought after product in some circles, used for a variety of purposes, and carries a very high profit." Ira's evasive answer irked Connor.

"Are you saying it's illegal?"

"In some locations, regulated in others, even disdained by those who don't understand its value—physical and mental."

Physical and mental. What did that mean? Connor wondered. Ira spoke in riddles that made no sense.

"How so?"

"My product brings peace of mind. It can change lives."

"What the hell does that mean, Walsh?" Connor was tired of the theatrics. He wanted specifics.

But Ira had finished. He wanted to throw out just enough to get Connor interested, but not enough for him to grasp the full impact of the import business. At least not yet. "We'll meet again tomorrow, Connor, and I'll tell you more." Ira looked at his watch and reached for his overcoat. "I'm late for a supper engagement."

Chapter Sixteen

Cold Creek, Colorado

"I'm going with you." Hands on her hips, Tess glared at the man in front of her.

"No."

"You need me. I can help." She insisted.

"Not this time. It's too dangerous. If we find the gang I don't want you there—I might not be able to protect you." The conversation was over as far as Drew was concerned.

"Protect me? You don't need to protect me. You taught me to shoot. You know I can help. Besides, you can't keep me here." She stomped away from him to the hooks holding her horse's bridle. Her body shook with frustration. He was being obstinate and she wouldn't have any of it.

Drew took a couple of calming breaths. He'd walked across his bedroom four times last night and hadn't waivered once, but only Jericho knew it. He was tempted to rise from the chair and physically restrain Tess from endangering her life. But he knew the anger he felt toward her would hinder his attempts to walk. No, he'd wait.

"Maybe I can't make you, but Grant will have a fit if he learns you rode out with us."

"You wouldn't." The words hissed out of her. She stopped midway through pulling the saddle off the rail.

He'd never seen her this angry. Why couldn't she understand? The other women weren't going. Both Kate and Amanda were better riders, better shots, yet they understood.

He lowered his voice in an attempt to quell his irritation. "No, but he'll find out, and when he does, there'll be hell to pay. Is that what you want?"

She wiped an arm across her forehead, more from agitation than the heat in the barn. Tess couldn't remember the last time the large, cavernous space had felt this hot. Her temper was getting the best of her and Drew was the cause. She never, ever, spoke in anger. Disappointment, fear, self-doubt had plagued her much of her life, but she was always capable of keeping the anger she felt tucked inside, hidden from those around her. But this man brought everything out. All the good and all the bad.

Tess raised her head to the ceiling and closed her eyes. She could lie to him. Say she'd stay, then follow at a safe distance. But that wasn't her way.

"Do what you feel is best, Drew. I won't stop you. I couldn't if I tried. At the same time, I won't allow you to tell me I can't ride along. It's my choice, not yours." A thought popped into her head. It was a risk but necessary. "Just like it was your choice to stay and help Will. None of us could have made that decision for you and no one faulted you the choice you made."

Drew's eyes turned to stone at her words. He swallowed hard. Yes, he'd made that choice, and he'd make the same one again. Stay to help his brother, Will. It had been an easy decision. That choice had cost him the use of his legs, and left him with the fear that the paralysis would be permanent. Even now, after thinking he'd never walk again, he knew he'd make the same decision.

He rolled his chair forward until it almost touched her dress. He reached out and took both of her hands in his, pulled them toward him, and turned them palm side up. He proceeded to place kisses on her soft, exposed wrists and the palms of each hand, then held them tight. His worried eyes turned to hers, an unspoken plea.

"Yes, you must make the decision that is best for you. I won't stop you. But losing you is not an option for me, Tess. I don't know that I can keep you safe if trouble finds us. And that same thing may hold true for you. Will you be able to stay focused if your attention is on me?"

Her heart pounded at his gentle touch and heartfelt words. She was conflicted. She loved him, didn't want to lose him, and felt that by being close she could keep him safe. What if she was wrong and her presence put him in more danger? She felt like screaming at the logic of his words—and she never screamed.

"I don't like you going without me," she confessed.

187

"I know."

"I don't want to lose you."

"I know that too."

She took a ragged breath, moved her hands to his shoulders, and leaned down to place a soft kiss on his lips. "You'll be careful?"

"I'll do my best. I am so close to my dreams, all of them, Tess. Believe me, I don't intend to lose even one."

She reached inside to compose herself. "Do you need any help getting ready?"

Jericho walked into the barn, stepped behind the wheelchair and grabbed the handles. "We're all set, Mr. MacLaren."

"I guess we're ready." Drew looked at Tess and a slight smile tugged at his mouth. "We'll be back before you realize we're even gone."

Tess watched the three groups ride out. Each going in a different direction and each searching for the same dangerous men who'd vandalized, beaten, and murdered.

As she walked up the front steps, Tess stopped and, for the first time, focused on his words. *I am so close to my dreams, all of them, Tess. Believe me, I don't intend to lose even one.*

She hoped she knew what those dreams were.

******

Denver, Colorado

Connor spotted Chester Mayfield, his contact who worked for Alexander McCann, from a block away. It wasn't hard. He seemed almost as round as he was tall, and appeared to jump over one mud hole, then another, in an attempt to keep his already ruined suit from becoming a rag. Connor would have chuckled at the sight if not for the reason he was meeting with him.

Connor's mind went to his sister. Meggie. Maybe today he'd learn what he needed to find her. He'd known Alex McCann for many years, worked with him for a time. McCann was Connor's age and had known Meggie, knew the misery her disappearance had caused him and his brother. After the numerous false starts, Alex was careful about potential leads and getting Connor's hopes up.

A scream pierced his thoughts. He snapped his head up to see a group of people surrounding something or someone on the ground. Panic seized him. Connor ran to the site and saw Mayfield sprawled on the ground, one leg twisted at an odd angle and blood streaming from his mouth. The owner of the rig who'd run him down was already by his side.

"The fool walked right out in front of me. I couldn't stop the horses in time." The driver's voice shook as much as his hands, which rested on Mayfield's arm

"Get a doctor. And a wagon," Connor ordered as he knelt to check for signs of life. He found a slight pulse.

Hours later he was still in the waiting room of Denver's Union Pacific Hospital, sometimes sitting, but more often pacing.

"Are you waiting for Mr. Mayfield?" The doctor had walked up without making a sound.

"Yes, I'm Connor, a friend."

"Well, we've done all we can at this point. His broken leg and arm are set. He's suffered a severe concussion but with rest, that will pass. Our main concern is additional internal bleeding. We've done what we can, but this accident was devastating to Mr. Mayfield's body. He's lucky to be alive."

Connor's slim hopes of learning about Meggie slipped away as the doctor spoke. "How long before he's able to talk?"

"I won't know for at least a day, maybe more. But we'll keep a close watch on him. He won't be left alone."

Connor shook the doctor's hand and trudged from the hospital onto the street. It was a clear, bright day. At any other time he might have found himself appreciating the crisp air and beautiful mountains near Denver. Today he didn't even notice them.

He'd telegraphed McCann's office the previous day and learned that his long-time friend, Mayfield's boss, had left on a ship for Europe. Alex had entrusted his man with delivering the latest news to Connor. Again, Connor felt despair snake around him and take hold. A despair that he'd never quite been able to shake.

******

Ira sat at his desk. Anger like he hadn't felt for years consumed him. The latest news had just been delivered and stared up at him in the form of a telegram. The words caused an almost manic hate. It was from a contact in New York who'd learned of a conversation among a group of businessmen the previous week. One man in particular had made a strong impression on the others. He'd talked about a businessman in Denver whom he and his peers suspected of grievous illegal actions.

When asked what the businessmen planned to do about it, he mentioned that they'd hired a Range Detective, a previous Texas Ranger, who'd also had a brief turn with Pinkerton's. The man from Denver felt they were close to obtaining what was needed to make an arrest for his various crimes. Crimes that stretched from rustling to smuggling illicit merchandise. Those final words were the ones that grabbed Ira's attention.

He crumbled the missive and threw it across the room. Who the hell was this man? This lawman who observed him without Ira becoming suspicious? He'd checked out each man and woman who worked for him. Their background, contacts, arrests, habits, and skills. He didn't hire anyone who didn't have some type of criminal past. That, it turned out, had been the easiest attribute to find. There were thousands of men out West who'd broken the law.

What had he missed?

His agitated mind didn't allow him to rest. He jumped from his chair and stalked to the wall safe, unlocked it, and checked inside. Everything was in its place, as it had been last night and yesterday morning, and each day since he'd taken over the Denver Rose.

San Francisco. That was the only time he'd been gone in months. Could someone have found his safe as well as the private ledger? He was so careful. No one knew of the safe. He kept the regular book on his desk each day, only putting it away at night. The other two were only brought out when he was alone. He slammed the safe door, rotated the knob, and again asked himself what he'd missed.

Ira ran both hands through his hair. His anger had subsided, somewhat, but the ball of fear in his gut grew. He had to find the person responsible. Find him and silence him. This might be one kill he'd make himself.

******

Cold Creek, Colorado

"See anything, Grant?" Jamie asked as they approached the small line shack.

They'd covered several miles on their trek up the mountain. Jamie had spotted tracks a few miles back—horse tracks—but lost them in the dense brush.

"Someone has been here, but can't tell how long ago. Fire's cold." Grant walked out of the eight-by-ten foot structure to look around the area. "Can't tell if Luther and his men were here at some point, but they sure aren't here now."

He and Jamie, along with Tinder and Hal—both men who'd worked at the Big G for years—had made a wide cut of the land on their way to the shack and found nothing.

Grant took off his hat and wiped his arm across his damp forehead. "I'd like to check one more place before we head back. I forgot about it last night. It's not far, a patchwork of caves up in the rocks, but it's worth checking."

It took them longer than anticipated to find the entrance. It had been twenty years since Grant had first discovered the group of caves that spidered off the entrance. There was a large central cave, which he'd always thought of as the main meeting room. Narrow passageways, branching off the core, led to smaller caves. All the ones he'd found years ago had shown signs of being inhabited at some point. He'd never stayed around long enough to run into anyone. From various markings he'd found, Grant guessed it had been used by the Ute Indians, trappers, and outlaw groups.

They spent an hour searching, but found nothing to indicate anyone had been living in or using the caves. "Nothing. Looks like no one has been here in years." Grant hoped the others were having more success. "Guess it's time to ride back."

Jamie didn't want to give up, but knew Grant was right. They were tired and had no idea where else to look.

The four mounted their horses and began the trip back to the ranch.

******

Frank had taken his group on a direct route to the old cabin. It surprised him that once they started he'd been able to recall the location. It was much the same as the last time he'd seen it. Dilapidated wood, crumbling roof, infested interior, and overgrown brush. Large trees surrounded it, but a small clearing had been made. For whatever reason the shrubs had never reappeared.

Niall rode Zeus in a large circle around the old cabin in one direction while one of Grant's men rode the opposite. They met in front of the cabin. Both had found evidence that someone had been at the cabin not too long before, but there was no telling who. Niall dismounted and followed some tracks away from the cabin.

Frank walked out with a small tin of coffee and an old blanket. The floor and walls had been cleaned at some point since he'd last seen it three months ago, but it didn't make sense that a gang of murderers would clean up their hole. Frank suspected that a lone person had discovered it, used the cabin for a short time, and then moved on.

"Frank, come over here," Niall called from several yards into the surrounding forest.

When Frank found him, Niall held a kerchief over his nose and was crouching, using a stick to push dirt back from the top of what appeared to be a hole. A man-sized hole. Both men began to dig in earnest and before long both could see fabric sticking through the dirt. They removed more dirt as fast as possible until they found the decomposing body of a man. He still wore his shirt and trousers, but his boots, hat, and any weapon he may have carried were missing.

"Do you recognize him, Frank?" Niall asked, choking from the odor. He noticed that Alts had also pulled a handkerchief from a pocket to ward off the smell.

"Might. He may be one of the missing wranglers from the Bierdan ranch, Hap Whidley. He disappeared just before Dave Dawson went missing. Dawson's body was found a couple of weeks ago. If this is Whidley, then at some point I'm guessing Luther and his men were here, but it appears they've moved out." Frank stood and brushed off his pants. "I'll get a blanket and wrap him up. We'd better get the body to Bierdan's to make sure if it's Hap."

******

"That's Hap," Jeff said when Frank pulled back the blanket. The Bierdan foreman had thought he'd seen a lot in the years since he'd fought in the War Between the States, but he never got used to seeing a dead body. Especially one ravaged from being in the ground. The skin was horribly deteriorated, but Jeff was still certain. "He always wore two kerchiefs, and that shirt is one his mother sent him a couple of months ago. God, I hate to be the one to send her a message that her son's not coming home."

Frank returned the blanket, masking the sight and some of the smell. "Give me her information, Jeff, if you have it, and I'll send the message."

"Yeah, I have it. He was a good kid. I was surprised when he just disappeared, but he was young, and those are the ones that move around more. I should've looked for him." Jeff shook his head and rubbed a hand on the back of his neck as he walked to the bunkhouse to get the mother's information.

Niall turned at the sound of the front door being opened. A young woman walked out and made her way down the steps to Frank. "Sheriff. What brings you out here?" Eloise asked.

"It's not good, Mrs. Bierdan. We've been out, searching for any place the men who've threatened you might hide. We found one possible place, but also dug up the body of Hap Whidley."

"Oh, God," she stepped back and placed her hand over her mouth. The men waited for her to digest the news. "He was such a young boy. Maybe seventeen. Why would someone do this to him?" Her voice had risen as the aching sensation in the pit of her stomach increased.

"I don't understand these kinds of men either. I just know that they exist and we have to learn to deal with them before the terror they create spreads." Frank took the piece of paper Jeff brought him and slipped it into his pocket.

For the first time Eloise Bierdan looked at the other man who'd accompanied Frank. "Hello, I'm Eloise Bierdan."

"Niall MacLaren, Mrs. Bierdan. I believe you've met my brothers."

Eloise felt the urge to step back. She knew there was nothing to fear from this man, but her instincts warred with her common sense. "Yes, Mr. MacLaren, I have met three of your brothers. I, uh, well, I'm sorry for the damage my late husband caused."

Niall watched her features as she spoke. She never broke eye contact and she sounded sincere. "I don't blame you—no one does. It happened. That's all there is to it."

She swallowed hard, and nodded, thankful for his gracious response.

Frank stood silent during the exchange. Seems the woman continued to be confronted with the past actions of her husband and the threats to her future. Over the last few weeks he'd come to see her in a different light. She wasn't the money-hungry, pampered woman that many assumed her to be. Eloise had impressed him with her determination, hard work, and commitment to her men. There were many who could learn a lesson from her.

"We'll take Hap into town, to Doc Wheaton's, if that's all right with you?" Frank asked Eloise. "I've suggested to Jeff that there be a meeting of all your men to let them know what we found. I know you've hired on extra men, and that's good. But you've had two hands murdered, two others threatened, your home vandalized, cattle slaughtered, and an attempt to burn down the barn. These men will do anything to get you to sell out to whoever has hired them."

"I understand, Frank. I just wish I knew who these men worked for, who I can trust. I've come to a point where I realize I'll most likely sell, but to who?" She looked toward the distant mountains as if reaching out to them for an answer. "What if I sell to the very man whose orders these men have carried out?"

Her use of his first name surprised Frank, but he decided to respond in kind. "Eloise, you have two honorable men who have an interest in your land. I know and trust both. Neither of these men would ever order the types of actions that have been taken against you. Meet with them. Hear their offers. If you want to meet with the third man, go ahead. But from where I stand, he's the one I'd be wary about." What else could he say? His gut told him Ira Walsh had hired these men to terrorize the ranchers, but he had no firm proof, just as he had no proof of any of the other illegal activities Walsh was suspected of organizing.

"All right. I appreciate you speaking your mind." She looked at Niall. "Will you be seeing Grant Taylor, Mr. MacLaren?"

"Yes, ma'am."

"Would you give him a message that I'd like to meet with him?"

"I'd be happy to deliver that message."

Eloise looked sad, but her back was straight, and her voice was firm. She would make the right decision concerning her ranch and the men. After that, well, she just didn't know.

Chapter Seventeen

Frank made a stop on his way to deliver Whidley's body to the doctor. The outlaw who'd been shot at Bierdan's had recovered enough to be moved to the jail. Deputy O'Dell was keeping a close watch on him, not wanting a repeat of what had happened to Vern Tyson. O'Dell was determined that no one was going to sneak in and murder this prisoner.

The front door crashed open. Frank walked in with what looked like a body thrown over his shoulder. The sheriff nodded at his deputy but continued his trek to the back cells and dropped the bundle in front of their prisoner and pulled open the blanket. The man jumped back when he saw Hap's wasted body.

"This is what Luther does to men who get in his way," Frank spat out. "Did you know he snuck in here and murdered Vern?" The look in the prisoner's eyes told Frank that he did know and may have participated. "You know he'll have no hesitation in coming after you. And since you've decided to not talk to us anyway, I'm thinking the deputy and I are going to head out to dinner, maybe stay for supper. Who knows? Maybe you'll have visitors." The sheriff knelt to roll Whidley's body back into the blanket. He picked it up and started for the front door.

"Wait," the prisoner croaked out.

"Yeah?"

"Luther was involved."

"How involved?"

"He didn't give the order. He said the boss wanted something permanent to be done about Vern. Luther made the decision to come in and kill him."

By now Frank had lowered the body back to the floor and pulled up a chair. "And the boss's name? And your name?"

"Mine's Dex Vixon. But I ain't telling you the boss's name. I don't care what kind of promises you make. He'll still find me and send someone to kill me."

"Uh huh. And who was the man killed at the barn?"

"Carl. Never knew his last name."

"Where's Luther now?"

"They move around, stay at different places almost each night. I've only been to one cave that the new guy found."

"What new guy? You know his name?"

"Mean sonofabitch. The boss sent him out from Denver. Luther gets orders from him now. He's the one that ordered us to slaughter the Bierdan cattle and sent us to burn down her barn—same as we did the Langdon place. You don't want to cross him, Sheriff. You'll never walk away." Dex had moved back to sit on the cot in his small cell.

201

His shoulders began to shake and Frank realized Dex was truly frightened at the thought of this new man.

"What's his name?"

"Drago. Sebastian Drago."

******

Niall walked into Grant's office to find Drew, Will, Jamie, and Jericho sitting around, discussing what they'd found, or more accurately, what they hadn't found. Neither group had seen anything indicating the band had stayed in either the line shack or the cave near the mine. At least Niall had some news.

Grant poured Niall a drink. "Have a seat. Tinder told us some of what you found at the old cabin, but it'd be best to hear it from you."

Niall sipped a small amount before throwing back the rest of the contents. He let the warm, amber liquid slide down his throat. "Found a body at the cabin. Jeff Burnham identified it as Hap Whidley, a wrangler they thought had quit, left the area. He didn't. He was murdered."

"That makes two," Drew said.

"That we know of," Grant added.

"We also found coffee, a blanket. Someone has stayed at the cabin recently. We can only guess it to be Luther since Frank's certain he murdered Whidley."

Grant sat forward and leaned his arms on the desk. "Where's Frank now?"

"Took the body to town. He said he had to talk with the prisoner, scare him a little, get him to talk. He's got his deputy guarding him. But hell, I'd just as soon use the prisoner as bait to lure Luther to the jail. Did you find anything?" He looked around the room.

"Nothing at either the line shack or mine. Doesn't appear that anyone's been to them in years," Grant spoke for the others in the room.

"A gang that size doesn't just disappear. They need food and a safe place to stay. Those men need rest like anyone else." Jamie looked at Grant." You don't suppose another rancher is letting them hide at his place, do you?"

"Hadn't thought of that, but it's a possibility. Don't know of anyone around here who'd let those men stay, although he might if they've threatened him and his family. Other than the old cabin, we sure haven't seen any sign of them."

"Besides Mrs. Bierdan, who's most vulnerable to threats? Maybe having problems like Langdon and needs cash but hasn't mentioned selling? Possibly a ranch further out, but close enough for the men to carry out their dirty work." Jamie seemed to be sorting through options as he spoke. "It'd have to be someone with a family, people he cares about so that the threats would mean something."

"Grant, you mentioned a family not far outside of Cold Creek a few months ago that was having problems but wouldn't consider help. As I recall, they have a boy Joey's age and the two had become friends." Will tried to remember the name but it was a passing comment Grant had made one day when Eleanor had left to take their son into town.

"Millers. Ted and Myrna. Their son, Philip, and Joey are good friends. We've had Philip at the house many times. There's also a daughter, younger than Philip, I believe. Eleanor would know her name." Grant stopped and tried to recall the last time he'd seen the Millers. "You know, I don't remember when I saw Philip last, or when Joey went for a visit. Problem is, I just don't see the benefit of threatening them. Their land doesn't have much value—poor grazing, little timber, average water access. He only has a couple of hundred acres. But his wife takes in sewing, and Ted also works for the smithy to make extra money."

"All right. I'll write down the Millers. Who else?" Drew asked.

"Manuel and Juanita Rosado have a small place not far from Langdon's. Does some ranching, enough to sell a few head each year. They're farmers and grow enough to sell to the mercantile and restaurants in Cold Creek. If I recall right, they have four or five kids, plus Juanita's mother lives with them." Grant thought about them. That one made more sense as their place was closer to where all the violence had occurred. "But their place is so small, I doubt there'd be any room for a gang to hide. Their horses would be noticeable to anyone. Manuel only has about five and he's only got one or two men who help him."

"Anyone else?" Drew continued to jot down notes.

"Well, Manuel's brother-in-law, Alonzo Ibarra, lives a few miles from him. He has a good-sized spread with good water, and is more of a cattleman than Rosado. Real good people. Alonzo's family came from Spain years ago. His sister, Juanita, married Manuel and they moved next to her brother. Alonzo may have been the one to sell them their land. They have several children, but I haven't seen any of them in a long time."

"So far there are three—Millers, Rosados, and Ibarras." Drew looked at the three names. His eyes kept going to the Ibarra family. Large spread, close to the ranchers who've been threatened, but remote enough that they wouldn't be spotted. "My first choice would be the Ibarra ranch. Manuel Rosado's place is close enough to check out at the same time. Let's ask Eleanor and Joey if they've see any of the Millers recently."

They were all silent as they thought through Drew's suggestion.

"I agree with you, Drew," Will said. "Let's speak with Eleanor and Joey in the morning. If they haven't seen or heard from the Millers, then we include them. But, we plan to ride to the Ibarra and Rosado homes tomorrow."

"Same groups?" Grant asked.

"If neither Eleanor nor Joey have seen them, I think you should go to the Miller place, Grant. Take a couple of your men. Jamie, Will, Drew, Jericho, and I can go to the Ibarra and Rosado ranches. At least we can warn them of what's been happening so they're prepared." Niall was still uncomfortable including Drew, but his brother made his own decisions.

"Makes sense." Grant took out his pocket watch. "It's late. We'll plan to start early tomorrow."

Everyone but Grant left before Niall remembered Mrs. Bierdan's request. He walked back into the office.

"Almost forgot. Eloise Bierdan asked if the two of you could meet. She's working through a decision to sell her place. Not sure she'll go through with it, but she'd like to at least speak with you."

"Not a problem, Niall. I'll ride by there on the way back from the Miller place tomorrow. That should give us plenty of time to talk."

******

Tess couldn't sleep. She'd tossed and turned for hours and was no closer to sleep than when she first lay down. Thoughts of Drew, their time in his room, and their possible future assailed her. She didn't know what the men's plans were for tomorrow, but knew that they'd decided to be aggressive and search out the outlaws—not wait for them to strike again.

She threw off the covers and covered her sheer night gown with a wrapper. Jericho had his own room next to Drew's. He would no doubt hear her when she knocked on Drew's door, but that couldn't be helped. Tess was also certain Jericho had an idea of what had transpired when he'd left them alone in Drew's room. She'd passed him in the hall when she'd left. He wasn't stupid. Her hair had been mussed and her dress still somewhat askew.

Tess's light tap on Drew's door echoed down the short hall. Who would have thought such a light tap could sound so loud? There was no answer. She tried again, but still no response. A door opened and she looked to see Jericho walk out of his room and stop.

He looked at her, deciding whether or not to comment. Making a decision, he took a slow breath. "He's in the barn." Jericho shut the door behind him.

Tess didn't hesitate but left the house and made her way to the barn. There was no lantern glow to suggest Drew was inside. The only hint was that the door stood ajar. He was either inside or someone had left it open. She stopped just inside to look around. She heard nothing. Tess took a few more steps, attempting to let her eyes adjust to the dark.

"Hello, Tess."

She jumped but knew the soft, deep voice belonged to the man she sought. Tess turned to see him in a stall. But her body stilled when the reality of the image hit her. He was standing, holding a rope in one hand while making loops in it with the other.

"You're practicing roping?" she asked, still stunned at the sight.

"Better than practicing my shooting at this time of night, don't you think?"

A smile lit her face, igniting a flame within Drew that halted him where he stood—without support or the security of his chair.

Tess ran up to him, looped her arms around his neck, and lay her head against his chest. "I guess you're right," she whispered.

Drew dropped the rope and let his arms wrap around her, holding her close, savoring the feel. He loosened his grip just enough to tilt her chin up and capture her mouth. He'd wanted to do this each minute of every hour since she'd left his room.

Tess eased her hold around his neck, letting her hands wander across his broad shoulders, down his arms, feeling his muscles tighten. The kiss became more ardent, hungry, fueling the heat between them.

His hands stroked up and down her back, following the curves of her body, and pulling her tight. He drew back from the kiss just enough to trace her lips with his tongue before plundering her mouth again.

Then he was lifting her, moving backwards inside the stall, and lowering them to the ground. They stretched out beside each other, not once breaking the kiss that bound them.

Drew rolled Tess to her back, keeping one strong hand behind her head as the knuckles of the other caressed her face, then moved down the soft column of her neck to her chest. He continued to place feather-like kisses across her face, until his mouth settled once more on hers.

He pulled the ribbon that held her wrapper in place and moved his hand down to cup a soft, lush breast. She gasped at the touch, but pushed into his hand, encouraging him. He continued to the other breast before easing down the top of her night dress to expose her to his view.

"Tess," he whispered. "You have no idea what you do to me, how beautiful you are." Then he took one round globe in his mouth and drew her in.

She squirmed against him, trying to get closer. The ache between her legs confused and excited her, but all she understood was that she didn't want him to stop. Ever.

He pulled the hem of her night gown up. She felt strong warmth as his hand moved upward along her calf, to her thigh, then higher, until he stopped and pulled away. He shifted his hand to her cheek and stroked the soft skin. "I want you, Tess."

"Yes."

"Do you understand what it will mean if I take you?" Drew wanted no confusion between them.

Tess's round, trusting, caramel-brown eyes gazed up at him, but she didn't speak.

"It will mean we belong to each other, forever. Is that what you want?"

"Yes, Drew. You're exactly who I want," and she pulled him down for another long, passion-filled kiss.

Chapter Eighteen

Ah, hell, Will thought as he walked into the barn early. It wasn't even light out, but he couldn't sleep, worried about Drew, and how he'd do if they encountered the outlaws. But then he saw the chair next to an open stall. Will moved closer. The edge of a woman's wrapper and bare feet peeked out at him. He drew back. *Shit.* He didn't want to be the one to find them, wake them up, but he sure as hell didn't want anyone else doing it.

Will turned his back to the stall and whispered, "Drew." No one stirred. He tried again, this time louder. His brother's legs moved. Moved! Was it just reflexes or had that been intentional, he wondered. This wasn't working. He backed into the stall, keeping his head turned away from Tess, and crouched beside Drew so that he could shake him.

Drew's eyes opened in slits, closed, then opened fully. He stared at Will.

"What the hell are you doing?" Drew hissed out.

"Me? What the hell are you doing?" Will replied and tried to incline his head toward the woman in Drew's arms.

Will's words hit their mark and Drew spun his head away to find Tess snuggled up next to him.

She looked wonderful, soft, the most beautiful image he'd ever seen. Then reality hit.

"Shit."

"Exactly," Will almost laughed. "Look, I'll keep watch until you can get you and Tess together. But hurry. I have no idea when someone else might be joining us. You need help getting in your chair?"

When Drew shook his head, Will stood up and walked out, chuckling at the scene he'd stumbled upon.

"Tess. Tess, honey, we have to get up," Drew whispered.

"Hmmm," Tess responded and reached for him. Her hand settled on his neck to pull him forward for her kiss.

This time it was Drew who chuckled. "No, honey, we have to get up, get dressed. It's morning." He gently pulled her arm from around his neck, then caressed her cheek once more. He heard Will talking with someone and knew they'd run out of time.

"What do you mean I can't go in the barn?" Grant's stern voice penetrated Tess's brain and she came fully awake with a start. It took Drew a moment of maneuvering, but he finally pushed himself up, stood, and held out his hand to Tess.

She grabbed it and scrambled to her feet. Her panic was obvious as she tried to right her gown, tie her wrapper, and brush the hay from her hair and clothing.

"What the hell!"

Tess heard Grant's hard voice and turned to see her father staring at her and Drew. His face red, contorted, as if he were choking on a bad piece of meat. He started toward them, but Drew stepped in front of her, shielding her, protecting her. From what he didn't know, since he was the one that Grant wanted to kill at that moment.

"It's not what you think, sir," Drew said and put a hand up to stop Grant from getting closer.

"Oh, I'm pretty sure it's exactly what I think, MacLaren," Grant raged and tried to look around the man shielding his daughter, but Drew continued to block him.

It was at that moment that it registered to Grant that Drew was standing. But that realization was over–shadowed by the rage he felt at finding them this way.

Tess had only heard her father bellow one other time, and that had been when her sister, Amanda, had put herself in danger. He was known for his calm control, the way he could stay composed when everyone else panicked. Well, he sure wasn't in control now.

"I love her, Mr. Taylor."

Grant put his hands on his hips, looked up to the ceiling, then down to the ground. He turned and paced a few steps away, getting himself under control. This was the last thing he'd expected to wake up to.

Eleanor raced into the barn, a worried expression marring her normally serene appearance. "Grant. We can hear you clear into the

213

house. What in the world..." But her words trailed off when she looked into the stall. "Oh."

"Yeah, oh," Grant repeated. He'd calmed but his voice was still hard as he glared at the young man before him. "You'll marry her."

"Yes, sir." Drew peeked over his shoulder at Tess and smiled. "If she'll have me."

At that Tess stepped forward and threw herself into his arms. "Yes, yes, yes!"

By now, everyone in the house had made their way to the barn, and stood in a semi-circle looking at Drew, standing, in his pants, no shirt, and Tess in her night clothes. All had heard Drew's question and Tess's response, and everyone noticed that Drew wasn't in his chair.

Amanda raced up and wrapped her arms around her sister. "Oh, Tess, I'm so happy for you."

Eleanor, Alicia, and Kate all followed Amanda's lead, hugging Tess, then turning to hug Drew.

Will, Jamie, and Niall all kept their distance, still stunned at seeing their brother out of his chair, standing. Then they looked at each other and started to move.

By the time Drew noticed their approach the three were upon him. Niall stepped behind him, Jamie to the left, and Will to the right. In one coordinated move, they lifted Drew, walked outside, and threw him into the horse trough.

Drenched, he sputtered, but pulled himself up to a sitting position and started to laugh. A full, stomach churning laugh that brought smiles and cheers from everyone.

******

Denver, Colorado

"How's he doing?" Connor asked the doctor who'd walked out of Chester Mayfield's room.

"We've got him on laudanum. He's in a great deal of pain, but he'll make it." The doctor took a moment to jot down some notes, then focused again on the visitor. "He's in no condition to talk to you. Maybe tomorrow. I'm sorry." The doctor turned and walked into another exam room, leaving Connor to ponder his choices. There were none. It was pointless to stay. He'd return tomorrow and hope Mayfield would be able to talk.

He made his way toward the saloon. Connor hoped to speak with Ira this morning to learn more about his import business. The suspicion that he wouldn't like what he learned nagged at Connor. He'd helped Ira get the backing for the saloon, which was a legitimate business and turned a nice profit. He had made sure of both. He'd also provided contacts to Ira when he needed to expand the silver mining operations. The money had come through as Connor knew it would, but Connor hadn't managed the Walsh side of the mine. Connor and his contacts had set someone else up to do that work—Ira just thought the work flowed from him.

He walked into the saloon and toward the stairs, but stopped when the bartender motioned him over. The man had been one of Connor's first hires, and one of his best. The barkeep knew his job, handled customers well, and kept the drinks flowing.

"Something's going on with Walsh," he told Connor.

"Why do you say that?"

"He stormed in about an hour ago, which is early for him, and went straight upstairs. Not a word to anyone. He just glared at Lola and pushed past her when she walked up to him. Never seen him treat her that way. Haven't seen him since."

Connor considered the barkeep's words. Ira's mood could mean anything. Problems with his legitimate cattle or mining operations? Connor doubted that either of those were the cause. His money was on Walsh's obsession with Cold Creek or his expanding import business—or both.

"Thanks for the warning," Connor threw over his shoulder as he started for Ira's office.

Ira looked up at the knock on this door. "What?"

Connor pushed the door open. "You have a few minutes?"

"Not now." Ira's harsh words weren't lost on Connor. Ira had always made time to speak with him. Whatever it was, it must be significant.

Connor wouldn't be pushed out. "Anything I can help with, Ira?"

Walsh raised his head and frowned at his saloon manager, a partner in the business. Connor had carried out his duties well, and linked Ira with the money needed to buy the saloon and expand the mines. He was sharp and controlled. At this point Ira couldn't afford to trust anyone, except perhaps Drago. However, he might be able to garner some information from Connor.

"You see anyone snooping around upstairs while I was out of town?" Ira asked straight out.

Connor's features remained fixed, nothing to indicate he was surprised or upset at Ira's question. "No one. Why?"

"Who checked out the ladies area during that time?" Ira already knew but wanted it confirmed.

"Pierce. The same man who checked all the areas including the hall outside your private quarters. You want to tell me what this is about?"

"I've gotten news that is unsettling. Seems there are rumors about me and my business operations. Disturbing comments. You hear anything?"

"You know I'd come to you if I had. Who told you about these rumors?"

Ira studied Connor. He wouldn't give a second thought to ordering his death if he learned Connor had betrayed him, set him up. He'd read through Connor's references and history twice last night after he'd gone home. Nothing jumped out as being out of place. He'd hired Pinkerton's to provide whatever they could learn. They'd confirmed that Connor had spent time in prison for murder, but had been pardoned when new evidence was presented exonerating him of the crime. The whole prison experience had been a plus for Ira. In his opinion, it hardened a man.

Walsh had also checked on Connor's contacts, which were considerable. One was the owner of New York's largest and most respected private detective firm. It wasn't as large as Pinkerton's, but handled similar work for those who held wealth in the extreme. That's how Connor had made many of his contacts, through his work with New York firm, the same contacts that had funded the saloon and silver mines.

"A contact back East heard about a meeting between some businessmen. One of the men was from here and mentioned that a certain Denver businessman was being investigated. He told the group that the man had interests in cattle, mining, a saloon, and timber." Ira's eyes turned to slits and he leaned forward, resting his arms on the desk. "There are few in Denver with interests in that many businesses. My contact was sure they were speaking of me."

"Did your contact say who was hired or why? Give you a name?"

"No. Names weren't mentioned, and my contact didn't know what motivated the investigation. Apparently the sonofabitch snooping around was a lawman."

Connor smirked. "That leaves everyone here out. You know our histories."

"I could find nothing showing any of my employees have been lawmen. That doesn't mean much. Lawmen go bad all the time. They're sometimes worse than the most hardened criminal."

Connor agreed—he'd seen it firsthand.

Ira leaned back, his eyes still focused on his visitor. "I've asked one of my men to watch Pierce. Something about him is amiss. Since you hired him, I didn't do the normal checks. I find I know nothing about his history."

"You're having him followed?"

"Starting today. Why? Do you object?"

"No, it's smart. He's done well here. I'd hate to lose him."

"Make no mistake, Connor. If I find anything at all that ties him to the rumors, he will disappear."

Chapter Nineteen

Cold Creek, Colorado

It had been a long day. Grant was still shaking his head at what he'd seen in the barn that morning. If it had been anyone other than Drew....well, it wouldn't have been anyone else. Both he and Eleanor had suspected their daughter had strong feelings for MacLaren, but they hadn't believed he returned Tess's interest. Now he understood why. Drew was determined to walk before he declared his intentions. Grant's respect for the young man had grown with that revelation, even if he wished Drew had kept his hands to himself a little longer.

After the late start, Grant and a few of his men had ridden to the Miller ranch. It was a relief when he saw Ted talking with his men, and Myrna with the children.

Grant had spoken with Ted for over an hour, explaining the concerns and what had transpired at the Langdon and Bierdan ranches. Although Ted had heard much about Warren Langdon's decision to sell his land, he wasn't aware of the numerous threats against Eloise Bierdan, nor the discovery of Hap Whidley's body.

They'd stayed longer than anticipated but Grant was grateful when Myrna had invited them all to stay for dinner. Now he was on his way to see Eloise Bierdan, for what he assumed would be another difficult conversation. He sent his men on as they approached the entrance to the Bierdan ranch, riding on toward the house alone.

Eloise answered the door and ushered him into the front room.

"May I pour you some coffee or a glass of whiskey?"

"Coffee would be great."

She returned within minutes with two cups. "Do you take anything in it?"

"No, black is good.

"Niall told you why I wished to meet with you?"

"Said you wanted to discuss selling even though he wasn't sure you'd made the decision to actually leave. Tell me what you're thinking, Eloise."

It didn't take long for her to go over the pros and cons of a sale, from her perspective. Grant added some additional factors for her to consider. He could see it was all quite over-whelming for the young widow.

"Let me assure you that I'm not here to pressure you to sell. But you need to confront the realities of running a ranch. It's hard work and requires attention twenty-four hours a day. It leaves little time for anything beyond the ranch boundaries. And there are no guarantees that anything you do will provide enough money to grow or break-even. Harsh weather, rustling, disease, disloyal ranch hands, and beef prices that fluctuate can wipe out any expected gain. It's a brutal business, Eloise." He finished the last of the second cup of coffee she'd poured. "But, it's my life and I wouldn't choose anything else. You'll have to ask yourself how much you want this, and if it's enough to risk everything to keep."

She walked to the window and pulled back the curtain. It had been a peaceful day. The weather was perfect and everyone moved about their business as if nothing odd was happening. She dropped the curtain and turned back to Grant.

"If I sell, would you have an interest?"

"Yes and no. It's no secret I'd like to purchase it if you're ready to sell. The issue is I've just committed myself to Langdon's ranch and don't know that I can manage another purchase. I'd need to check with a couple of banks. I use the one here and one in Great Valley. You have any idea what you'd ask?"

She named a number.

"That's quite reasonable, Eloise. To be honest, I'd expect to pay more."

"I appreciate your honesty and all of your time. It's a hard decision for me but everything you've said makes sense. I know you're anxious to get back, but let me know if you're able to arrange something. As much as I'd like to keep the ranch, have a place of my own, I lack the skills and money to continue."

The disconsolate look she shot Grant ate at him. He'd wondered many times how his family would do if they lost him and if he had done what he could to let them continue the ranch if they chose. He cursed Gordon Bierdan once more for his poor choices and insistence on vengeance.

"I'll get back to you as soon as I can, but you decide if selling is what you want. If you do, I'll help you work something out."

Grant thought of their conversation all the way back to the ranch. He knew it would be hard to pull off another purchase. Most of his capital was now committed to his existing operations and improving those at the new property.

As he glanced at the darkening sky, a new idea began to materialize, one that, on the surface, felt right. He rode up to the barn, unsaddled and groomed his horse, then took his time walking toward the house. By the time Grant entered the front door he felt certain he had a plan that Eloise would accept and that would be beneficial not only to him, but to others.

******

Denver, Colorado

Connor left Ira's office and walked down the street to a restaurant for dinner. He sat down and looked out the window toward the street. He was surprised to spot one of Ira's enforcers, Glen Stiles, who appeared to be following him. Walsh employed the enforcer for instances such as the one concerning Pierce. Connor watched as Glen crossed the street, walked into the restaurant, and scanned the small space. He spotted Connor and took a seat a few tables away.

The waitress took Connor's order, then walked over to where Stiles sat. Connor could hear the waitress laugh at something Glen said, then saw her walk away.

Connor fumed at the realization that Walsh suspected not just Pierce, but him as well. He'd spent months building his credibility, growing the saloon business, and making Ira a handsome profit. That appeared to mean little to someone like Walsh.

He suspected they already knew where Pierce lived, which was a problem. Connor had intended to go there himself. He didn't want someone with an incentive to rough Pierce up doing anything before he had a chance to see him.

Connor finished dinner and stood. He made a show of looking around until his eyes landed on Glen.

"Stiles. Didn't know you were back in town."

"Connor," the hired gun eyed him and shifted in his seat.

"You back for a reason?"

"I am. Ira's got a new job for me."

"And that would be?"

"You'll have to speak with him about it." Stiles sat back in his chair, exposing his gun. It was more for show, not a real threat. This piece of slime wouldn't draw in public. No, he'd wait to catch his target unaware and shoot him in the back. Fair play wasn't the killer's style.

Connor's face hardened. He bent low and spoke in a soft voice. "Stay out of my way, Stiles. I'm not like those you murder from behind. If it ever comes down to you and me, rest assured you won't like the ending." He straightened and walked out to the street without a backward glance.

******

Cold Creek, Colorado

"What do you see, Niall?" Jamie asked. The group was positioned behind some large boulders hidden by a stand of pine, a couple hundred yards from the Ibarra ranch house. The day had not gone as planned.

The first hour Niall, Jamie, and Will had rotated shifts, watching Drew. They knew Jericho kept a constant watch, but they needed to know the extent of his recovery themselves. It seemed total. They didn't know the pain he'd endured getting to this point, but they were proud of him and stunned at his recovery.

They'd first ridden to the Rosado property, but no one was there. Not one person, nor one animal. Will and Drew checked inside while Jamie and Niall walked the property. The house was a mess. That could mean nothing given their large family. Jamie found dried blood in the barn. It could've belonged to an animal, but they doubted it. Beyond that, nothing. The five then rode to the Ibarra ranch.

Niall had climbed to the top to get a better view of the barn and house. Like the Rosado's place, he saw nothing—no one working, no activity at all. That made no sense. It appeared to be a large ranch. The barn was close to the size of Grant's, the house was one story, but spread out. He estimated the building covered over half an acre.

"I don't see much of anything. Some horses in a back corral, but nothing else." He climbed down and faced the open area between them and the house. Wide open, no cover, nothing to protect them if they rode straight in.

"I don't like it," Jamie announced. "Both places appear deserted, with no one on guard. Makes no sense."

"We only have one choice as I see it." Will had been studying the terrain, looking for ways to enter or leave the property without being seen. "We ride in as far as we can along the tree line to the north to see if we spot anyone. The cover on that side will conceal us. The house is built real close to the rock and trees where we'd approach. If we're careful, no one will see us until we've confirmed if the family is all right." He looked at the others.

"Sounds like a good plan," Jamie offered. "Personally, I don't like the thought of leaving without knowing about the family. I'd rather do as Will says and ride on in. Confirm what's going on."

"I agree. We just can't just leave if we suspect there may be trouble. Who knows what's happening in that place." Niall hated the thought of riding out without knowing if the family was okay. The scene at the Rosado's had the group on edge. No one believed that nothing had happened at that ranch.

"Or, we can do both." The others shot a look at Drew, waiting for him to continue. "One rides back, gets together as many men as possible, and returns. The other four follow the tree line and go in from the other side. Will's right. It appears the forest and rock cover comes up to the back of the property on that side. It should only take a couple of hours if we start now."

Niall's gaze cut from Drew to the trees and mountains. They'd need to travel north, then west. It would take time, but that route would protect them if anyone was keeping a lookout. "Makes sense." He studied the four other men. Niall knew the skills his brothers had. All were good shots, all calm under pressure. They were confident in their abilities. He didn't know about Jericho. "Mr. Jericho, would you be willing to ride back and organize a group to return?"

"I can do that, Mr. MacLaren. Best to keep the four of you together."

Niall took one more look toward the ranch. Nothing had changed—still no sign of life other than the few horses they'd seen. "I realize we may be pulling in more fire power than needed, but knowing what that gang has been up to, I'd rather have more men than less." He pulled his Colt from its holster and checked the barrel. Then he walked to Zeus and checked the rifle. Reaching in his saddle bags he withdrew several more rounds of ammunition. His brothers did the same.

Jericho watched the men work, then checked his own weapons. He'd rather stay with them, but someone needed to head back and he was the logical choice. "I'll start back. With luck I'll have men back here by morning." He mounted, then turned his horse toward the others. "Where do you want us?"

"I'd suggest a small group stay back here. It's the main exit to the east and town. The rest should follow our trail and group up with us on the other side." Jamie had considerable experience tracking and arresting outlaws from his years as a U.S. Marshal. He looked to Will, the other brother with experience against ruthless killers.

"I agree. We need to have a few men here to cut off any who'd try to escape. They could ride out going south, but it's tougher terrain than going east." Will mounted his horse, a clear indication he was through talking.

"Good luck, Mr. Jericho," Drew called out as he followed his brothers.

"Same to you, Mr. MacLaren. I'll see you on the other side." Jericho nodded toward the Ibarra barn. His gut told him the brothers were riding into a horde of trouble. The sooner he got to the Big G and back, the better he'd feel.

******

Denver, Colorado

"Pierce, you in here?" The brother looked around but the place seemed empty.

The back door pushed open and Pierce walked in, gun drawn, ready for trouble.

"What's going on?" his brother asked.

"Had a visitor earlier today. Didn't knock, just came in, took a brief look at me, and started rifling through my stuff. I'd just put the ledger and other materials away. Funny thing was, I'd just loaded my gun and laid it on my lap. When he turned to look at me he was staring right down the barrel of it." Pierce chuckled at the memory of the look on the man's face. He'd known he was a dead man if he reached for his own weapon.

"He tell you his name?"

"Greg Stiles. You know him?"

"Works for Walsh. We need to get out of here. Now. No time for explanations. Take everything you have and pack up. You have a horse?"

"No, but I'm sure I can get one pretty quick," Pierce replied.

Thirty minutes later the two were at the stables, paying for Pierce's horse and loading his gear in the saddle bags.

"You head out of town to the west. Don't stop until you reach Frisco. Wait for me there."

"Hell no. I'm not leaving you here to face Stiles and any of Walsh's other men. I'm staying." Pierce cinched the last saddle bag and turned to his brother, anger flowing from him.

"I have to get a message to our boss, let him know what's going on. Walsh suspects you're involved in something to discredit him and he hired Stiles to follow you. The gunman doesn't care if you're guilty or innocent. All he cares about is the money Walsh pays and moving on to his next job. Your death will make that easier," his brother ground out, then stepped within inches of Pierce. "Besides, you have the evidence to convict Walsh and the others. The information you decoded will put a lot of people out of commission for a long time. There's no way to prove anything without that ledger."

"Shouldn't I get it to the boss?"

"Too late for that now. Best to get it out of town."

Pierce placed his hands on his hips and stared down at the dirt floor. This job was to be quick. Decode, hand over the evidence, and get out. They had been a day away from that happening, until now

His brother walked to the stable door and peered out. "Stiles is on his way with two others. You have to leave, now," he ordered.

Pierce jumped on the horse and reined it around toward the back door. He glanced over his shoulder once more as his brother strode to a doorway behind the supply shed.

"I'll see you in Frisco," he called out.

Connor only nodded and slipped outside.

Chapter Twenty

Cold Creek, Colorado

Jericho had ridden non-stop to the Big G. It was late, after suppertime, but lights were showing through the windows. He dashed up the front steps, knocked twice, then opened the door to see Grant walking out of this office.

"There's a situation at the Ibarra ranch, Mr. Taylor," Jericho managed. He was tired and hungry, but determined to ride back tonight.

"What happened?" Grant was already walking to the gun cabinet to grab a rifle. Eleanor and the other women had heard Jericho's voice and joined them.

"Nothing yet, but we think the outlaws may be holed up at the Ibarra place. We went to Rosado's and no one was there, and I mean no one. All their animals were gone. The house was a mess and we found dried blood." Jericho scrubbed a hand over his stubbled face. "We rode on to the Ibarra ranch but stayed a ways back. Again, no sign of life other than a few horses. We watched for a while but nothing. The MacLarens are making their way around the north end of the property, trying to get to the trees and rocks behind the house on the west. But if there's trouble, like we all expect, they'll need help." Jericho noticed the anxious looks on the women's faces. "The men were fine when I left them," he added for their benefit.

Grant didn't wait any longer but bounded down the steps and marched to the bunkhouse. "Jake! Everyone up. We need to ride out!"

Fifteen minutes later Grant, Jericho and eight of the Big G men were saddled and on their way. They didn't spare their horses but rode flat out toward the Ibarra ranch.

******

"You see anything, Jamie?" Niall was behind him, holding the reins to Zeus and Jamie's horse, Rebel.

"I can just make out three men with guns. They're in the office. Another man is in there with them. Looks like he's in a chair, tied to it." He looked at his brothers. They'd found what they'd hoped they wouldn't.

"Any women, children?" Niall asked.

"Can't see any from here, and that's a problem. We can't go in until we know where they are and how many men Luther has. I need to get closer." Jamie slipped down from the rocks, walked to Rebel, and pulled out a knife and another gun from his saddle bags, then grabbed his rifle from its scabbard. "I'll be back as soon as I can," he whispered before Niall grabbed his arm and spun him around.

"Wait a minute. You're not going alone. Let me get my gear and we'll go together."

"No. This is a one man job. Two of us may draw attention." Jamie ignored the concern he saw in Niall's eyes. "Trust me, Niall. I'll take a look and get back before you miss me."

******

Frisco, Colorado

Pierce settled into the small hotel room on the top floor. He checked the window but saw no evidence that he'd been followed. It had been hours since he had left Denver. He was exhausted. The owner had gone to the kitchen and found some leftover stew. Pierce had thanked him, wolfed it down, and trudged upstairs.

He thought of Connor.

Had he gotten the message off to their boss? Had Stiles found him? Connor was a survivor—a man with many lives. Pierce had seen him get out of more difficult situations than he cared to count. If Connor said he'd be here, he would.

Pierce removed his boots and sat back on the bed. The ledger was hidden in a place he believed no one could find. The code used was more sophisticated than most Pierce had seen. Decoding was quick once he'd found the key, except for one word in the ledger. Walsh hadn't used the code for it. He'd made up a word using a mix of letters and numbers. It had taken time, but Pierce had figured it out the day before, and that one word brought it all together. Opium.

Pierce was aware of the laws prohibiting the importation of the drug into San Francisco. Ironically, opium dens weren't illegal—importing it into the city was. Ira's suppliers were in British Columbia. It was legal to import the raw opium into that city, although there were steep import duties imposed.

Walsh had chosen to import into one the few cities who had enacted laws making it illegal instead of cities where it may have been tolerated. The reason, of course, was the number of opium dens and users in the large California bay city. Walsh had chosen a city which could make him rich or would send him to jail if his involvement was discovered.

Pierce closed his eyes and drifted off.

******

Denver, Colorado

"What do you mean, gone?" Ira bellowed at Stiles when he delivered the news that Pierce couldn't be found. "I told you to frighten him, but not enough to run him off."

"He had help, Boss."

"How's that?"

"Your man, Connor, helped him get away."

Connor? The red began on Walsh's neck and crept up toward his face, although the color turned a sickening purple as it surrounded the skin around his eyes and made its way up his forehead. "You're sure?" Ira bit out.

"We found this in a hidden storage closet where Pierce lived." Stiles spread out the documents he and his men had found when they searched the abandoned room.

Ira stared down at copies of two of his ledgers. Other papers showed notes, scribbles that Walsh recognized as parts of his code. He pushed them aside, scrutinizing the other documents Stiles had recovered. His hands shook as he picked up and studied each scrap of paper.

"And you're sure Connor was involved?"

"We watched them leave Pierce's building together, but lost them. I figured Connor was trying to get Pierce out of town and went to the closest livery. We saw Connor slip out at the same time Pierce rode away through the back. Believe me, they acted together."

"And you didn't follow them?" Ira tried to control the almost debilitating rage he felt.

"Pierce got away before we could get to our horses. We followed Connor but he disappeared. One minute he was fifty feet in front of us, the next he was gone." Stiles watched Ira attempt to bring his anger under control. He'd seen him take out his fury on others. Stiles rested his hand on the butt of his gun. One could never be too careful around Ira Walsh.

"There's more." Stiles reached into his coat and extracted a few more papers from the inside pocket. He threw them on the desk.

Ira picked one up, then another. Dates, names, amounts. These could have come from just one place—the third ledger. He crumbled the document in his hand and threw it across the room. The original was still in the safe. He'd used it not long before Stiles entered his office. Someone had a copy and the means to decipher the entries. Pierce or Connor. Or both. The realization that he'd been manipulated gripped his chest, squeezing until it became painful to breathe. His hate-filled eyes lifted to Stiles.

Stiles cleared his throat. "I've had men watching the train station. Neither has shown up. We know Pierce is on horseback, but Connor..." He trailed off, not wanting to anger his boss further.

Ira looked around his office. The lavish furnishings, artwork, cigars, and expensive liquor. He thought of the enormous mansion he owned in an exclusive part of Denver, and the actress he kept in a fashionable apartment near the theatre. Ira came to a decision. "Get us on the next train to Great Valley. Load horses and plenty of ammunition. They'll head to Cold Creek, but they'll be on horseback. If we leave tonight we'll arrive ahead of them." Ira paused and looked at the papers on his desk. "Then we'll kill them."

******

Louis Dunnigan looked at the note he'd been handed when he returned to his office. It was a note from his associate, Connor. Pierce had deciphered the final sections of the ledger. Cattle rustling, embezzling, instructions to intimidate, orders to kill, and illegal shipments of opium. Although he knew Walsh was dirty, the extent of his crimes staggered Louis. The activities had been going on for years without consequence. But now they could stop him.

Connor wrote that Walsh had issued another kill order, this one against Pierce as Ira had discovered his involvement. A man name Greg Stiles had been brought in to eliminate him. Connor and Pierce were headed to Cold Creek with the ledger.

"Terrance," Louis called from inside his office.

"Yes, Mr. Dunnigan."

"I need a message sent to Grant Taylor in Cold Creek. Without delay."

******

Cold Creek, Colorado

Jamie moved with silent determination toward the Ibarra house. He was fortunate. It was a dark night with heavy clouds that obscured the small sliver of a moon. He'd seen no dogs, no guards. Judging by the number of horses he'd seen during his brief look in the barn there could be as many as twelve men. Their animals were easy to spot, all kept in stalls on one side of the barn, compared to the high-grade horse stock that Ibarra kept. Jamie moved around the house and stopped.

He was close enough to hear conversations. Men's voices, laughing. A woman's voice, pleading. His stomach tightened. Jamie crept forward to stop beneath an open window and peered over the ledge. Two men were holding a woman down, tying her to the bed posts, while another man, arms folded, ankles crossed, leaned against a wall, and smirked at the scene in front of him. Eight men so far.

"Enough," the man against the wall called out. "Leave us."

The men stopped and stared at the woman. "Sure, Drago, but when you're done, we want a turn," one of the men snorted before walking out, shutting the door behind them.

Jamie eased up in small increments until he could see into the room once more. Drago was sitting on the bed, stroking the woman's face while his other hand moved up one leg. She tried to move her head away, tears streaming down her face.

Drago grabbed the woman's hair and yanked her head back around, holding her in place. The other hand left her leg and moved to the bodice of her dress, gripped the top edge, and ripped the fabric away.

Jamie eased down. He had to do something, now. The sound of movement around the corner caught his attention. He smelled smoke, heard voices. At least two men were outside, smoking. It was the opportunity he needed. The woman in the bedroom screamed. Jamie moved fast.

The outlaws turned at the sound of Jamie's boot landing on broken twigs. The closest man lifted his rifle to shoot. Jamie threw his knife, imbedding it in the one holding the rifle. The second went for his gun, but it never made it out of its holster. Jamie's shot drove straight through the man's heart.

Yelling erupted from inside. Jamie moved away from the house and back into the dark, returning the way he had come. He didn't stop to watch. Curses pierced the night. He knew they'd found the bodies. Someone was yelling out orders. He assumed it was the one they called Drago. Jamie needed to get back to his brothers and formulate a plan. The outlaws now knew they'd been discovered. Time was short.

Niall, Drew, and Will heard the shot, then the yelling, and drew their weapons.

"Stay down," Niall whispered as his gaze focused on the path Jamie had taken. Not more than a minute later Jamie appeared and joined them behind the rocks they were using as cover. Niall looked at him. An unspoken question passed between them.

"As far as I can tell, there are at least six left," Jamie said and slid a bullet into his pistol to replace the one he'd used. "I could see one woman, a couple of kids, and one man. Probably Ibarra and his family."

"And the Rosado's?" Drew asked.

"Don't know."

They heard voices moving toward them from the direction of the house. The sound of boots crunching the rocky dirt path indicated that several men were searching for the intruders. The brothers fanned out and took positions that allowed them to pick off the outlaws as they emerged from the brush.

A tall, slender gunman emerged only yards from Will, holding his pistol in front of him. One shot and the outlaw lay on the ground, writhing in pain.

"Shit," another called out. "Think they got Clem."

Two others appeared to the left of Drew, guns ready. Drew aimed and squeezed at the same time another shot rang out. He'd hit his man, as had Niall.

"Let's get out of here, Luther," someone hissed.

"Back to the house. Now!" another voice commanded.

Niall made his way toward Jamie. "You hear that?"

"Yeah," Jamie replied. "Looks like Luther is part of this group." He stopped at the sound of the barn door being opened. "We'd better get moving if we hope to get them before they ride out."

The four stalked toward the house in silent, quick steps, keeping low, guns at the ready. Niall motioned for them to spread out. Drew reached the back of the house first and crouched below the open kitchen window. He edged up. A man was tied to a chair, trying to break loose as the chair tipped and swayed below him. He dropped down and moved to the next window. A woman tied to a bed. He cursed in disgust, but didn't stop, moving on to the next opening. He heard crying, whimpering. He looked in to see several children, another man, and two women. These must be the Rosados.

He spun at the sound of someone approaching to see Will kneel beside him at the same time yells sounded from the barn and seven riders took off to the south. They rode fast and low, making for a difficult target.

The sound of gunfire split the night as the brothers emerged from around the house to aim and shoot at the retreating men. One shot was true as an outlaw grabbed a shoulder and fell to the ground. The other six disappeared into the dark.

"Did any of you get a good look at those men?" Niall asked.

"One was the man they called Drago." Jamie reloaded and holstered his revolver.

"The largest one was probably Luther. We'll know when we check the other bodies," Drew added.

They split up, with Drew and Will walking out to the rider who'd fallen in his attempt to flee. Niall and Jamie walked into the house to check on the families.

"Are you Ibarra?" Niall asked as he knelt to loosen the ties on the chair. He helped the man stand and stepped back.

"Sí, I am Alonzo Ibarra," he said as he hurried to the bedroom where his wife had been held.

Jamie heard crying in the back bedroom, pulled his gun, and slowly opened the door. He saw no gunmen, only a frightened family. "Are you the Rosados?" he asked as he holstered his weapon.

"I am Manuel Rosado. This is my family." He looked at Jamie in confusion. "Who are you?"

"Jamie MacLaren, a friend of Gordon Taylor," Jamie replied and gave them a brief summary of the events leading up to tonight. "Do you know anything about a man named Drago?"

"Sí, he is a mean one. Ordered his men to take us and bring us to Alonzo's home. We've been here four days. Are Alonzo and Sophia all right?"

Manuel's question was answered when the Ibarras ran into the room. Niall stood in the doorway and surveyed the site. Five adults and six children, the oldest no more than fourteen. It must have been terrifying for them.

"Jamie, we best grab our horses and check the men out back, make sure none are still breathing."

None of the three men were alive, and none looked like the description they had of Luther. Jamie and Niall flung them over the horses and walked to the house, dumping the bodies near the barn.

Drew and Will had returned with the one who had tried to leave. He was alive, but unconscious. They laid him on the porch while the women went for water and bandages. Perhaps they could find out where Drago and Luther were headed.

Chapter Twenty-One

Frisco, Colorado

Pierce awoke in his darkened hotel room, illuminated only by a small ray of moonlight streaming through the curtains. A sound drew his attention. He rolled over, grabbed his gun, then stood, and pointed the weapon at the sound. Connor.

"Hell, I could have shot you," Pierce hissed.

"Except that you would've already been dead," Connor replied. He'd been in the room for just a few minutes, but Pierce hadn't stirred at all when he'd entered.

"Shit, what time is it?" Pierce pushed his hands through his hair, and scrubbed his face in an attempt to wake up.

"Just after midnight. Time to leave." Connor started to gather Pierce's belongings and stuff them into his saddlebag while his brother threw on his shirt and boots.

They rode non-stop toward Cold Creek.

Connor wasn't certain Ira would realize he and Pierce were traveling to the small Colorado town. Walsh had insisted Connor concentrate on the saloon and mining business—his involvement in activities at the Bierdan and Langdon ranches had been limited. But Ira wasn't stupid. If he couldn't locate his ex-employees in Denver, the next logical place would be Cold Creek, where Walsh had sent Drago and Luther, two men prominently mentioned in the damning ledger.

******

Cold Creek, Colorado

"You sure you'll be all right riding over alone?" Alicia asked as the three younger women prepared to depart for the Bierdan ranch. Amanda and Tess thought they should've paid a social call on Eloise sooner, but there hadn't been time. Kate decided to join them. The visit would take their minds off the men who'd ridden out to find the outlaws.

"It's daylight and there are three of us. We'll use the road instead of the shortcut through the trees. I'm sure we'll be fine." Amanda didn't mention that each of the women carried handguns with them, plus the rifle Amanda always had tucked in the scabbard on her saddle. "And we'll be back in plenty of time for supper." She hugged Alicia. The other two were outside, saddled and ready to leave.

Eloise was surprised but pleased when she saw them ride up before noon. She seldom had company these days, except for the sheriff.

"I hope we're not intruding," Amanda leaned in and gave the young woman a warm hug. "You know Tess, of course, and this is Kate MacLaren. She's Niall's wife."

Within minutes the four were chatting, catching up on the activities of late. Even though Tess, Kate, and Amanda were aware of Eloise's troubles, the impact intensified when described by Eloise herself.

"Are you going to stay?" Amanda placed the empty coffee cup on the table. She knew if it were her she would fight to the end. But Amanda had been born to ranch, loved the life and the challenges. Eloise hadn't.

Eloise looked at the three women, each so different, but each strong in their own way. She wasn't sure where she fit with women like them—if she did fit.

"I would like to stay but I'm not sure that's possible. Running a ranch requires so much more than I'd realized. Skills I never learned, money that isn't available. I just hope to make it through this season, then I'll decide." Eloise stood and picked up the empty cups. "I hope you can all stay for dinner. There's plenty and I'd love the company."

The hopeful expression on her face just about broke Tess's heart. She knew Eloise had struggled with not only running the ranch but the consequences of her husband's decisions. She realized that Eloise would be interested in what was happening with Drew.

"Oh, Eloise, I have some wonderful news for you," Tess said and explained how Drew had been working to walk again, and finally had succeeded. "It is so wonderful," she finished.

"My God, Tess, that is wonderful news. You don't know how many times I've thought of him and prayed that he'd walk again." As far as Eloise was concerned, that was the best news she'd heard in a very long time.

"Plus Drew has asked Tess to marry him," Kate smiled at the woman seated next to her. "Of course she accepted."

"I'm so happy for you, Tess!" Eloise hugged her friend, wishing her the best in her marriage. "Come on, you can all help me in the kitchen."

******

"Where to now?" Luther asked Drago. They'd ridden all night, first south, then east. He was sure Drago had a plan. His moves were never impulsive. They'd pulled up to rest, eat jerky and hardtack, and water the horses.

Earlier they'd watched a large group of men riding toward the Rosado and Ibarra ranches. Drago had recognized three of them—Grant Taylor, his foreman, and the large man who always escorted Drew MacLaren. He'd only seen Grant Taylor twice when he'd snuck onto the Big G. Taylor's place was the next one on Ira's list. Walsh wanted all the ranchland that had good timber, and the Big G was one of them.

"We ride north from here and pay a visit to the lovely Widow Bierdan. The woman will agree to sell the land to Walsh before we leave."

******

Ira and Stiles stepped from the train and waited in impatient silence for their horses to be unloaded and saddled. The men were determined to reach Cold Creek before Connor. As far as Walsh was concerned, Connor was a walking dead man.

He'd been retracing his decisions since he'd hired Connor several months before. Connor had been recommended by several sources, including his contact in New York who'd alerted Ira of the inquiries into his businesses. If his contact was an associate of Connor, he wouldn't have warned Ira, would he? No, his contact must have been just as blind to Connor's true reasons for being in Denver as Ira had.

And who was Pierce? Connor had to have hired him at the saloon for only one reason—to find the ledger and decode it. Walsh had sent a telegram to contacts in Boston, New York, and Philadelphia when he'd made the decision to bring in Stiles to follow Pierce. The response from Boston finalized his decision. Pierce was an accomplished thief and decoding expert. One of the best. Ira cursed himself for the hundredth time for being such a fool.

When Pierce had ridden out of Denver, Ira had had no doubt where he would go—Cold Creek. The man had made a copy of his ledger, decoded it, and knew the extent of Ira's activities, knew of Drago and Luther's involvement, and knew both men were in Cold Creek. Walsh also realized there was no way the two could reach the Bierdan ranch before him and Stiles. He'd visit Mrs. Bierdan and wait for Connor and Pierce to arrive. Then he'd kill them.

******

"I wish we'd figured things out before you and your family went through this," Grant said as he and the rest of the men prepared to leave for the Big G.

"You sent men, Grant. Without their help we would not have survived. There was no reason for Drago and his men to keep us alive—we meant nothing to them. My home was just a safe place for them to stay." Alonzo Ibarra held out his hand to his neighbor and friend. "Thank you. I will be forever in your debt."

He walked over to the MacLarens. "Thank you. I wish there was more I could do to show my gratitude." He shook each hand, then stepped back.

"No thanks needed, Mr. Ibarra. We're glad to have helped," Drew said, expressing the thoughts of everyone.

"Let's go, men." Grant tipped his hat once more to the Ibarras. He hoped he and his men found Drago and Luther before they harmed anyone else. At least the MacLarens had put a hole in the size of their gang. Now only six were left.

******

"I'm so glad all of you came. It's been the nicest day I've had in a long time." Eloise hugged each of the women, sorry to see the day end.

"It's been a wonderful day for all of us. I'm hoping we'll be able to see you again before we leave for Fire Mountain," Amanda said as she picked up her riding gloves. They'd stayed later than intended. She was glad the ride home wouldn't take long.

She grasped the handle of the front door, pulled it open, and almost walked into a tall, bronze-skinned man standing at the threshold. Her eyes must have shown her surprise.

"Sorry to have frightened you, Miss....?"

"Uh, Amanda. Amanda MacLaren."

"Ah, a MacLaren. How nice to meet you." He extended his arm and for the first time Amanda noticed it held a gun. A gun now pointed at her. "Please, step back into the house, Amanda MacLaren."

She walked backyards a few feet and ran into Kate, who'd come up behind her. "What's going on?"

"Another beautiful woman. I am a lucky man today." The stranger pointed the gun toward the front room. Two other men followed him and began to check each room in the house.

The women turned as a loud crash came from the kitchen. Amanda and Kate's eyes shot to where Tess and Eloise had been talking and heard a man's voice.

"Move into the front room, ladies, and don't say a word," the harsh voice commanded. Tess and Eloise walked through the doorway, a large, brutal looking man behind them, pointing a gun at their backs. Another man stepped into the kitchen and closed the door, leaving their last comrade to watch the horses.

"Well, it appears we are very lucky indeed." Drago told the others. "Did you seen anyone else?"

"One, but he is no longer a concern to us," Luther sneered.

Eloise gasped at the knowledge that another of her men may have been murdered by these men. Jeff had debated whether or not to leave just the one man today. Eloise had insisted one was enough. She'd been wrong.

"Which of you is Mrs. Bierdan?" Drago asked.

Each looked away from him or let their eyes fall to the floor, but no one spoke.

"Let me remind you ladies who holds the gun. I'm sure you're all aware that I have no qualms about using it." His cold stare washed over the women. "Now, which one of you is Eloise Bierdan?"

"I am," Eloise said in a calm voice that masked her inner fear. She glared at the man but didn't back away.

Drago studied the four and made a decision. "Take these three into separate rooms and tie them," pointing to Amanda, Kate, and Tess. "And gag them. This one will stay here." He focused his gaze and gun on Eloise.

Luther and two others escorted the women away from the front of the house. Tess was deposited in a downstairs bedroom while Amanda and Kate were securely tied to bedposts in rooms above.

Drago sat in a chair across from Eloise.

"Where are all your ranch hands? Surely there is more than the one that Luther found?"

Eloise raised her chin and glared at the foul creature before her. "They're wranglers. Where do you think they are?"

He let her comment go. "So, they are gone for the entire day. You and your friends are alone." It was a statement.

Eloise said nothing.

"You are a very stubborn woman, Mrs. Bierdan. You have no husband, no experience in ranching, yet you continue to hold on to a ranch you know you will lose. Why?" No one had suspected the young woman would be so difficult to persuade. Her determined nature and strong will had held her fear at bay. She never even asked how much Walsh was willing to pay. Drago had to admire her spirit even though he knew she'd make the right decision—or disappear.

Eloise stared at her captor, not understanding how anyone would think she'd react to threats and killings by giving up. She knew few people in this part of the country who responded well to intimidation.

Eloise knew Jeff and her other men were working at the far end of the ranch today, sorting and branding cattle, and checking for disease. He'd told her it would be a long day. She could only pray that they'd finish early and return. Her mind buzzed with anything she could say or do to stall for time. "You have me at a disadvantage. You know my name but I don't know yours."

"Ah, my apologies. My name is Sebastian Drago."

"And you work for?"

"I work for myself, Mrs. Bierdan, and my partner." Drago bent to rest his forearms on his thighs, the gun still pointing her way.

"And is your partner Ira Walsh?" She'd reasoned it could only be the other buyer from Denver. No other buyer had surfaced and she was convinced that neither Grant Taylor nor Louis Dunnigan would use the tactics of men such as the one who sat before her.

Drago ignored her. He stood and walked to the small cabinet that contained two decanters and a bottle of whiskey. He holstered his gun, certain Eloise would not try anything stupid while her friends were his hostages. Drago poured a drink and threw it back, then poured another. "You have not answered my question. Why stay when you will lose the ranch anyway?" This time his eyes trailed over her, making their way up her dress to her chest, and settling on her face with an appreciative gaze.

The scrutiny made her skin crawl. She stood and walked within five feet of the repulsive man. She couldn't force her body to move closer.

"It's my land, Mr. Drago, and my decision whether or not I sell. It's too bad your partner had no patience, because, as you say, I may very well lose the ranch. But I assure you, if I sell, it won't be to men like you or Walsh." Eloise had no idea where the words came from. She was angry, outraged at what these men had done. The lives they'd wasted and damage they'd caused.

He set the glass down, never taking his eyes from her. The menace in his face sent chills up her spine and she forced herself not to back away. To her astonishment, he laughed. It was a sinister sound, not the type of laugh that caught others and made them join in. No, this was a laugh of disbelief, threatening in its harshness, by a man who thought she would cower under his threats.

Drago walked up to within inches of her and stared into her eyes.

His eyes are soulless—blank and predatory, Eloise thought as she worked to not glance away.

His hand snaked up, wrapped around her neck, and squeezed. She grabbed at his wrist, arm, anything that would loosen his hold. Eloise wasn't a match for his strength. Her efforts made his fingers tighten further until she was unable to draw a breath.

Drago's grip relaxed and he pushed her away. Eloise stumbled backwards, falling to the wood floor. He stared down at her but made no effort to help her stand.

"You are an ignorant woman. One that I will enjoy humbling later. But for now, I want you alive." He walked to the hall and called for Luther to bring one of the other women into the room. "It is much easier to make a decision when friends are around, don't you think?"

Luther walked in pushing Tess in front of him. Her hands were still tied but the gag had been removed.

"Sit, Miss...?" Drago asked.

Tess looked at Eloise, who now stood a few feet away and nodded. There was no point in keeping their names a secret. He'd use force to learn them.

"Tessa Taylor."

Surprise registered on Drago's face. "So you are Grant Taylor's daughter?"

She ignored him, tried to take a step back, and bumped into Luther's solid chest.

As Drago considered this, he heard the back door open, then close. Two more men entered from the kitchen.

"I thought I recognized your horse, Drago," Ira Walsh said and looked at the two women. Greg Stiles moved to the side, surveying the room.

"There are two more upstairs, tied and gagged," Luther offered.

"And what are your plans for them? You cannot kill four women and expect to walk away." Ira poured drinks for him and Stiles.

"You've known me too long to think I would simply kill these beautiful women. No, we will get what is needed then find more useful ways to fill their time—and ours."

Drago introduced the two to Ira. Knowing the connections between the Taylors, MacLarens, and Gordon Bierdan, the man was surprised that a Taylor was in the home.

"Who are the other women?" Walsh asked.

Drago looked at Eloise.

She clenched her hands in front of her and cleared her voice. "Amanda and Kate MacLaren." As soon as she'd said the names she knew it was a mistake. The glee in Walsh's eyes was hard to miss.

"Outstanding, Drago. Your choice in women is excellent." Ira sat down to enjoy the liquor and crossed one leg over the other. "Where are all of our men?"

"The MacLarens discovered us at the Ibarra ranch. Some of the men were killed, but six of us got away. Luther and I saw a group of men from the Big G ride towards the Ibarra's. It should take them awhile to clean up the place and return to their ranch. That's when they will realize their women have not returned. Even so, we have plenty of time," Drago chuckled, understanding the meaning behind his partner's question.

Ira turned to Stiles. "Bring my saddle bags into the kitchen."

Drago was sure he knew what was coming. It was one of Ira's dirty secrets, known to few.

When Stiles returned, Ira left for the kitchen, drew water into a pan, and began to heat the liquid. He walked to a cabinet and pulled down two cups before opening a saddlebag and extracting a pouch. He opened it and reached in to snatch some of the substance inside. He placed the pulp in the hot water and stepped back. A few minutes later he strained the liquid into two cups and added the sugar he'd found in a cupboard. Ira tasted one—perfect. He grabbed the other cup and strolled back to where the women were seated. They would, of course, have no idea what was about to happen.

Chapter Twenty-Two

It had been a long day. Everyone was exhausted. The men took care of their horses before trudging into the house and removing their gun belts. Eleanor and Alicia sat, working on needle point, Eleanor drinking tea and Alicia a cup of coffee.

"Where is everyone?" Drew threw his hat on a nearby chair and stretched his arms above his head, enjoying the feel of standing and moving at will. He looked toward the dining room but saw no one. There wasn't the female chatter that usually greeted everyone when they walked in.

"Amanda, Kate, and Tess left this morning to visit Eloise Bierdan. We expected them early afternoon." She walked up to Grant and placed a soft kiss on his cheek. "Did everything go all right?"

"Turned out okay but could've been disastrous for the Rosados and Ibarras. Luther and his men were using the Ibarra ranch as their headquarters—were holding the two families hostage. Drew, Will, and Niall forced them out, killing a few in the process."

"There were six we missed. One was Luther and another named Drago. They rode south. Don't know where they are now," Drew added and accepted the drink Niall offered him.

Will stood back, looking pensive. Something wasn't right. "You say the ladies left this morning?"

"Yes, around nine," Alicia replied, noting the concern in her nephew's eyes.

"It's no more than an hour each way, even if they took the road and not the back trails. That means they've been visiting Eloise for over eight hours. That seem right?" Will persisted.

Eleanor looked to Grant. "That's a long visit, yes."

"What are you getting at, Will?" Niall asked.

"Something doesn't feel right. We know Luther and Drago rode south. These men work for Ira Walsh, and Ira wants Eloise's land. It wouldn't be hard for them to backtrack, head west, then north to the Bierdan place."

"Let's go," Drew snapped as all of the men grabbed their guns and left at full speed for the Bierdan ranch.

******

"Got a message for you, Sheriff." The telegraph clerk walked into Frank's office and plunked the paper down on the desk. "Should've gotten it to you this morning but got busy. Sorry about that."

Frank picked up the telegram from Louis Dunnigan and scanned it briefly. It was short and clear. "Shit," he ground out and thought of Eloise. "Eddy," he called to his deputy, "I'm riding to the Bierdan ranch. You handle things here."

Sweat beaded on his forehead as he pushed his horse into a full run. The message had been ominous in what it didn't say. *Walsh and Stiles riding to Cold Creek. Sebastian Drago already there. Be prepared.*

Drago. Frank didn't believe he'd met a more evil man. He'd run up against him twice while a Colorado Ranger and once as a U.S. Marshal. Could never make any charges stick. The man was as slick as slime.

He didn't know Stiles, but he didn't need to. If he worked for Ira, then he was bad news.

******

Connor and Pierce sat on a hill overlooking the Bierdan ranch. It gave them a clear view of the barn, ranch house, three horses tied in the front, four horses tied at the back. A neighbor had given them directions as well as coffee after they'd provided him with their names. The man hadn't asked further questions, just wished them well.

"What do you think?" Pierce handed the field glasses back to Connor.

"One of the horses in the back is Drago's black stallion. The others I don't recognize, but it's my guess they belong to Ira, Stiles, and Luther, if he's still alive." Connor looked at the three horses tied in front. "I don't recognize any of the horses out front, but we know there are at least seven people in the house." He studied the layout once more. What he saw surprised him. Other than the horses, there was no other movement around the property. It was late, close to supper time. There should be men and activity all around.

"We'll leave our horses here. Take what you need and plenty of ammunition. The men in that house won't quit without a fight."

"What about the ledger?"

"Wrap it in a blanket and take it over there." Connor pointed to the base of a large pine and walked toward it. The tree was surrounded by smaller shrubs. He pushed the low branches aside and began to dig. Pierce watched as the fabric covered ledger was placed in the shallow hole and covered with dirt, then twigs and leaves. With luck, they'd be back for it tonight.

******

Tess and Eloise held the warm cups in their hands. They'd refused the vile concoction when it was first offered. Ira explained the tea would relax them, allow a civil conversation about the Bierdan property and its sale. The women knew otherwise, and in defiance of his command, dumped the liquid onto the carpet.

Ira became incensed and slapped Tess, hard, causing a bruise to form and blood to trickle from her mouth. She sat ramrod straight in her chair, wiped the blood away, and didn't flinch when he threatened to slap her again. Instead of hitting her he returned to the kitchen and poured two more cups. These he'd handed to them with the threat

261

that if the cups weren't empty within a few minutes, he'd let Drago do whatever he wanted with the women upstairs.

Tess lowered her arms to her lap and cradled the cup. She'd followed Amanda and Kate's lead and placed her gun in one of her boots. She could feel the metal against her leg, wished she could reach down and grab it. At this range she couldn't miss, but neither would the men in front of her.

The liquid had cooled enough to drink. They started to take small sips with the encouragement of Ira—and Drago's gun. Neither had the will to subject Kate or Amanda to anything Drago might choose to do. They'd drink the brew and hope they could handle the effects of whatever was in it.

The tea wasn't anything either had tasted before, and it wasn't pleasant. Tess felt a warming sensation that traveled throughout her body. She reached up to touch her forehead but it felt cool, not warm like the sensations moving over her.

She noticed that Eloise had mirrored her actions by touching her own forehead, then her neck, rubbing it as if that would dispel the sensations. Tess understood her friend was having the same reaction to the tea.

They looked toward each other, seeking strength and reassurance that all would be fine. After a while, a feeling of calm followed by pleasant sensations confused both women's minds and bodies. The effects of the tea were too strong.

Ira looked at Drago. "Have the men leave us with the women. Post them around the house, but do not let them disturb us."

Drago gave the instructions and returned to the room where his partner sat, eyeing the two women.

Ira leered at Tess. He would take her first and let Drago have the Bierdan woman. Then they'd bring the two down from upstairs. "Please, finish your drinks, then we can start our discussions about the future of the ranch."

"Now," Drago ordered and tapped the gun against the edge of each cup. As he did, his hand rested on Eloise's knee and began to massage it. She pushed his hand away but her actions seemed slow, sluggish. Drago chuckled at her attempts to ward off the effects of the drug.

"If you refuse, I will ask Luther to bring your friends downstairs so that you can watch how Drago persuades reluctant people to do as we ask." Ira stood and walked to the bottom of the staircase. He glanced once more at Tess, who sat motionless.

"Luther," Ira called out.

"Wait," Tess whispered and finished the last of her tea, reached out to place the cup on a table but missed, and watched it fall to the floor.

Drago looked at Ira and gestured toward the bedroom.

"Miss Taylor, why don't I help you to the back where you can lie down? You don't look so well." Ira wrapped his fingers around her arm and lifted her to stand. Tess wobbled a little, but steadied when Ira put his arm around her. He walked with her to the office door and looked in to where Stiles stood guard at a front window. "I want to know if you see anything," Walsh said.

Eloise heard a door close and looked at the man in front of her.

"Now, Mrs. Bierdan, let's talk about the sale of your land."

******

Amanda had worked without stopping to untie the rope that held her secure to the bedpost. The gunman had tied her arms above her head and the pressure to her neck and shoulders increased as she worked the restraints. Her wrists were chafed, bleeding in some places, but she could feel the rope loosening.

He hadn't tied her ankles. She used her feet to push against the bedding and supply leverage. She'd heard nothing from downstairs in a long time.

Without warning, the rope gave way. Amanda looked up to see it dangling on one end. She hurried to work it off of her wrists and scrambled off the bed.

Amanda made her way to the door and peered out. She heard a sound, then saw a man holding a rifle walk out of another room and move to the next door. She closed the door and reached down to retrieve her pistol, glad that she'd decided to bring it inside. Now she had to find a way to slip into Kate's room without being spotted.

Kate had been placed in the room closest to the stairs. Amanda waited and glanced through the small opening in the door once more. Again, the gunman walked out of a room and moved back to where he'd come from. This was her chance.

She crept out of the room, keeping her back against the wall as she made her way down the hallway, and pushed open the door to where Kate was held. Her sister-in-law was almost done removing her own bindings in the same manner as Amanda. They're eyes met. Amanda's finger touched her lips—a signal for Kate to stay quiet.

******

There hadn't been time to gather more Big G men before Grant, Jericho, and the MacLarens rode out. They were after six men. Grant figured the odds were still in their favor.

It was dusk when they reached the fence line that signaled the ranch's entrance. It was perhaps a quarter mile to the house. The men could see the women's horses tied out front, but no other movement around the barn or the bunkhouse.

"It's quiet," Niall said.

"Yeah, too quiet," Jamie replied and reined Rebel around so that he could check out the back of the house. A few minutes later he rejoined the others.

"What'd you see?" Drew had almost followed Jamie. He kept telling himself that his older brother was the expert in this and to follow his lead but not knowing if Tess was all right was torture.

"Eight horses. One large black stallion, much like Justice," he looked at Will who sat atop the magnificent stallion he'd had since the colt's birth at Fire Mountain, "and like the one that Drago rode when he left Ibarra's."

Grant swept a hand down his face and rubbed his eyes. "Eight. They must've met up with two more. I don't like this."

"Neither do I. My guess is that the men are holding the women hostage, either hoping to get Mrs. Bierdan to sign over the ranch or ..." Will's voice trailed off as he pulled out his Colt Peacemaker and checked the cylinder. It was loaded.

The others did the same with their pistols, then repeated the process with their rifles.

The six dismounted and hid the horses behind a copse of dense trees. Niall walked a few feet away, knelt in the dirt, and brushed away the dried leaves. He sketched a house, barn, bunkhouse, and corrals in the dirt, then looked up at the other five men.

Five minutes later, their plan set, the six eased through the darkening night toward the house and the women inside.

Chapter Twenty-Three

Frank saw the horses hidden outside the entrance to the Bierdan ranch, recognizing that one belonged to Will and another to Jamie MacLaren. He left his horse near theirs and started a circular route toward the house. As he got closer he could see three horses in front, none that he recognized. There were few lights on in the house. All the curtains were closed.

Frank moved in closer, coming in from the back, and saw eight more horses. He dropped behind a bush and tried to get a better view.

"Don't move. Drop the gun." A stern whisper came from behind at the same time Frank felt the cold barrel of a gun against his skull. "Turn around," the voice commanded.

Frank raised his hands and turned in a slow, fluid movement.

"Shit," Niall said and lowered his gun.

"Are the others here?" Frank reached down to pick up his discarded sidearm.

"Spread out all over. I'll show you." Niall drew a quick diagram, indicating where each man hid, waiting for the signal from Jamie. The last thing they needed was for one of them to shoot Frank in error.

"Where do you want me?" the sheriff asked.

"You're good where you are. Keep an eye on Jamie. He'll give the signal to move in." Niall pointed to a spot near a front corner of the house. "You should have no problem seeing it." Niall clapped Frank on the back and returned to his position.

******

"Make yourself comfortable, Miss Taylor." Ira helped Tess to the bed, pushed her back with a gentle movement, and lifted her legs up onto the mattress so she lay flat. He looked down at her, her eyes and body movements indicating she still struggled against the effects of the drugs. Ira had seen the same look in the eyes of other women. In the end, they'd all done what he asked.

He'd given Tess enough opium to provide a pleasurable feeling, ease all inhibitions. The effects would last for hours, allowing him ample time to do whatever he wanted. It was time.

Ira removed his jacket and loosened his shirt. He set the belt he'd worn on a chair, then turned to the woman before him. He sat on the edge of the bed and leaned forward. "You will be more comfortable with your dress loosened," he said as his fingers began to open her dress, exposing the chemise below. Her body protested little, but her hands moved up to stall his actions. He pushed them away.

"So, you are Grant Taylor's daughter. You are the younger one, yes?" His soothing voice washed over her, caressing her as the drug continued to break down her defenses. He slid the back of his knuckles down her neck, over her chest, and moved to the swell of her breasts. "Ah, Miss Taylor, I will enjoy this very much." He leaned down, his mouth inches from hers.

******

Jamie watched through slits in the curtains and listened from his position near the front corner. He noticed papers on a nearby table, but couldn't make out Drago's words as he spoke in soft tones. The lights were low. Eloise was reclined on a settee, Drago on a chair in front of her, his hands resting on her legs. Jamie watched for another moment, trying to detect if the woman was encouraging the actions or being forced. He couldn't tell from his position but noticed the vacant look in her eyes. They stared beyond Drago, not at him. At least she was alive. He looked towards the back at Niall, who crouched low behind a group of rocks.

Luther had been standing outside when Niall first knelt behind the rocks. The large, imposing man looked around and, satisfied nothing was amiss, disappeared into the kitchen. The outlaw watching the horses had disappeared into the trees. Jericho had been charged with taking care of the guard. Niall watched another minute until Jericho appeared and nodded, then signaled to Will at the other corner.

269

Will moved along the side but saw nothing. There were no windows or door at this end. He suspected there were more men upstairs, but couldn't tell from his position. He joined Drew at the far front corner of the house.

Drew turned and moved toward the front. He passed what appeared to be a bedroom but moved on to the next window. He stayed close to the house and didn't move when he saw a figure approach the window.

The man inside was alert, watching, but he didn't spot Drew.

Drew retraced his steps several feet and knelt below the window he'd passed, then raised up to peer through the slight opening in the curtains. What he saw sickened him. Tess was on the bed, Ira standing over her. Her head moved toward the window, but she didn't see Drew. She had a vacant look in her eyes, blank and staring into space. Her eyes moved back to Ira. Her hands weren't bound. Drew cursed. He wanted to jump through the window and wrap his hand around Ira's throat. Squeeze the life out of the miserable human who stood, leering at Tess. But he held his anger. If he acted on it others could die, including Tess. He looked toward Jamie's position. They had to move fast.

Drew signaled to Grant, now hidden just inside the barn. Instead of signaling to move in, he gave him the sign to wait. He moved toward Jamie's position. They needed to regroup.

Drew slipped under the windows to the side where Jamie knelt. Niall had joined him. He was momentarily stunned to see Frank Alts, but acknowledged the lawman with a nod. Will had made his way along the back of the house and now knelt next to Drew.

"Drago has Eloise in the living room," Jamie informed them.

"Ira Walsh has Tess in a back bedroom," Drew hissed in frustration then took a deep breath. "There's another man in the office. I didn't see Amanda or Kate. My guess is they're upstairs along with at least two of Ira's men."

"Luther and one other are in the kitchen. Looks like Jericho took care of the one watching their horses." Niall glanced behind him and saw Jericho's large form standing next to a group of pines.

"I saw no one, but heard movement upstairs. Could be Amanda and Kate, but my guess it's the other two men," Will added.

"All right. We know that Ira's in the bedroom, one's in the office, Drago's in the front, Luther and another are in the kitchen. Jericho got one, so that leaves two upstairs, correct?" Jamie asked. They all nodded.

"Frank, you keep watch on Drago from here. Shoot him if he makes any move to hurt Eloise. I'll go in the front with Drew. Drew, as soon as we get in, you go after Ira." Jamie looked at his brother. "You okay with that?"

"Oh yeah," Drew answered, eager to kill the man who held Tess.

"Good. I'll get the one in the office."

"Will and Niall need to take care of Luther and the other man, then go upstairs to find Kate and Amanda. We need to move fast, before they try to use the women as shields. As soon as the shooting starts, Grant and Jericho will scatter the horses then be prepared to fire if any of the men get past us."

Each man absorbed their assignment.

Jamie looked at Niall and Will. "Move in as soon as you hear my shots. All right, let's go." Jamie moved toward the front of the house, Drew right behind.

******

Unaware of what was happening outside, Ira touched his mouth to Tess's for a brief moment before traveling his lips down her neck, settling at the base of her throat. His hand moved up her stomach. She didn't try to push him away this time. Instead, her hand covered his and moved it higher, encouraging him to cup her breast. Tess arched her body into his hand, attempting to tell him what she wanted. Her breath became labored. Glassy eyes, a mellow stare, and soft smile told him she was ready, eager for him. He shifted and began to lower his mouth to hers when a gun blast split the night.

Walsh jumped from the bed and grabbed his gun. He started out the door and looked over his shoulder at the woman on the bed, knowing she was unaware of what was happening around her. Two more shots rang out and Ira eased into the hall.

He looked toward the kitchen and saw a man on the floor, his legs twitching. Luther. Another stood with his arms in the air, his back to Ira.

"Stay where you are or I'll put a bullet in the woman." Ira recognized the voice as Drago's.

Ira wondered if Stiles was alive or dead. Didn't matter, he had to get out while he could. He slid back into the bedroom and closed the door.

"There are four of us, Drago, and two more outside. There's no chance you'll get out of here alive, with or without her. She's an innocent—let her go." Jamie walked closer as he spoke to the outlaw who used Eloise as a shield. He wanted to distract the gunman, let Frank get into position outside. Jamie knew Drago would never leave the house alive.

******

Kate and Amanda heard the gunshots and prayed that help had come. They moved to the door and looked out. One man stood at a window at the end of the hall, the other had just walked out of one of the rooms. Kate aimed and fired. One man fell as the other pivoted and pulled the trigger. Kate and Amanda ducked back into the room as the gun blast split the wood around the door.

The men glanced up when they heard shots from upstairs. Niall, Drew, and Will stood in place, not wanting to provoke Drago, but anxious to get to the other women. Drew's hands clenched at his sides, the chamber of his gun still full. Jamie had dropped Stiles with his first shot. Niall looked across the room at Will. Their wives were upstairs, they were sure of it. They wanted to go after them, now.

Jamie realized that Drew stood outside of Drago's view. His eyes shifted to his brother and he gestured with his head a fraction, but it was enough for Drew to know what was needed. He slipped out the door and made his way to the outside of the bedroom where Ira held Tess.

******

Connor and Pierce watched as the men outside circled the house, preparing to enter. When the shooting began, two other men untied the horses and let them go. One of them was Jericho, Connor's colleague, friend, and another employee of Louis Dunnigan. Connor and Pierce made a path to Jericho. The man turned just as they were within a few feet and pointed his gun.

"Wondered when you boys would show up." Jericho lowered his weapon.

"See Ira?"

"Drew says he has Tess Taylor in a back bedroom. He's going after him."

"I'd like to get in there, but not go through the doors. You see a way?" Connor whispered to his brother.

The ex-thief glanced at the roofline and cocked his head to one side, then the next before he pointed to a spot near the other corner. "Right there. Easy as anything."

They moved through the trees and Pierce helped Connor up, then watched as he slid through an upstairs bedroom window.

Connor dropped inside without a sound. Gun drawn, he made his way to the door and peered out down the long hallway. He heard movement to his right and turned to see a man crouched, his rifle pointed at him. Connor didn't hesitate. Before the man knew what had hit him, he was on the ground, a bullet through his heart.

"Never hesitate," Connor whispered as he grabbed the dead man's rifle and made his way down the hall. He passed one door and opened it. A narrow staircase, the type often used back East for servants. It looked as if it hadn't been used in years.

He walked toward the main stairway, checking doors as he went. Four empty, one left to check. He had just reached for the knob when the door cracked open and he stared at the softest blue eyes he'd ever seen. Blond hair fell in strands from atop her head. She started to scream, but he pushed her back into the room, covered her mouth, and positioned himself against a wall with her in front of him. He saw the second woman, another beauty with ink black hair, similar to his, but eyes the color of a dark blue sea. And they were raging at him.

"Don't scream," Connor muttered. "I work for Louis Dunnigan."

The black-haired woman continued to glare, unsure if he told the truth or not.

"He hired me to spy on Ira Walsh. I'm here to help." He let his hand slip from the blond woman's mouth. "I'm Connor."

Kate turned to stare at the man and froze. *My God, he looks like Niall.* They shared the same hair, eyes, skins tones, height.

Connor saw the confusion on the woman's face. "I promise I'll explain as soon as I'm sure your men downstairs have everything under control." He turned and slipped out into the hall, leaving Kate and Amanda to gape after him.

Connor went straight for the back staircase and made his way down. He doubted anyone but the owner knew it existed. He came out in a small alcove, invisible from the other rooms, and waited.

******

Drew crouched below the window then leaned up to look inside. Ira Walsh moved in his direction, toward the window, his eyes narrowed, focused. Tess lay on the bed, her clothes mussed. Drew's stomach tightened. He couldn't think about what had happened between the two before he'd arrived. He had to focus on Ira and stopping him.

Ira moved the curtains and peered out. He opened the window just as Drew stood and rammed the butt of his rifle into Ira's gut. Walsh slammed backwards and lost his footing, his gun discharging into the floor.

Drew dropped the rifle and vaulted into the room, his Colt pointed at Ira.

"Don't move, Walsh," Drew ordered.

Ira ignored the warning. He lifted his gun toward Drew when he felt a sharp pain cut through his chest. Ira looked down to see blood covering his shirt. His wide eyes found Drew, then he slumped against the wall and slid to the floor.

His gun still smoking, Drew moved toward the dead man.

Connor heard a gunshot in a room next to the alcove where he stood. Connor moved to the other side, behind the main stairs to get a better view and saw Jericho enter the kitchen from the back followed by Pierce, both with guns drawn. They saw Connor, nodded. Connor moved to the bedroom doorway and peered in. He saw Ira laying in a pool of blood.

Drew hadn't checked for a pulse, but there was no need. The man was dead. His eyes traveled up to the bed and the woman he loved. *What happened here tonight*, he wondered. His eyes sought hers. He saw no recognition. It was as if she was in some sort of dream, only her eyes were open.

Drew walked to the other side of the bed and sat. Tess's breathing was somewhat labored. He noticed a slight bruise on her cheek, courtesy of Ira, he was sure, but nothing to help him discover what had transpired in this room.

He laid his gun on the spread and traced the slender column of her neck with his fingers. They stopped at one corner of her mouth. He traced her lips, then ran his thumb over the lush bottom one. The one he would capture between his teeth when they made love. He bent and placed a kiss on her mouth, then one on each eye.

He felt a hand come up and caress his jaw and cheek, then move up into his hair. She pulled him more fully into her for a kiss that was passionate and bold, given that their families were just outside the door. He enjoyed the feeling a few more moments before he pushed away on a ragged breath.

"Tess, we can't do this here, now."

"Yes," Tess responded in a throaty, sexy voice that had Drew confused. She looked down his body, her hand following the path of her eyes, and placed it on the bulge he couldn't hide. "Yes, Drew. Make love to me. Now." Her whispered plea was followed by her hand reaching behind his neck and drawing him down. He followed her lead for an instant before grabbing both of her wrists in his hands and holding them above her head.

"Tess, we have to stop..." he began. Then he heard a gun cock and turned to see Ira Walsh supporting himself with his arms on the bed, one hand holding Drew's Colt.

"So, she is your woman," Ira choked out. His face was ashen and his hand wasn't steady, but Drew's gun was loaded and a mere two feet way. "I wondered," he coughed again, began to topple, but caught himself and continued to point the weapon at the man who now held the woman Ira wanted. "Too bad you'll never have her again."

Ira's gun began to rise, his arm extending toward Drew. The end came with one shot. Ira slumped to the floor, a bullet hole placed neatly above his left ear.

Drew's eyes swung to the door to see Ira's man, the one he'd met in the saloon, who'd taken him back to his office after Luther broke his wheelchair, staring at the body with a satisfied expression.

Connor holstered his gun and walked over to Drew, extending his hand. "Nice to see you again, Drew. You may not remember me. I'm Connor MacLaren." The two men stared at each other. "Your cousin."

Chapter Twenty-Four

Jamie stood in the doorway, his gun trained on Drago. Will and Niall stood at the entrance to the kitchen, both their pistols aimed at the same man. The only thing stopping them from shooting was the woman Drago used as a shield. Eloise. The outlaw was unaware of Frank's rifle pointed at his head.

"I'm leaving, with the woman. Don't be foolish and try to stop me or you'll never see Mrs. Bierdan again. At least not alive," Drago said as he shifted his gaze from Jamie to Niall, then to Will. The brothers glanced at each other, all three aware that Frank stood outside, positioned to drop Drago with one shot.

Frank sighted the rifle, took a calming breath, and squeezed the trigger.

Jamie rushed to grab Eloise before she hit the floor while Drago pitched to the side, toppling a table, and landing with a dull thud.

Frank dashed around front and into the house, gently taking Eloise from Jamie's grasp. She looked into his eyes and sighed, then wrapped both arms around his neck. He sat with her while the others carried the bodies out and brought Amanda and Kate downstairs. Amanda and Kate hurried to help Tess and Eloise, but had no idea what to do with women who'd been given opium.

As soon as Jamie spotted the saddle bags and pouches, then put a finger in the cold tea left in the pan, he knew what had happened. Jamie told them it would run its course within eight to twelve hours but that they should take them both to the Taylor's and send for the doctor. No one asked about his knowledge of the drug.

Jeff and the men had returned in time to see bodies being carried from the house and two women, wrapped in blankets, being laid in the back of a wagon. Jeff dismounted and ran over, moving the blanket enough to see that one was Eloise Bierdan.

"What happened? Is she hurt?" Jeff's eyes were filled with worry.

"No," Frank responded. "Not the way you mean. I'll explain, but I need someone to ride to town and bring Doc Wheaton to the Taylor's. You got someone?"

"Jay and Stan, ride to town, get the doc, and make sure he gets to the Taylor ranch. Both Mrs. Bierdan and Miss Taylor need his help."

"Yes, sir," both men responded. They were dog tired, but either would do anything for Eloise Bierdan.

Frank looked at Jeff. "I know you've had a long day, but why don't you get your men settled and ride over with us. You need to hear it all."

******

The doctor spent a couple of hours at the Taylor's then, echoing what Jamie had told them, said Tess and Eloise would be tired but fine the next day. He'd seen the use of opium during the war. Whoever gave the women the tea knew enough to not overdose them.

Eloise asked Frank to stay, which he was glad to do. He held her hand until she fell into a fitful sleep, then slept in the chair next to her bed.

Drew refused to leave Tess alone. Her reaction to the drug seemed more pronounced than Eloise's. He sure as hell wasn't going to leave any of the other men with her. He and Frank had sat in the back of the wagon with the two women on the way back. Amanda and Kate had ridden in the front with Amanda driving. Tess had opened her eyes several times, looked toward him and reached out. She had tried to pull him down to her, but he took her hand, and held it tight.

When they'd arrived at the ranch, Eloise had wrapped her arms around Frank's neck and quietly let him take her inside. Tess had wrapped her arms around Drew, then snuggled in, nuzzling his neck, and placing soft kisses on his face. His brothers had stood back and watched. He could still hear their laughter as he walked into the house with her. Bastards.

******

Everyone was in bed, asleep. It was after midnight, the four brothers and their cousins sat in the dining room with Aunt Alicia, sipping whiskey or coffee, and coming to grips with the fact that there were two more MacLarens. Men they'd never met, yet who seemed to know everything about them.

Connor and Pierce MacLaren.

When they'd ridden in that night, Aunt Alicia had walked out of the house, down the steps, and straight up to them. She'd stood before the men a moment, as if inspecting each, then turned to Connor. "I know we met in Denver, but who are you, Connor?"

He'd known who she was the minute he'd seen her. It had been hard not to tell her of their connection, but his job with Louis had prevented it. Now it was over and he could let the truth come out.

"I am Connor MacLaren and this is my brother, Pierce. Our father was Hugh MacLaren." He watched as Alicia absorbed his words.

"Stuart and Duncan's cousin? Hugh MacLaren." Yes, she knew of Hugh. He'd written to Stuart for a while. The letters had ceased a few years before Stuart died. They'd never known what had happened to him or his children.

"Yes."

She stood on her toes and wrapped her arms around each man in turn, then stepped back, wiping tears from her eyes. "I wish Stuart could've been here to meet you. He'd be so pleased." She hadn't noticed Niall, Will, and Jamie walk up behind her. Each bore a decidedly confused expression.

Niall sized up the men before him. Drew had mentioned that the two were related, but there'd been no time for questions. Now he wanted answers.

"I'm Niall MacLaren. These are my brothers, Jamie and Will. You've met Drew."

Aunt Alicia could feel the tension, the confusion. "This is Connor and Pierce MacLaren, boys. Their father is Hugh MacLaren, Stuart and Duncan's cousin." The men shook hands then continued to peruse each other, the way men seemed to do.

"Was. He died several years ago, along with our mother," Connor clarified.

"Oh, I'm sorry to hear about that. We suspected as much when he didn't respond to Stuart's letters."

When the house was quiet, they all settled around the table, learning about each other for the first time.

Connor sipped his whiskey and began to answer the unspoken questions. "We came to this country twelve years ago. Our parents sent us as our prospects in Scotland were slim. They wanted a better life for us. The letters they received from Duncan and Stuart made it sound so grand. There were opportunities for everyone and work for all." He sat back, remembering the trip over, and the rude realization when they landed that they knew no one and had little money. "We tried to find Duncan and his family in Ohio," he nodded at the brothers, "but they were gone. Someone else was settled on their farm and no one knew how to contact anyone. We knew you and Stuart were in Arizona, but we had no funds, no way to get a message to you. So we returned to New York."

"And what have you done all these years?" Alicia asked.

"Whatever we could to live," Pierce replied. He'd stayed quiet most of the night, following his brother's lead, absorbing what he could from the MacLaren cousins. It was obvious to him they were slow to warm to them. He hoped that would change.

"I see." Alicia studied the cold coffee in her cup. "I know that Connor is a Range Detective. What do you do, Pierce?"

Connor laughed at the question. Pierce could do whatever he wanted. He had brains, motivation, and a desire for adventure. The combination often got him in trouble. Everyone glanced at Connor then turned their eyes back to Pierce.

He narrowed his eyes at his brother before answering. "Right now I'm a decoder."

"And thief," Connor interjected.

Pierce ignored him and continued. "I figure out coded communications that don't fit the normal patterns." He paused a moment. "Yes, and sometimes it does involve borrowing a document or ledger in order to copy it for decoding."

"So you're the one who deciphered Ira Walsh's ledgers, found out about his illegal actions?" Drew asked. A message from Dunnigan had indicated he'd used a decoder to find out about Ira.

"Yes. Connor worked for Louis, but brought me in when it was suspected that Ira had another set of ledgers. One that documented transactions that were important but that he didn't want discovered."

"Did Dunnigan know you were related to us?" Jamie asked.

"Yes. He knew all about our background." *The good and the bad*, Connor recalled.

"I'll be damned. And he never said a word to you, Drew?" Niall asked.

"No."

"He didn't want you involved," Connor said to his cousin. "You had enough to worry about, plus your work for him. It was better that way." They all knew that Connor was referring to Drew's efforts to walk.

"What are your plans now?" Will asked. He wondered if they'd be traveling back to Fire Mountain, building a life with them.

"We travel around, but would like to see the ranch, if that's all right with you?" Connor asked Alicia, speaking for both Pierce and himself.

They were grown men. Proud. They'd made a life for themselves. Why did she feel like she wanted to wrap her arms around them and insist they live in Fire Mountain?

"You're family. Of course you'll come to the ranch. Whenever you want." She looked at her four nephews. "And there will always be a place for you if you ever decide to settle down."

******

"Don't be ridiculous. Of course you're going to see him, talk to him. That boy hardly left your side. Wouldn't let anyone else help you," Eleanor said as she helped Tess into her dress the next evening. "You've made excuses all day, but tonight you will come to supper with the rest of us." Eleanor didn't know everything that had transpired. She was woefully ignorant of the effects of opium, and cursed Ira Walsh over and over for his part in her step-daughter's misery.

Tess sat on the bed and placed her hands over her face. A face red with embarrassment. She wanted to hide in her room and never come out each time she recalled what she'd done while under the effects of the drug. She'd made a complete fool of herself. In front of everyone. In front of Drew. How could she ever look at him again and not feel embarrassed?

"Is Eloise still here?" Tess asked.

"Yes, and so is Frank. He'll take her back after supper. Now there's a man who's smitten." Eleanor folded Tess's night dress and closed the chifferobe. "It wasn't your fault, Tess. There's no reason to feel bad about anything that happened."

An hour later, Tess sat at the supper table between Amanda and Eloise, across from Drew.

She hadn't looked at him or even acknowledged his presence, but Tess knew he continued to stare at her, trying to get her attention.

She'd fought the effects as long as she could, but her body and mind had failed her. It had been as if she were floating above, watching the scenes unfold beneath her, powerless to stop herself from wanting to play along. Ira was repulsive, a murderer, but the opium made her crave his touch, just as she'd craved Drew's later that same night. Ira had been eager for her. Drew had pushed her away, tried to stop her advances. She knew Ira's responses were vile, meant to destroy her, as she knew Drew's were meant to protect her. Thinking about it, she couldn't help but believe her actions disgusted him.

"Tess?" Drew's voice penetrated her thoughts. She looked up to see his beautiful hazel eyes trained on hers. "Are you feeling better?"

"Um, yes. Tired, but much better. Thank you." She looked away and pretended to concentrate on the food before her.

Drew continued to watch her. She'd refused to see him since he'd left her room early this morning. He thought he knew what was bothering her, but until she'd agree to talk, there wasn't much he could do. He loved her. There was no other woman he wanted. They would work through this, he was certain of it.

He'd spent his day with Grant, preparing an agreement concerning the Bierdan ranch. Drew had been somewhat surprised at the complexities of the transaction, and the people involved, but he thought the plan was brilliant. They expected the other party to the transaction to arrive the following day. He doubted the final negotiations would take long—it was too beneficial to each party involved.

"You're welcome to stay here another night, Eloise. You too, Frank. You don't have to go back to the ranch tonight." Eleanor didn't like the thought of the young woman staying at the house alone.

"Thank you, but it's best to get back. Jeff and the men planned to take care of the house today, clean it up, and fix what was broken. Now it's my turn to help. I can't leave it all for them." Eloise glanced at Frank. His eyes caught hers and held.

"I plan to stay over one night, Eleanor, make sure she's all right. Her foreman is real protective. After what happened, I'm sure he'll keep extra men posted." Frank definitely planned to stay with Eloise tonight, and maybe the next. Talk some things through.

Niall pushed back from the table and wrapped his arm around Kate's chair. "We need to start back, too. Not tomorrow, but the next. Jamie's anxious to see Torie, and we all need to get back to business. Can't leave Gus and Pete to have all the fun." He reached over and kissed his wife on the cheek.

Grant stood and pulled out Eleanor's chair. "I don't know about the rest of you, but tomorrow's a busy day. I'm having one drink before I turn in. Anyone care to join me?"

All the men but Frank and Drew followed Grant into his office. Frank helped Eloise up and walked her down the hall to grab her things.

Drew sat patiently, waiting for Tess to acknowledge him, and accept that he wouldn't go away. She hadn't moved since everyone had left. "You realize, of course, that I'm not leaving here without you," Drew said.

"What?" Tess's confused eyes pulled at Drew's heart. This might be worse than he'd thought.

"Leaving here, the Big G, without you. We're getting married. Either here or in Fire Mountain, makes no difference to me. But when I leave, you're going with me, Tess."

"You still want to marry me?" Her question stunned him.

He stood, walked around the table, and sat on the chair next to her. He grabbed her shoulders, gently turned her towards him, then took her hands in his.

"I love you. Of course I still want to marry you."

She stared at their joined hands. His thumbs drew small circles on her hands as he spoke. It distracted her, aroused her. Tears came unbidden. She tried to make them stop, without success. She took a deep breath and looked up at him.

"I tried hard to stop what was happening, but couldn't. The drug kept seizing my body, controlling my mind." She pulled a hand from his and swiped at a tear. "I'm sorry, Drew. It must have been humiliating for you to see me like that. I guess I'm not as strong as I thought I was. Not as strong as you. I tried to be, but I'm not."

The tears in her eyes almost broke him. It wasn't her fault. He had to make her understand. He wouldn't lose her to the actions of a murderous lecher or the effects of an illicit drug.

He reached out to her but she pulled away. Drew took a deep breath and tried again. "You're the strongest woman I know. Many women would've broken down, given up. But you did everything you could. You went against Ira even though he made you suffer for it." He looked at the small laceration at the edge of her mouth and traced the bruise on her cheek with his thumb, both the outcome of her efforts to defy Walsh. "You're beautiful, smart, funny, and passionate."

At the use of that word she placed her hands over her face and tried to turn from him. He grabbed her arm and spun her back around to face him.

"Yes, passionate. You were before what happened. The opium did nothing to change your response to me, our love making." He pulled her close, not letting her pull back. "I love you, Tess, and I'm not losing you. Ever."

He lifted her from the chair and settled her on his lap. She wrapped her arms around his neck and laid her head on his shoulder. "Where?" he asked.

His question confused her. "Where?" she whispered.

"Are we getting married here or in Fire Mountain?"

Her heart pounded so loud she almost couldn't make out what he'd said. Almost.

"Here."

Drew let out a breath, then tightened his hold. He never planned to let go.

Epilogue

Eleanor, Alicia, Amanda, and Kate pulled off a beautiful wedding three days later. Since most everyone was already at the Big G, Drew and Tess decided not to wait. Besides, Drew didn't want Tess focusing on the past. He wanted her firmly in the present, with him.

How the women got a small band, decorations, food, and the minister together in that short amount of time astonished the men.

Tess was stunning. Eleanor brought her wedding gown down from the attic. It took very little to adjust it. The women added pearls and small amounts of lace. It was perfect.

Grant surprised Drew with the gift of a beautiful chestnut stallion with a wide white blaze. "To help your breeding program," Grant said. Drew named him Freedom.

Tess danced with Drew as well as the other five MacLaren men. She saved a dance for Jake, Frank, Jericho, and Louis Dunnigan. The best one, however, was with her father.

"I'll miss you, Tess," he said as they danced slowly on the small floor. "But I'm glad you'll be with Amanda. It'll give Eleanor a place to go when she wants to get away from me." He smiled down at her.

"And you. You'll come to visit also, right?"

"Of course."

Grant handed Tess to her new husband and stepped back.

Drew took her in his arms and spun her around the floor, then pulled her away from the crowd. He wrapped his arms around her, kissing her face, nuzzling her neck. "It won't be long before we can disappear upstairs," he whispered.

Tess pulled back and ran a finger up his arm, over his chest, and behind his neck to pull him down for a beautiful smile. "Don't keep me waiting," she whispered back, then started to laugh.

Drew laughed with her as he took her hand to return to the party. "Vixen," he murmured.

******

It was dark and the guests had gone home. The women helped Tess change her clothes and pack her things. The MacLarens would be leaving tomorrow for Fire Mountain.

Afterwards, everyone gathered in Grant's office as Drew explained the complicated transaction that had brought Louis to Cold Creek.

Eloise had agreed to sell her land to a new entity called Taylor-Dunnigan Cattle & Timber. That got the attention of all in the room. Louis had agreed to buy the land with his cash, including purchase of a home for Eloise in Cold Creek.

Grant had agreed to merge his ownership of the Langdon ranch into Taylor-Dunnigan. Most surprising was that Grant accepted Dunnigan's offer to purchase half of the Big G. The three ranches sat side by side, creating the largest cattle and timber property west of Denver. Taylor-Dunnigan Cattle & Timber would do just what the name implied. Raise cattle, provide timber to the mills, and within a year, build the largest lumber mill in this side of the state with distribution throughout the country.

Grant would be in charge of the cattle business, Louis in charge of the timber and lumber mill operations. Dunnigan had an idea about selecting and cutting timber in a planned method, with re-planting following soon after the trees were removed. It was something he had heard about while back east, and he was anxious to try it. He called it the never-ending-supply-of-timber concept.

The best news to all was that no jobs were lost. There was to be a place for everyone who wanted to stay, and that included Connor and Pierce. Both Grant and Louis saw a place for both men in their business. It was up to them to decide.

One surprising offer was to Drew, after everyone else had left the office. "I know you've given me your resignation," Dunnigan said, "but let Grant and I make you a counter offer. One I think you'll like."

"All right." Drew was willing to listen to them. He respected them both. Hell, one was his father-in-law.

"We need a lawyer for Taylor-Dunnigan. This will be a big operation. We'll need someone who knows cattle and understands business. You can do it from Fire Mountain and it shouldn't detract from the horse breeding business you and Tess have planned. In fact, we may even find a way to combine the breeding program here with yours. What do you say?" Dunnigan sat back and waited for Drew to digest the offer before adding, "And you'll make the same pay as at Dunnigan Enterprises."

Drew's eyes widened. He was a good negotiator, used to keeping a straight face. The first offer was a coup, the second...Well, he'd have to be a fool to pass it up.

"I'll accept, but under one condition."

The two older men looked at him, waiting.

"You pay me as part of the MacLaren Ranch business, not to me personally. You do that, and we've got a deal, gentlemen."

Louis and Grant looked at each other then burst out laughing.

"Best damn deal I ever made," Louis said and held out his hand.

Louis spotted Connor as the three left the office. "Excuse me, there's one more person I need to speak with."

Louis walked outside and down the front steps.

Connor stood by the barn, holding a piece of rope, tying and retying knots, killing time. He was glad to have met the other MacLarens. They were a good group—one he'd be proud to be associated with if he were a different man. But he wasn't. He'd understood years ago that the demon that haunted him could only be extricated in one way— by finding Meggie. Except that dream had died a little more with each passing year. He looked up to see Dunnigan walking toward him.

"Connor," Louis greeted him. He hoped the man would consider the offer from Grant and him to work for Taylor-Dunnigan. He was a good man, even if he wouldn't acknowledge it.

"Mr. Dunnigan."

"You and I discussed a deal if you helped me with Ira. You did and I'm here to make right that deal."

Connor's eyes lit up.

Louis pulled out a slip of paper and held it out. "It's as of two days ago."

Connor took the telegram and read it through. "They've tracked her to Salt Lake." He looked at Dunnigan. "That's only a couple days ride from here." He took a couple of steps away, then turned back. "It's sounds like they're sure."

"Yes, it does," Louis answered.

"I need to let Pierce know."

"You'll stay in touch?" Dunnigan asked. He knew Connor would be gone now that he had news. And Pierce might go with him.

"Yes. And thank you, Mr. Dunnigan." Connor shook the man's hand then left to find his brother. Pierce was in the back, talking with Jamie and Will. He'd told Connor that he planned to go back to Fire Mountain with their cousins, maybe work at the ranch. He wanted to give it a try. Connor didn't know if the latest news would change his plans or not.

Connor nodded at his cousins as he joined them. "Pierce, you got a minute?"

They walked a few feet away. Connor handed him the telegram.

Pierce's eyes grew wide. "Damn, they've found her. After all this time."

Connor stood, watching Pierce, deciding how to phrase his thoughts.

"I'm leaving in a few minutes, and I'm going alone."

Pierce started to protest but Connor stopped him.

"Don't argue with me. This is my quest. I know you love her, want to find her, but I'm the one who lost her. It's my fault she's been missing all these years."

The pain Pierce saw in his brother's eyes cut through him. Connor had blamed himself too long, and it had never been his fault. Finding Meggie was the only thing that could bring him peace.

"You have an opportunity in Fire Mountain. I want you to go. I'll find Meggie and come to you."

Pierce felt his eyes water—for his brother and for his missing sister. He knew he had to let

298

Connor do this his way. He held out his hand and when his brother took it, he pulled him into a hug. "Swear to me you'll make it to Fire Mountain," Pierce said in a low voice.

Connor pulled back. "I swear."

Thank you for taking time to read Stronger than the Rest. If you enjoyed it, please consider telling your friends or posting a short review. Word of mouth is an author's best friend and much appreciated.

Please join my reader's group and sign up to be notified of my New Releases at www.shirleendavies.com.

About the Author

Shirleen Davies writes romance—historical, contemporary, and romantic suspense. She grew up in Southern California, attended Oregon State University, and has degrees from San Diego State University and the University of Maryland. During the day she provides consulting services to small and mid-sized businesses. But her real passion is writing emotionally charged stories of flawed people who find redemption through love and acceptance. She now lives with her husband in a beautiful town in northern Arizona.

Shirleen began her series, MacLarens of Fire Mountain, with Tougher than the Rest, the story of the oldest brother, Niall MacLaren. Other books in the series include, Faster than the Rest, Harder than the Rest, Stronger than the Rest, and Deadlier than the Rest. Book six, Wilder than the Rest, is due for release in early summer, 2014. Her contemporary romance series, MacLarens of Fire Mountain Contemporary, opened with book one, Second Summer. Book two, Hard Landing, released in April 2014, and Book three, One More day, is scheduled to release in midsummer, 2014. Book one of her newest historical western series,

Redemption Mountain, will release in the fall of 2014.

Shirleen loves to hear from her readers.

Write to her at: shirleen@shirleendavies.com

Visit her website: http://www.shirleendavies.com

Comment on her blog:
http://www.shirleendavies.com/blog.html

Facebook Fan Page:
https://www.facebook.com/ShirleenDaviesAuthor

Twitter: http://twitter.com/shirleendavies

Google+: http://www.gplusid.com/shirleendavies

LinkedIn:
http://www.linkedin.com/in/shirleendaviesauthor

Other Books by Shirleen Davies

Tougher than the Rest – Book One
MacLarens of Fire Mountain Historical Western Romance Series

"A passionate, fast-paced story set in the untamed western frontier by an exciting new voice in historical romance."

Niall MacLaren is the oldest of four brothers, and the undisputed leader of the family. A widower, and single father, his focus is on building the MacLaren ranch into the largest and most successful in northern Arizona. He is serious about two things—his responsibility to the family and his future marriage to the wealthy, well-connected widow who will secure his place in the territory's destiny.

Katherine is determined to live the life she's dreamed about. With a job waiting for her in the growing town of Los Angeles, California, the young teacher from Philadelphia begins a journey across the United States with only a couple of trunks and her spinster companion. Life is perfect for this adventurous, beautiful young woman, until an accident throws her into the arms of the one man who can destroy it all.

Fighting his growing attraction and strong desire for the beautiful stranger, Niall is more determined than ever to push emotions aside to focus on his goals of wealth and political gain. But looking into the clear, blue eyes of the woman who could ruin everything, Niall discovers he will have to harden his heart and be tougher than he's ever been in his life...Tougher than the Rest.

Faster than the Rest – Book Two
MacLarens of Fire Mountain Historical Western Romance Series

"Headstrong, brash, confident, and complex, the MacLarens of Fire Mountain will captivate you with strong characters set in the wild and rugged western frontier."

Handsome, ruthless, young U.S. Marshal Jamie MacLaren had lost everything—his parents, his family connections, and his childhood sweetheart—but now he's back in Fire Mountain and ready for another chance. Just as he successfully reconnects with his family and starts to rebuild his life, he gets the unexpected and unwanted assignment of rescuing the woman who broke his heart.

Beautiful, wealthy Victoria Wicklin chose money and power over love, but is now fighting for her life—or is she? Who has she become in the seven years since she left Fire Mountain to take up her life in San Francisco? Is she really as innocent as she says?

Marshal MacLaren struggles to learn the truth and do his job, but the past and present lead him in different directions as his heart and brain wage battle. Is Victoria a victim or a villain? Is life offering him another chance, or just another heartbreak?

As Jamie and Victoria struggle to uncover past secrets and come to grips with their shared passion, another danger arises. A life-altering danger that is out of their control and threatens to destroy any chance for a shared future.

Harder than the Rest – Book Three
MacLarens of Fire Mountain Historical Western Romance Series

"They are men you want on your side. Hard, confident, and loyal, the MacLarens of Fire Mountain will seize your attention from the first page."

Will MacLaren is a hardened, plain-speaking bounty hunter. His life centers on finding men guilty of horrendous crimes and making sure justice is done. There is no place in his world for the carefree attitude he carried years before when a tragic event destroyed his dreams.

Amanda is the daughter of a successful Colorado rancher. Determined and proud, she works hard to prove she is as capable as any man and worthy to be her father's heir. When a stranger arrives, her independent nature collides with the strong pull toward the handsome ranch hand. But is he what he seems and could his secrets endanger her as well as her family?

The last thing Will needs is to feel passion for another woman. But Amanda elicits feelings he thought were long buried. Can Will's desire for her change him? Or will the vengeance he seeks against the one man he wants to destroy—a dangerous opponent without a conscious—continue to control his life?

Stronger than the Rest – Book Four
MacLarens of Fire Mountain Historical Western Romance Series

"Smart, tough, and capable, the MacLarens protect their own no matter the odds. Set against America's rugged frontier, the stories of the men from Fire Mountain are complex, fast-paced, and a must read for anyone who enjoys non-stop action and romance."

Drew MacLaren is focused and strong. He has achieved all of his goals except one—to return to the MacLaren ranch and build the best horse breeding program in the west. His successful career as an attorney is about to give way to his ranching roots when a bullet changes everything.

Tess Taylor is the quiet, serious daughter of a Colorado ranch family with dreams of her own. Her shy nature keeps her from developing friendships outside of her close-knit family until Drew enters her life. Their relationship grows. Then a bullet, meant for another, leaves him paralyzed and determined to distance himself from the one woman he's come to love.

Convinced he is no longer the man Tess needs, Drew focuses on regaining the use of his legs and recapturing a life he thought lost. But danger of another kind threatens those he cares about—including Tess—forcing him to rethink his future.

Can Drew overcome the barriers that stand between him, the safety of his friends and family, and a life with the woman he loves? To do it all, he has to be strong. Stronger than the Rest.

Deadlier than the Rest – Book Five
MacLarens of Fire Mountain Historical Western Romance Series

"A passionate, heartwarming story of the iconic MacLarens of Fire Mountain. This captivating historical western romance grabs your attention from the start with an engrossing story encompassing two romances set against the rugged backdrop of the burgeoning western frontier."

Connor MacLaren's search has already stolen eight years of his life. Now he is close to finding what he seeks—Meggie, his missing sister. His quest leads him to the growing city of Salt Lake and an encounter with the most captivating woman he has ever met.

Grace is the third wife of a Mormon farmer, forced into a life far different from what she'd have chosen. Her independent spirit longs for choices governed only by her own heart and mind. To achieve her dreams, she must hide behind secrets and half-truths, even as her heart pulls her towards the ruggedly handsome Connor.

Known as cool and uncompromising, Connor MacLaren lives by a few, firm rules that have served him well and kept him alive. However, danger stalks Connor, even to the front range of the beautiful Wasatch Mountains, threatening those he cares about and impacting his ability to find his sister.

Can Connor protect himself from those who seek his death? Will his eight-year search lead him to his sister while unlocking the secrets he knows are held tight within Grace, the woman who has captured his heart?

Read this heartening story of duty, honor, passion, and love in book five of the MacLarens of Fire Mountain series.

Wilder than the Rest – Book Six
MacLarens of Fire Mountain Historical Western Romance Series

"A captivating historical western romance set in the burgeoning and treacherous city of San Francisco. Go along for the ride in this gripping story that seizes your attention from the very first page."

"If you're a reader who wants to discover an entire family of characters you can fall in love with, this is the series for you." – Authors to Watch

Pierce is a rough man, but happy in his new life as a Special Agent. Tasked with defending the rights of the federal government, Pierce is a cunning gunslinger always ready to tackle the next job. That is, until he finds out that his new job involves Mollie Jamison.

Mollie can be a lot to handle. Headstrong and independent, Mollie has chosen a life of danger and intrigue guaranteed to prove her liquor-loving father wrong. She will make something of herself, and no one, not even arrogant Pierce MacLaren, will stand in her way.

A secret mission brings them together, but will their attraction to each other prove deadly in their hunt for justice? The payoff for success is high, much higher than any assignment either has taken before. But will the damage to their hearts and souls be too much to bear? Can Pierce and Mollie find a way to overcome their misgivings and work together as one?

Read Wilder than the Rest, another heartening story of duty, honor, passion, and love in book six of the MacLarens of Fire Mountain.

Second Summer – Book One
MacLarens of Fire Mountain Contemporary Romance Series

"In this passionate Contemporary Romance, author Shirleen Davies introduces her readers to the modern day MacLarens starting with Heath MacLaren, the head of the family."

The Chairman of both the MacLaren Cattle Co. and MacLaren Land Development, Heath MacLaren is a success professionally—his personal life is another matter.
Following a divorce after a long, loveless marriage, Heath spends his time with women who are beautiful and passionate, yet unable to provide what he longs for . . .

Heath has never experienced love even though he witnesses it every day between his younger brother, Jace, and wife, Caroline. He wants what they have, yet spends his time with women too young to understand what drives him and too focused on themselves to be true companions.
It's been two years since Annie's husband died, leaving her to build a new life. He was her soul mate and confidante. She has no desire to find a replacement, yet longs for male friendship.

Annie's closest friend in Fire Mountain, Caroline MacLaren, is determined to see Annie come out of her shell after almost two years of mourning. A chance meeting with Heath turns into an offer to be a part of the MacLaren Foundation Board and an opportunity for a life outside her home sanctuary which has also become her prison. The platonic friendship that builds between Annie and Heath points to a future where each may rely on the other without the bonds a romance would entail.

However, without consciously seeking it, each yearns for more . . .

The MacLaren Development Company is booming with Heath at the helm. His meetings at a partner company with the young, beautiful marketing director, who makes no secret of her desire for him, are a temptation. But is she the type of woman he truly wants?

Annie's acceptance of the deep, yet passionless, friendship with Heath sustains her, lulling her to believe it is all she needs. At least until Heath drops a bombshell, forcing Annie to realize that what she took for friendship is actually a deep, lasting love. One she doesn't want to lose.

Each must decide to settle—or fight for it all.

Hard Landing – Book Two
MacLarens of Fire Mountain Contemporary Romance Series

"The author really gets into the hearts and souls of her characters in this book, which is probably why I fell in love with the story the way I did. Wonderful, wonderful story." - Authors to Watch

Trey MacLaren is a confident, poised Navy pilot. He's focused, loyal, ethical, and a natural leader. He is also on his way to what he hopes will be a lasting relationship and marriage with fellow pilot, Jesse Evans.

Jesse has always been driven. Her graduation from the Naval Academy and acceptance into the pilot training program are all she thought she wanted—until she discovered love with Trey MacLaren

Trey and Jesse's lives are filled with fast flying, friends, and the demands of their military careers. Lives each has settled into with a passion. At least until the day Trey receives a letter that could change his and Jesse's lives forever.

It's been over two years since Trey has seen the woman in Pensacola. Her unexpected letter stuns him and pushes Jesse into a tailspin from which she might not pull back.

Each must make a choice. Will the choice Trey makes cause him to lose Jesse forever? Will she follow her heart or her head as she fights for a chance to save the love she's found? Will their independent decisions collide, forcing them to give up on a life together?

One More Day – Book Three
MacLarens of Fire Mountain Contemporary Romance Series

Watch for One More Day, Cameron and Lainey's story, in the summer of 2014.